Shrimply
Dead

Shrimply Dead

A Seafood Caper Mystery

MAGGIE TOUSSAINT

Shrimply Dead
A Seafood Caper Mystery
Book 3

Print ISBN 9780999705445
COPYRIGHT © 2021 by Maggie Toussaint

Contact information: maggietoussaint@darientel.net
Cover art by Maggie Toussaint
The series logo from Henery Press is used by permission.

Muddle House Publishing
1146 Tolomato Drive SE
Darien, GA 31305
Visit us at www.muddlehousepublishing.com

Published in the United States of America

Dedication

This one's for Craig.

Acknowledgments

Critique partner Polly Iyer helped sharpen this manuscript. Henery Press allowed me to use the series logo from book one in this series, Seas the Day. Thanks also go to my editor, Jaden Terrell, who helped add the sparkle.

Chapter One

"Show time," I said to my trio of servers. They looked so professional in their black pants, white shirts, and striped Holloway Catering aprons that I got a little choked up.

Food for this crowd of 120 covered every square inch of kitchen counterspace. This was the first time I'd catered in this lovely new Parish House, and another first to cater for the Nature Coalition. The arched windows and the stained glass swag-style lighting in the dining room's circular rotunda dressed up the space, as did the flickering candles and greenery on every table.

The kitchen's central island worked well for staging the two meal choices, so we passed the plates assembly-line style down to the serving trays. One side held rosemary potatoes, broccoli, and pork tenderloin, while the other side had oven-baked "fried" green tomatoes, roasted cauliflower, and killer three-bean salad. Cornbread had already been served with lightly dressed spring mix salad.

Easy peasy.

I'm River Holloway Merrick, and Holloway Catering

is my business. My assistants tonight included my husband of five months, Pete Merrick, proprietor of Island Creamery; my brother, Doug Holloway, owner of Doug's Pro Home Repair; and Patsy Wilson, a recent hire, as Doug's wife Viv was too busy with their kids and her pending delivery next month.

"Rumor has it Jasmine Garr is up for an award," I said. "Since I cooked for her mom all summer, I'd like to serve her table, and then Patsy and I will continue loading plates for you guys to serve."

"Let me carry that heavy tray for you," Pete said, lifting it out of my hands.

I had been carrying loaded trays this size for years, but my husband couldn't help himself. Our eyes met with a rush of love. "Thanks."

From the side of the room, I carried two veggie plates to Jasmine's table. She paused her conversation with real estate broker Milton Wainwright to flash me a smile. I started to serve the other veggie plate to the pest removal guy.

"Wait. I'm having the pork tenderloin," Ash Braswell said, pointing to the blue dot on his name tag.

"Sure." I nodded through my embarrassment. "I apologize for not checking. I assumed since you rescued wild animals for a living you were vegetarian."

"Not hardly," he said accepting the pork tenderloin meal with a grin. "Some animals are meant to be eaten."

"Enjoy."

He lifted a fork. "Thanks. I will."

After that, I scrupulously checked for name tag dots, but Ash was the only carnivore at this table. The next hour passed in a blur of entrees and chocolate desserts. We circled the room with carafes of coffee serving both regular and decaf, while removing the empty plates.

As the speeches began, we cleaned the kitchen and loaded the van. Doug left to be with his family, while Patsy opted to stay with Pete and me to see who won the Coalition's Volunteer of the Year Award.

The three of us nibbled on leftovers in the kitchen and listened to the program. Emcee Milton Wainwright announced speakers, narrated a slideshow of the organization's accomplishments, and gave a pitch for donations for the coming year's efforts. Finally, one item remained on the agenda.

"The Volunteer of the Year," said Milton, pausing theatrically, "is Jasmine Garr. Come on up here, Dr. Garr."

The room exploded in applause as Jasmine made her way to the podium.

"Despite her busy schedule as a supply veterinarian throughout the region," Milton continued, "Dr. Garr volunteered on all of our initiatives this year and still found the time to terraform two acres of land surrounding her home into a native plant sanctuary. During the year, she led tours for third and fifth grade students through those sustainable plantings, sending each child home with a wildflower seedling. Dr. Garr made a significant difference in connecting residents with local habitats. Her extraordinary dedication empowers people to be stewards of our natural environment. Her leadership serves as a beacon for all who follow in her footsteps."

"Thanks! Y'all don't know how much this means to me," Jasmine said as she hoisted the clear Lucite trophy at the podium.

I felt happy for her as she thanked everyone for the

award. She'd done all those things while caring for her late mother during her losing battle with breast cancer. This honor couldn't have come at a better time to lift her spirits.

"This award is for my mom." Jasmine hugged her trophy high. "I'm sorry she didn't live to see it. At least it would've given her some satisfaction since, despite my logging kazillion hours in forests all over the tri-county area, I never found a trace of the elusive *Franklinia alatamaha*."

Polite laughter rang out. From Georgia History class way back when, I knew that the Franklin tree, as it is also known, has been extinct in the wild for two hundred years or so, though cultivated plants from botanist John Bartram's collected seeds resulted in biological specimens. Many had searched the Altamaha River delta in vain for this tall flowering shrub in the tea plant family first identified here in the eighteenth century.

Jasmine concluded her remarks and received a standing ovation. Fellow veterinarian Linette Nelson, Ash, and Milton clustered around her, offering congratulations, before yielding to other well-wishers.

I saw Jasmine frequently this summer when I brought weekday lunches to the Garr homestead. After her mother's death six weeks ago, the catering contract ended, but I'd enjoyed the peaceful serenity of their wooded property. It felt safe and tranquil, like my place did.

While people streamed out of the awards ceremony, Pete, Patsy, and I hauled out the trash and sanitized the counters again. I believed in leaving a place cleaner than we found it.

Milton Wainwright lagged behind to lock the door.

"That was so nice, what you did for Jasmine," I said. "I'm glad to see her out and about and smiling again."

"She earned that award. None of the other nominees matched her passion for native habitats. On another note, if I could give an award for best catered meal ever, I'd give it to you." Milton handed me a check for the remainder owed on the meal. "The food was excellent. People will be talking about this banquet for years to come. If I have any say about the caterer next year, you've got the job."

"Thank you," I said. "It was a delight to be here. The bonus for me was seeing Jasmine's face so full of joy."

Soon Pete and I were winding our way home. With Shell Island being only 12 miles long and one to two across, it was a short drive, especially since traffic was scant this time of night. I felt exhilarated but I'd crash as soon as I got home and unloaded. It was always this way after an event.

"I always appreciate your help, but you don't have to work every catering job," I told Pete. "Now that you're so busy with your company, I'd understand. Patsy has a cousin who's looking for work, so I could fill your spot easy enough."

"I'm right where I need to be," Pete said from behind the wheel. "I enjoy seeing people respond to your cooking. If you ever decide to get out of the cooking business, I could use your organizational skills in my business."

"Well, thanks. I'm happy to help out at your end too," I said. "Now that our renovation is complete, I'm looking forward to soaking in our tub."

Pete's smile lit his gaze. "Good thing we got one big

enough for two."

~*~

"Jasmine glowed with happiness when she won that award," I reminisced, sipping morning coffee with Pete two days later on our deck. We sat side by side on padded loungers. My black kitty, Major, purred contentedly in my lap. "I know what it's like to be a caretaker and how harried you feel when your time is not your own. She probably had to put her dreams on hold for a few years. I'm sure that once upon a time she expected to establish a private veterinary practice."

Pete frowned. "Jasmine created a niche job as a supply vet, and she kept the same soft career focus after her mother passed, most likely because it allowed her time to do other things. In fact, her career reminds me of yours."

I took that remark as a compliment. "I get why she didn't commit to a practice once she had more time. It's nice being accountable only to yourself."

Though it was October, our Indian Summer temperatures felt more like summer than fall. Dark clouds cloaked the sky, giving an ominous sense to the day. I didn't have any special intuition, but the heavy air felt brooding, dangerous even. Only what could it be? Shell Island had been a tranquil place for months.

Would this be a rainy Monday? I had paperwork to finish and a check to deposit after Saturday's banquet, not that rain would interfere with those activities.

"Along the same lines," Pete said, "have you thought more about expanding Holloway Catering? I know you're considering several options, including my suggestion to make cookies for Island Creamery."

"I've made a decision," I said. "My preference is to

make bakery items for your shop, that is, if you'll have me. Our respective markets dovetail at desserts. You've got the best ice cream, I've got the best baked goods. It's win-win for both of us."

Pete whooped and drew me onto his lounger. "This is the best news I've had all day. Except for that good morning kiss. That was spectacular. Wow."

"Glad you approve," I said, nibbling his ear a bit.

"Take it easy on a guy. I've got a staff meeting in thirty minutes. Since I called the meeting and I'm the boss, I have to be there." He nuzzled my neck. "But I can reschedule."

"Not on your life, bud. I've got a busy day ahead too. Just so we're clear on the business collaboration, let's start with one day a week of cookies and cakes at the ice cream shop. How about Friday or Saturday?"

"Let's shoot for Friday noon. That way, they'll have that fresh-baked taste on Saturday too."

Which meant rising before dawn on Friday to get everything done, but working early hours wasn't a big deal, and taking this on meant that I could pay Patsy more each week. "I love how you think. What should we start out with?"

"Surprise me."

"What about white chocolate macadamia nut, oatmeal raisin, and iced cookies? For the cakes, an ice cream cake of your choice, one Death by Chocolate Cake, and a pan of brownies."

"Sounds great. Can you start this Friday?"

"I can."

We sealed our bargain with a kiss, then Pete headed off to work. I finished up at home and decided to swing through the Post Office before depositing my earnings.

7

Major wanted a ride, so I drove my Mom's Buick. Despite its many years, this older car rode like a dream and I loved it. The owner's manual had twelve years of vehicle registrations in the front pocket, eleven with Mom's name on them. Hanging onto the car helped me feel less alone in the world, since my birth family had narrowed down to just my brother and me. I loved being able to ask Mom for advice before she got too sick. With her passing, I'd become the family matriarch.

So far, no grandchildren for her resulting from my marriage, though we'd been trying since Valentine's Day. Pete and I both wanted children, but other than an early miscarriage, I hadn't conceived. I put on a brave face, but my failure in this area worried me. Though I'd never met a challenge I couldn't overcome, this was out of my control.

Control.

That word dogged me these days, triggering misgivings where there should only be bliss. Marriage involved his, hers, and ours, and each side in that triangle supported the other. I'd married the man of my dreams, and we loved each other. If I couldn't carry a baby to term, would love be enough for Pete?

I knew couples who'd divorced when children failed to arrive naturally, and I didn't want that for us. The only help for it was to believe it would all work out, but, oh, how I wanted to be assured of that outcome.

Meanwhile, we'd become surrogate aunt and uncle for Doug's adopted children, and his daughter by blood would make her presence known in the next few weeks. So the Holloway line would continue. Maybe that birth would relieve some of the pressure and apprehension I felt.

My thoughts drifted as I passed under live oaks shaped by two hundred years of sun and wind, their branches gnarled and bent at odd angles. Some biannual azaleas bloomed as did a few early camelias, the floral fragrance mixing with the earthy forest scent and the ocean-fresh sea breeze. Ah, the smell of home!

A herd of vehicles gathered at the Post Office's overflowing parking lot. That didn't bode well. Something must've happened, and everyone headed for Gossip Central to hear the news. I took a deep centering breath, remembering my earlier misgivings. What kind of foul play had visited our fair shores?

Chapter Two

Leaving the Buick's windows down for my cat, I hurried inside the post office lobby's tight quarters. As expected, Ola Mae Reed and her sister Valerie Slade held center court by the mail drop. I squeezed around people to hear the news.

Ola Mae appeared deep into postmortem of another gruesome island tragedy, but she didn't mention any names. I asked one of Mom's bridge lady friends, "What happened?"

"Jasmine Garr died," Lizzie Collins whispered back.

Shocked, I rewound Lizzie's words in my head. Yes. She'd said Jasmine died. "Oh, no. I don't know what to say. She's in the prime of her life. Could this be a mistake?"

"No mistake. Happened yesterday, bless her heart."

"But she just won an award Saturday night." I realized how stupid that sounded as soon as the words left my mouth. An award wouldn't prevent death. An argument could be made that getting passed over for the honor provided motive for retaliation.

You're getting ahead of yourself, River. You don't even

know how she died. It could be natural causes or a snake bite or something.

"The Chicken Lady found her round about sunset yesterday," Lizzie continued. "She was long gone by then."

"How?" I asked, my curiosity demanding an answer right now.

"River Holloway, come on over here," Ola Mae boomed.

The crowd parted as people glanced over their shoulders at me. With just enough room to thread my way through, I made it to Ola Mae's side. "Yes?"

"Folks, this gal is smart as a whip. River's solved two homicide cases already, cases the Riceland County Sheriff's Office mangled. Well, we're working on getting a new sheriff in office, and I'll give a shout out to Deputy Gil Franklin right now. Everybody needs to vote for him next month if you want a change in how our county is policed. Anyway, Jasmine was a hometown gal. I knew her mom, Holly Garr, and her grandmother, Zinnia Drummond. They're good people. If anyone can figure out what happened to Jasmine, it's my friend River."

All eyes turned to me. Guess I should say something. "Thanks for the vote of confidence, Ola Mae, but this is the first I've heard about Jasmine dying. What makes you think it was foul play?"

"The coroner's assistant's second cousin is married to my mechanic's wife. She works at the office over there. Anyhow, I went in for an oil change and got the scoop. Jasmine was found in her yard, shot in the back, lying in a pool of blood. Whoever shot her left her there to die. On purpose. We can't have that on our island."

The crowd burst into acclimation until Ola Mae held

up her arms to silence everyone. "Now, now. We're gonna do what we're supposed to. We're gonna go out in pairs and keep an eagle eye out for gunmen. We're gonna keep our doors locked in the meantime and stay away from strangers."

"And eat a lot of ice cream," a man yelled from the back of the lobby.

At that point, the postal clerks came out from the back. I thought sure they'd shoo us all out because we were blocking traffic, but no, they wanted the scoop, so I heard the story all over again.

The facts of the case were few. Jasmine was killed in her yard, most likely early morning yesterday. The bullet didn't exit her body, and she bled out on the ground.

A man I didn't recognize called out, "What kind of yella-bellied snake shoots someone in the back? That's what I want to know."

The crowd buzzed with conversation.

After a minute of commotion, Ola Mae raised her arms again, and the group calmed. "Look here, we've got a plan. River's the best amateur detective this side of the Atlantic. If anyone can figure out the truth, she can. Meantime, we're all on the buddy system. Call your friends and neighbors and warn them we've got a killer on the loose."

"And go home," one of the post office workers shouted. "Nobody else can fit in here, and we're violating the fire code right now. Let's not add another incident for Ms. Holloway to investigate."

My cheeks burned with heat. Everyone expected me to work a miracle. I'd been lucky enough to solve two murder cases, sure, but I was highly motivated to solve those cases. Who was I kidding? Jasmine needed justice same as the other victims. Of course I'd ask questions about what happened to her.

The first person on my list of folks to question was the Chicken Lady, Cora Radley.

~*~

After I banked my check, I drove to Cora's place on Emmeline Drive, but her truck wasn't there, nor did she answer the door. Not a single chicken squawking anywhere. Must mean they were on a road trip. Somehow this woman trained her chickens to fly into the bed of her pickup truck so she could haul them all over the island to forage for worms and insects. She took cage-free living to a whole new level.

Which left me with a few ideas about where she might be. The cops might've run Cora in for questioning because they often suspected the person who reported a crime. If so, her truck would likely be at Jasmine's place. On the other hand, if they'd given the spry, petite woman a pass, she could be anywhere on this island with her beloved chickens.

As far as I knew, Cora was a widow with no children, only her chickens. I'd never met anyone related to her. Some folks assumed she was simple because she kept chickens, but I'd bought plenty of eggs from her, and she'd seemed fine to me. Some people preferred their own company is all. I understood that completely.

Since I was nearby, I cruised further down Emmeline Drive to Jasmine's place, but I couldn't turn down her driveway due to a cop car blocking the way. Deputy Gil Franklin and Deputy Jenny Zillo were probably collecting fingerprints and more from Jasmine's house. No chickens and no sign of Cora or her truck. I'd have to wait until it wasn't an active crime scene to do my own snooping.

I had faith in the deputies to do their jobs with the forensic evidence, but I had more faith in me talking to the right people. Of course, there was always the chance that the sheriff wouldn't rush to justice this time.

Yeah, right. The election was only a month away.

Chapter Three

Stymied with the investigation, I returned home and took inventory of my baking supplies for the Big Cookie Caper. I'd completed a bulk order with my supplier when I received a call from my friend, Rosemarie. She'd forgotten to call me for help with her rental property cleaning today. Was I available?

I had time and energy to burn, so I made lunches for both of us and headed over to the rental. The work and the retro nineties music Rosemarie favored settled my thoughts. Housecleaning wasn't glamorous, but it was an honorable profession, and there'd always be a demand for it. Rosemarie was picky about her clients, and in general, the people who rented this property were older couples with grown children, so we'd never happened upon a disaster.

My part was stripping the beds and washing all the sheets while I vacuumed and mopped the floors. Rosemarie dusted everything and deep cleaned the bathrooms and kitchens. She was fanatical about mold and mildew and did not tolerate them. People could eat off any surface in the houses she cleaned, and if she thought I'd missed a spot, she'd do an entire floor all over again.

When we finished two hours later, we sat on the back steps as was our custom. Our conversation turned to Jasmine's shooting.

"Did you hear about it on the police scanner?" I asked. "My source was the post office grapevine, so I wonder if I you might have better information."

Rosemarie bit into an egg salad sandwich and rolled her eyes in bliss. "I don't know how you make this taste so good, but I love your egg salad. It's just right."

"Duke's Mayonnaise is my secret weapon," I said. "About Jasmine, what went out on the scanner?"

"Deputy Zillo caught the call and carped about the Chicken Lady. She thinks the woman's a few chickens shy of a full coop, if you know what I mean."

Zillo dropped several notches in my good graces. "Can she defame citizens on the radio? Doesn't she worry about slander?"

"Doubt the Chicken Lady will find out. In any event, it's the truth, right?"

"No way. I go there for eggs when I can. Cora's chickens are like children to her. She has names for each of them, and she makes sure they have everything they need. If reincarnation is a thing, it would be good to come back as her pet chickens."

Rosemarie shuddered. "Doesn't she eat them?"

"No-o-o-o. She's vegetarian. She would not eat her chickens, even if she were starving. But getting back to the case, what did they say about Jasmine on the radio?"

"First off, her cat wouldn't let anybody near her. They called the dogcatcher to remove the cat, but the pound was full so Deputy Zillo took the cat to that

Happy Paws Vet Clinic. Once that happened, the coroner determined Jasmine was good and dead. Many hours' worth of dead, in fact."

"And?"

"Single entry bullet wound to her back. Bullet clipped her heart and they think it must've lodged in a rib since there's no exit wound. No gun at the scene. They're working this case as a homicide."

I mulled things over for a few bites of egg salad. Jasmine had been murdered. Who would do such a thing? "It feels so strange. I saw her at the banquet Saturday night where she won the Volunteer of the Year Award. Everyone applauded her win, and her tablemates were all smiles and hugs. I don't get it."

"Who did she sit with?" Rosemarie asked, her tone a smidge brittle.

"Linette Nelson, Milton Wainwright, and Ash Braswell."

"Hmmm. You didn't mention her cousin, Iris O'Brien."

The gunmetal gray clouds pressed down on us. "Iris? I haven't thought of her in years. Didn't she nearly smother some guy with love letters once upon a time?"

"Uh-huh. Ash Braswell. When he finally told her to get lost, she married Billy O'Brien on the rebound. Had two kids back-to-back and then found out he'd used their marriage to keep his parents from guessing his true sexual preference. She kicked him to the curb, with a healthy alimony as long as she keeps her mouth shut."

I stilled. "Wait a minute. How'd I miss all this drama? William O'Brien, the timber baron?"

"That's the guy. You never see him without his foreman. Word is they've been a couple for years."

"He's twenty years older than Iris. Why'd she marry him in the first place?"

"Did you miss the part about O'Brien being rich and Iris being on the rebound from Ash?"

Gossip wasn't my thing normally, but I was intrigued. "Holy cow. What does any of this have to do with Jasmine's homicide?"

"My police buddies have taken Iris home many a night from various hotel bars. She's trolling for a husband again, still carrying a torch for Ash apparently."

"Ash was with Jasmine on Saturday night. They sat together. Were they a couple?"

"Ash wanted to be her guy, but Jasmine didn't have time for a steady relationship. Ash wants to settle down, and they both love animals. He must've thought it was a match made in heaven."

"I believe I see where you're headed with this." I watched a male cardinal chase another bright red cardinal away until my thoughts gelled. "Iris wants Ash, but Ash wants Jasmine. Jasmine enjoyed Ash's company, but she wouldn't commit."

"That's about it."

"That's a lot. Do the cops know about all the unrequited love going on? Iris would be jealous that Ash gave his affections to Jasmine, and Ash would be angry that Jasmine wouldn't commit to him. Both had motive to kill Jasmine."

Rosemarie shrugged. "That's your department, girlfriend. Ring up that cop that always orbits in your vicinity, Bill something."

"Deputy Gil Franklin. He likes my cooking."

"You just keep on believing that."

I didn't like the turn this conversation had taken. "You're way off-base. He's never indicated a romantic interest."

"Not much point when you and Pete are so obviously in love and happily married. Plus Pete wouldn't take kindly to any male poaching on his territory. He's had his eye on you since third grade."

"It's mutual. I fell in love with him at the same time."

"Lucky ducks. The rest of us flail around the dating pond and hope to survive the gators and snakes."

The tension eased from my shoulders. "You'll find someone, Rosemarie."

"Thought I'd found somebody twice, but both choices were of the snake and gator persuasion."

"Hang in there. Your prince will come."

"Sure. Tell me about Operation Cookie at the ice cream place."

I collected our trash. "How do you know about that?"

"I helped Pete decide on a cookie display case when I dropped in for ice cream. He wanted a woman's opinion."

"Wow. He sure moves fast. I only decided to provide cookies for him today. Did you have ice cream for breakfast?"

"No. It was Saturday afternoon. My sister visited the island, and ice cream's her thing. He must've been hoping you'd agree."

"Maybe. He's a strategic planner, and it's a good thing because I hadn't even considered product presentation in his shop."

"I've never had a thing for Pete, but he's the standard by which judged all my dates: he's good looking, caring, considerate, respectful, hardworking, and has a killer smile."

My natural inclination upon hearing this was to gape like a beached fish, however, I did no such thing. Mom would've been proud of my iron jaw. "I had no idea."

"Not every day I can stump you. Have to do it now before you're too busy cooking to give me the time of day."

"That'll never happen."

Chapter Four

On Tuesday morning, I decided to try the Chicken Lady, Cora Radley, again. I wanted to talk with her, but I also needed two dozen more eggs for all the baking I planned to do on Friday.

When I arrived at her place, her truck was parked on the lawn. I hoped that meant she was home. I knocked on the door and waited. Didn't hear anything.

I knocked harder and called out, "Cora, it's River Holloway. I came to buy eggs."

Inside I heard a noise then footfalls coming toward the door. I repeated my name and intent. The lock disengaged, and the door swung partway open.

Cora looked like she hadn't slept a wink, and she had the shakes. Her thin hair was a scraggly mess, her eyes looked red, and her stomach growled before she said, "River."

It took all of a single heartbeat to decide to waltz into her house and fix this woman a meal. Finding Jasmine's body must've traumatized her. I'd been rattled the time I'd found someone I knew who'd been murdered.

"Cora let me help you," I said, guiding her by the

21

shoulders inside her house. Her normally strong body trembled under my hand. "Gracious. I don't know what's wrong, but we can fix it. Let's get you a blanket and something to eat."

I grabbed a crocheted afghan from the padded rocker, wrapped it around her shoulders, and propelled her to the kitchen. My guess was that whatever frightened her happened recently. Everything looked tidy throughout the small cottage, so no one had ransacked her place. Chicken and rooster figures occupied every tabletop and shelf. They were of wood, metal, ceramic, and several kinds of plastic, some fixed up true to life, some more abstract.

"I don't deserve comfort because I'm a bad chicken mother. Something ate my Birdie Sue, and I can't stop thinking about it." She opened her clenched left fist to reveal three tiny feathers. "This is all that's left of her. A few feathers. I raised her from a chick."

She broke down in tears, and I hugged her close. Poor woman. She'd had too many shocks at once. She certainly needed comforting, and I was glad to provide it. Gradually her tears subsided, and the shivering ceased. I settled her in a kitchen chair, with the afghan tucked around her narrow shoulders, and squatted beside her chair.

I took her hand. "I'm sorry this happened. I know those chickens are your world."

"They's like family to me. I done buried all my kinfolk, and the chickens are good company."

"Islanders care about you. I want to help. What can I fix you for breakfast? You like coffee or tea?"

"Iced milk, buttered toast, and an apple is what I usually eat."

"Coming right up." The toaster and the bread sat on the counter, right beside a small basket of pretty red apples. I started the toast, sliced an apple, and prepared her milk.

I put the glass of ice milk on her placemat. "My mother liked milk this way. She claimed it tasted better really cold."

"Your mom was one smart cookie. She gave me my first rooster figurine. Once word got out that I liked it, everybody and their brother started giving me those things. I didn't mind. People say chickens bring you good luck, and that certainly seemed true for me. I never minded being called the Chicken Lady either, but here lately I've been so lonely. Folks don't come around for eggs much anymore. Easier for them to go to the store and get all their groceries at the same time."

The toast popped up. I took the top off the chicken-shaped butter dish and slathered her toast with butter. Cora dove into the food, eating voraciously like my cat Major. I fixed myself a glass of water from the tap and sat with her.

When she pushed back from her plate, her color looked better. "That was good eatin'. You oughta be a caterer or something."

I smiled at her, enjoying the fresh breeze wafting through the open windows. "Glad you're feeling better. I'm concerned for you, Cora. Do you have someone who checks on you on a regular basis? A friend or a relative?"

"Nope." She pursed her lips. "Don't want anybody's nose in my business. I been taking care of myself for a long time, and I'm not one to run to a doctor for every scratch. I had a setback, that's all. Losing Birdie Sue and finding Doc Jasmine dead in her yard were two bitter reality pills to swallow."

I interlaced my fingers and gentled my voice. "Do you need to talk to a professional about your feelings?"

She shook her head real fast, followed by a teeth-rattling shudder. "Nope. Ain't no head doc gonna lock me up, no way, no how."

"Sorry, I meant no offense. You've been through so much lately. I wanted to make sure you had coping strategies to process what happened. I can listen and offer insights, but I'm no doctor."

"You lost your mom, so you know what it's like when there's a hole in your heart." A stormy expression flashed across her face. "I know what to do. Just put one foot in front of the other and keep going. The hurt burrowed in yesterday after the cops questioned me. I couldn't get away from it, so I tried to go to bed. Only every time I closed my eyes, I saw her. Got to where I walked the floors all night long so I wouldn't go to sleep."

I nodded, compassion welling for this plucky woman who faced life's trials alone. "I know it's hard. My mother's death was a blessing, but the grief didn't hit me like a tsunami. I grieved all the months and weeks she lost ground. Life has challenges, but a slow death is heartless."

"You're a good person, River, and I admire your strength," Cora said, her voice cracking. "I hope you find who hurt Doc Jasmine. She didn't deserve a bullet in the back." Her shoulders rose and fell as she sighed. "Whoever shot her had a dog because I saw dog prints around her body."

I filed the dog-print tidbit away. "I'll do my best, and

I came here hoping you could tell me more about your neighbor."

"She loved animals and her plants. Her searches for *Franklinia alatamaha* were epic. On her days off, she'd pack up and search wetland or forests for the plant. She never worried about rabid foxes, stray gators, or poisonous snakes. I know she had all kinds of training to be a vet, but that woman could melt into a forest like an army commando."

An odd trait, for sure. "I didn't realize she searched in stealth mode. I wonder if she was in the wrong place at the wrong time."

"Could be." Cora trailed off for a moment, her fingers worrying with the afghan's tassels. "What you reckon will happen to her cat?"

"I heard they took her kitty to the Happy Paws Vet Clinic. Maybe somebody will adopt her."

"It's an older calico named Ivy. They tell me kittens get adopted but cats aren't as adoptable. Plus this one's got personality quirks. I can't take it because it chases my chickens. You could adopt her."

I shook my head. "I've already got a cat with personality quirks. Good chance they wouldn't get along."

Her eyes bored into mine. "Maybe you could foster Ivy, you know, take her out on a trial run."

"Two cats. Having one cat doesn't imply crazy cat lady but having two is a step closer."

"Wouldja think about it? I hate for any animal to be cooped up. Speaking of which, I thought those deputies would lock me up. They questioned me for hours because I found my friend lying on the ground." She fixed me with a watery gaze. "What if they come back?

What'll I do?"

"If they don't charge you with a crime, they can't hold you at the station. Stand up and walk out."

The corners of her mouth turned up. "Just like that?"

I nodded. "Just like that."

"You're all right, River. Now, let's see. You said something about needing eggs."

I nodded. "I'm starting a new venture with my husband, baking cookies and cakes one day a week for Island Creamery. I need more eggs to fill that order. If all goes well, I could place a standing weekly egg order with you."

Cora pointed toward her refrigerator covered in rooster magnets. "I've got three dozen now. Take as many as you like."

"I need two dozen. Will that leave you with enough for your regular customers?"

"Yeah. There's more in the laying boxes. Haven't collected eggs since Monday. But the eggs keep just fine. Without washing them, mine'll keep three weeks on the counter at room temperature. Remember to wash these eggs before using. Fresh eggs are different that way."

"I remember." I stood, dug in my pocket for egg money, and handed her the correct amount.

She swatted my cash away. "Your money's no good here. What you did for me today meant more than you'll ever know. How 'bout if you bring me some of your cookies next time? I can't remember when I last had cookies baked from scratch."

"Will do." Touched by her generosity, I thanked her and handed her a business card. "Call me anytime, okay? We islanders have to look out for each other."

"Sure."

I walked down the narrow walkway flanked with metal chicken sculptures. Wonder what the living chickens thought about these decorations?

It felt good to help Cora, and I'd learned something new about Jasmine. Why did she do her plant searching in a secretive manner? Nobody liked being spied on or having trespassers on their property, especially if they were up to no good. If someone ill-willed discovered Jasmine's presence, that could be a motive for murder.

Only, how did the dog prints around Jasmine's body fit in?

Chapter Five

Jasmine Garr's occupation involved taking care of cats and dogs. The logical place to ask if she ever had a dog or took one home for rehab would be her place of work. Since she substituted at vet clinics all over, those inquiries could take a while.

How discouraging. Were the deputies calling every vet clinic to find out where she'd recently worked? Or maybe they found her work schedule. I didn't have the luxury of viewing Jasmine's electronic calendar or searching her place for a paper one, if she kept track of appointments that way.

All wasn't lost. I knew a vet who must be friends with Jasmine as they'd seemed friendly at the banquet. With that realization, I pointed my van in the direction of Happy Paws Vet Clinic where Dr. Linette Nelson worked.

Every parking space in the clinic's lot held a vehicle. One patron walked a very large dog on the lawn. I pulled into the real estate company lot beside the clinic and parked in an out-of-the-way location.

With so many clients waiting, Linette would not have

time to see me, but I'd come this far. I may as well continue. Maybe all these people were here for an obedience class.

Shouldering my purse, I made my way to the main entrance. Chaos reigned in the waiting room. Leashed dogs barked, cats in crates hissed, people talked loudly. It smelled like wet dog and cat urine. Two people stood in line at the vacant receptionist desk. Good gracious. What a mess.

Tracie Barthole, a beauty stylist who used to do Mom's hair, stood last in line. "What's going on in here?" I asked.

"Hey, River," Tracie managed over the commotion. "Apparently the receptionist called in sick. They booked appointments for two vets, but the regular vet had hernia surgery and Dr. Garr died, so they're shorthanded today."

"I came by to speak to the vet about Jasmine Garr, but it looks like a lost cause."

"Yeah. The people who're seated said Dr. Nelson checked them in. I don't want to sit down with my kitty until I get checked in, otherwise I might lose my place in line."

"Hmm. I don't have any place to be this afternoon. Wonder if I could help?"

"If you could check me in, that'd be great," Tracie said. "I spend enough time on my feet as it is."

I glanced over the receptionist's counter. "How do they do it here? Is it computerized or a manual process?"

"On the computer."

"It's probably password protected." My hopes plummeted. "I can't help with that, but I can make a paper list of those of you in line. That would at least allow you guys to sit down."

"Please do that," the man in front of Tracie said. "I've been standing here fifteen minutes for flea medicine."

It was risky to insert myself into an employee position, but what harm would there be in taking a few names?

So, I edged around the desk and searched for a piece of paper. Nothing in the desk but two empty clipboards, so I took a blank page from the printer's paper tray. I drew a few columns and lines across the page and headed the columns with name, time of arrival, pet's name, and notes. Securing that page and a pen to a clipboard, I set that on the counter.

"If y'all sign in, you can have a seat," I said.

Both people standing in line eagerly signed in. As Tracie was filling in her information the phone rang. "Aren't you going to get that?" she asked.

"I shouldn't. I've probably overstepped already."

"Go for it, River," Tracie said. "Dr. Nelson needs a helper today."

"You're right." I picked up the phone. "Happy Paws Vet Clinic, how may I help you?"

"Thank goodness, somebody picked up," a man said, wheezing for breath. "This is John Brennan. I've been calling all afternoon trying to cancel my appointment. I'm too sick to bring Pumpkin in for his check-up today. I need to reschedule."

"I'm not an employee, Mr. Brennan," I said, introducing myself. "The clinic is short-staffed today. I can take the message you're canceling today's appointment, but please call back another day to reschedule. I don't have access to the appointment calendar."

"All right. I'll do that."

The call ended, and I grabbed another sheet of paper from the printer and wrote the message. A woman with a crated cat came out of an exam room, followed by Dr. Nelson.

The vet paused and blinked when she recognized me. "Ms. Holloway. What are you doing here?"

"I came to talk to you, saw the overflow crowd, and thought I could help. I hope you don't mind. I've made a list of people who were standing at the desk when I arrived, and I took a phone message for you."

"Great. I need another set of hands around here today." The vet bustled around me and unlocked the computer screen with a password to check the client out. It didn't take long. "My receptionist had root canal surgery complications, and my vet tech's kid came down with strep from preschool. Can you stay and handle the chaos out here?"

"I can try, but I don't know your software. However, at a glance it looks like the program they have at the beauty shop. Maybe Tracie Barthole knows how to work this software."

"Good idea." She waved Tracie over and explained the situation. "Can you lend a hand for the next two hours?"

"That's how long until my appointment?" Tracie asked, setting her animal crate near the counter.

"Afraid so, unless you'd like to reschedule," Dr. Nelson said.

"No. I don't want to get behind on her shots. Let me take a look at your software. Yep. Looks like what we have at Creative Cuts. I can handle this end, but make sure I have a password in case the screen times out."

Dr. Nelson created a login and a password for Tracie. "Your appointment will be on the house."

"Super," Tracie said, settling in her chair.

"If any of them want to reschedule, book them at least a week out. And anybody who's here for any of the products we sell, go ahead and process them."

Dr. Nelson turned to me. "If you can stay until I clear out these appointments, I'll have a free moment."

"Sure. I can help with the appointments if you like."

Dr. Nelson squinted at me. "I know you cook like a dream. How are you with dogs and cats?"

"I'm fine with them. I have a cat now, and I've always liked dogs."

"Good answer. I hereby deputize you as my extra set of hands in the exam room. Come on back, and I'll get you a lab coat."

What a relief to leave that noisy lobby. I donned the lab coat she offered and followed the vet into the empty exam room. She showed me how to sanitize the exam table and where to put the used supplies, with instructions to join her in the next room when I was finished cleaning the empty room.

The afternoon passed in a flurry of cats and dogs and shots. I stepped and fetched and cleaned, including wiping up a few pet accidents. We worked out a nice rhythm with Tracie, once I knew to press the call light to show the room was ready for the next pet.

After we gave Tracie's cat her shots, Tracie offered to stay until closing. I noticed the packed lobby seemed tranquil when I brought out some medicine for a client's pet. Much later, after Tracie out-processed the person, I asked about the peaceful atmosphere. "How'd you do it?"

"Simple. I reminded people that cats are on the left side of the room, dogs the right."

"Makes sense. You're a natural at this."

"So are you. People say their appointments went super smooth."

"I have another career," I reminded her.

She grinned. "So do I."

The last patient departed, and Dr. Nelson turned to me. "One more thing before I'm free to talk with you. We need to feed the in-house animals. I'll take the dogs, and you can do the cats. Check the cage cards for the amount per cat."

The last cat hissed at me. I glanced at the name on the card, Ivy, and then I noticed the cat's calico coat. I turned to Dr. Nelson and asked, "Is this Dr. Garr's cat?"

She finished the dogs on her side of the pet hospital area. "It is, though I can't keep her indefinitely. This a recovery area for surgery or sick animals. We're not a kennel, but the shelter was full when Ivy needed a place to stay."

"Why's she afraid of me?"

"She's afraid of everybody but Jasmine. Someone dropped off a batch of kittens here about eight years ago. We offered the free kittens to our customers. All of them went except for Ivy who liked to hide behind the ivy plant we used to have. Jasmine had a big heart and a truckload of patience and took the frightened kitten. Now she's homeless again." She eyed me speculatively. "Say, you're good with pets. If you take Ivy, I'll comp you the cost of her next routine appointment."

"My outdoor cat Major has personality quirks and skittish behavior. It took weeks for him to trust me.

Adding another cat to the mix might be a very bad idea."

"Or a great idea. They could be companions for each other."

"Let me talk it over with my husband."

Dr. Nelson reached over and wrote my name on Ivy's card. "Wait," I protested. "I said I'd think about it."

"You think all you like. That cat is yours. Turn around slowly."

I did and the cat had moved to the front of the cage and regarded me steadily. "Huh."

"You are a cat whisperer. I thought as much when we didn't have trouble with Mr. Green's Maine Coon cat or Ms. McMurphy's Siamese. You ever want a job here, you got it."

Indecision and pride whirled around each other in a silent dance. I wanted to help Ivy, but right now I'd committed to helping find out who killed Jasmine. Focus had never been more important.

"Thanks but no thanks," I said. "I stay busy with my catering company most of the time. I came to talk with you about Jasmine. Would you share your thoughts with me, Dr. Nelson?"

"Please call me Linette, and yes I'll tell you anything you want to know after the way you pitched in here today. I'm happy to pay you or comp your other kitty a routine healthcare visit."

"I'll take the visit comp, and thanks. About Jasmine?"

"She was top of her class in vet school but taking care of her mom put her behind the curve with establishing a private practice. Then once she started being a supply vet and her mother paid off her school loans, she decided having irregular hours and a flexible schedule more than made up for the lower pay. Tell you the truth, I envied her freedom."

"Did she have any enemies?"

"Not that I know of. People and pets loved her."

"Did she own a dog?"

"Just Ivy. The two of them suited each other. Both liked keeping their own company."

"What about boyfriends? Did Jasmine break up with anyone recently?"

"She never chatted about her personal life. Mostly, she talked about plants and Ivy."

Rats. The only thing I had to show for my afternoon was the possibility of adopting another skittish kitty. "What about men who wanted to date her? I saw Ash Braswell and Milton Wainwright hug her after she won the award."

"Ash and Jasmine frequently worked together." Linette gathered an armload of file folders. "Because she wasn't tied to clinic hours all the time, she freelanced on some of his wild animal cases. In my opinion, Ash wanted to move out of the friends category with Jasmine. Something about the way he looked at her."

I kept my expression bland, but inside I silently cheered. Confirmation of the unrequited love motive. "I see. What about Milton? He have a thing for her too?"

"My gut says no. Milton is all about whatever deal he's working. He had a spaniel for about a year, said he inherited the dog from an aunt. He brought the dog here for a few visits, but the dog had poor manners and a ton of energy. They weren't a good fit, and then we didn't see him anymore. I assumed he found another home for that dog."

"Oh." The exclamation slipped out in an unguarded moment. If Milton still had that dog, he could be the killer. "How large was the spaniel?"

"Probably weighed sixty pounds."

I didn't know much about pawprints, but surely a medium sized heavy dog would have deep mid-sized prints. I filed that away.

"Thanks, that's all very helpful. Anything else you remember about Jasmine?"

"She had a YouTube channel."

"Wow. What did she talk about?"

"Some were vids about pet care but most were about her search for that plant."

"The *Franklinia alatamaha*."

"Yes. Her favorite topic."

Her sharp tone caught my ear. "You didn't approve?"

"I wished she'd stuck to pet care."

An odd response. "Why?"

"Because her posts are popular. Now there's a bunch of people tromping around in the woods searching for a plant that's extinct in the wild. They're wasting their time."

Chapter Six

As I baked a creamy spinach and mushroom lasagna dinner, I mulled over Linette's statement that Jasmine's videos incited others to search for that rare plant. Why did it upset Linette that people were on a wild goose chase?

Pete stuck his head in the kitchen. "They're here."

My brother, Doug, and his pregnant wife, Viv, and Viv's niece and nephew they were adopting, joined us for dinner. I'd tried making homemade chicken nuggets for three year old Harry and nine month old Zoey before, but they would only eat a certain brand from the freezer case. I'd caved to avoid the fuss they made, though it went against the grain to serve prepared food to anyone in my household.

Harry thought the world was his playpen, while baby Zoey wanted to taste everything. Ever since the kids started visiting a few months ago, I'd moved every cleaning supply I owned to lofty heights. I'd also put away fragile items, covered electrical plugs, and filled a toy bin with classic toys for them to play with. Even so, for an evening here, Doug carried in a highchair, a diaper bag, and a fat bag of toys.

Pete lifted Harry and tossed him in the air a few times, much to his delight. We cooed over little Zoey until she squirmed to get down. In the moment it took to hug Doug and Viv, Zoey found the cat's water dish, flipped the bowl, and smacked her hands in the puddle happily. The cat had been in and out lately, more out than in if truth be told, but I'd shown him the door today on purpose. As shy as Major was around adults, he would not do well with these noisy and active kiddos.

Viv picked up her new daughter and rinsed her hands in the sink. "These kids have so much energy. If only they could share it with me."

Harry and Zoey's parents were unable to care for them. In fact, a few months back, their mom nearly added me to her murder list and their dad, Viv's brother Darry, had a mental breakdown after being shanghaied for months. Hence Viv and my brother had custody of her brother's kids.

"Elevate your feet," I said. "That's what I always do after a big catering job."

"I should help you finish making dinner," Viv said. "It smells amazing, by the way."

"Please, sit. I got this. Only a few more minutes in the oven for the lasagna. I hope this tomato-free recipe doesn't give you indigestion."

"Oh the joys of pregnancy. Seems like I have new minor issues every day. I'm sure you don't want to hear about my swollen ankles or bathroom woes. Tell me about your day."

I brushed the chopped celery off the cutting board into the salad bowl. "I visited a vet clinic where Jasmine Garr had worked and ended up acting as a vet tech for nearly three hours." I moved the salad fixings to the center island so I could chop veggies and face Viv.

"Sit for a bit, hon, and y'all have a visit," Doug said, reaching for Zoey. "Pete and I will take the kids to inspect the new shower."

Viv relinquished the baby and sat with a big sigh, rubbing her rounded belly. "I'm glad to have the night off from cooking, though I readily admit most nights Doug and I eat chicken nuggets with the kids. It's easier to cook one meal. But enough about us. Tell me about Jasmine."

"According to Cora Radley and Linette Nelson, many of Jasmine's searches for the *Franklinia alatamaha* were covert, suggesting she may have trespassed. That makes me wonder if she saw something she shouldn't. Jasmine had a YouTube channel of podcasts, but I haven't had time to view them."

"I can help you watch podcasts. I have random bits of time here and there when the kids are playing or asleep and I have my feet up. Should I start at the beginning?"

"I don't know how many there are. Use your best judgement. When I get time, I plan to start at the most recent video and work backward."

"Will do, and I'm glad to be helping. What'd the vet tell you?"

I paused my herb mincing. "What makes you think she revealed anything?"

"Your superpower is putting people at ease so they share information freely. I know she told you something."

"You make me sound nefarious." The thought made me laugh. "As it happens, Jasmine's cousin, Iris O'Brien, had a crush on Ash years ago, only he wasn't interested.

She married someone else but is single now and hankering after Ash again. Meanwhile, Ash wanted to date Jasmine. Perhaps Iris viewed Jasmine as competition for Ash's affections."

Viv wrinkled her nose as if she smelled a dirty diaper. "Sounds like third grade do-you-like-me-I-like-you notes passed in class."

I finished the herbs, added my light vinaigrette dressing, and tossed the salad. "Maybe, but Ash sat beside Jasmine at the awards banquet. I thought he was her date for the occasion."

"She purposefully led him on?"

Doug and Pete wandered back into the kitchen with the kids in tow. "Sounds like we missed the juicy bits," Doug said. "Do tell."

I waved him toward the table. "Perfect timing. The children's plates are ready, and I'm about to serve our plates."

Viv repeated a kid-friendly version of our conversation, while Doug got the kids situated with food and I plated the lasagna and tossed salad for us, nuggets and fries for the kids. Pete helped with drinks and soon we were all eating.

"Funny you should mention Iris O'Brien," Doug said. "I saw her in the hardware store this morning buying locks. She said the family homestead was hers now that Jasmine had passed."

"Iris inherited the property?" I asked. "That could be a motive, two motives if you count the unrequited love scenario."

Little Harry swallowed a sip of milk. "What's a motif?"

Little pitcher ears. Huh. I caught Doug's eye with a

glance I hope broadcasted the word help.

"It's why you do something," Doug said. "For instance, you pick up a nugget because you want to eat it."

"Cool," Harry said, filling his mouth with a nugget.

Crisis averted, we cycled through topics of weather, work, and my cookie and cake commitment to Island Creamery.

"Here's to your new endeavor. May you find much success." Viv raised her water glass to me as she made a toast. Each of us raised a glass, even little Harry and said, "Hear, hear."

"If I didn't know being too full would cause indigestion," Viv continued, "I'd get seconds and thirds of this lasagna. Thank you for making it for us. It's delish."

"No digestive worries on my end about seconds," Doug said, rising for more. I was heartened to see him also select more salad.

Soon we were tidying up, and Little Harry slipped away from Doug. The boy ran toward the kitchen table, tripped over his feet, and went down hard. We rushed over, but the tyke was inconsolable for a few minutes. His sister joined in the crying. Luckily, I had matching ice packs and popsicles that helped them both settle.

"We need to get these two home and start our bedtime ritual," Viv said, reaching for Zoey. Doug scooped up Harry. After a flurry of goodbyes, Pete and I shared a glance.

"That was intense." Pete rubbed the back of his neck. "How many children are we planning to have?"

"It's different when it's your own kids. Those little ones had a rough start. An absentee dad, a murderess of a mom, and now Viv and Doug are learning parenting the old-fashioned way. Zoey did fine tonight until Harry lost it. And Harry didn't once run his trucks over the furniture or walls. He only played trucks on the floor. The kids are learning too."

"You knew what to do when trouble happened."

"All those teenage years of babysitting finally paid off. Plus I'm getting a lot of on the job training."

Chapter Seven

I began baking Friday morning long before the sun rose, starting with a batch of devil's food cake in two eight-inch pie pans. Next, I rolled out two bowls of cookie dough that I'd prepared last night. I dotted the round cookie tops with white chocolate and chunks of macadamia nuts and popped those bad boys in another oven.

Meanwhile the cake timer rang. As those layers cooled, I slightly thawed the cookies and cream ice cream tub from the Island Creamery began mixing up my Death by Chocolate cake. The pile of bowls, measuring utensils, and dirty pans mounted. Not my usual "clean as you go" M.O., but the time pressure to get everything freshly made urged me to keep cooking. The cake went in the oven, and I made a batch of fudge sauce.

The sky had completely pinked up by the time Pete popped over. "Smells good," he said, handing me a big mug of coffee and an egg omelet rolled in a wrap.

I thanked him and wolfed down the food. "I'm on schedule. Next time, I'll hire someone to help get all this prepared. It's a lot for me to do in one day."

"People will love everything you make. I'm 100 percent certain of that."

"I sure hope so."

"Gotta run," he said with a quick glance at his watch. "See you at noon."

Once the fudge sauce got to the soft ball stage, I cut the heat and let the mixture cool. The rich aroma in the air assured me of success. This would be the best fudge sauce ever. I smushed chocolate cookies to go in the fudge sauce and set them aside.

I pulled sugar cookie dough I'd premixed yesterday out of the fridge to warm slightly. I couldn't take the tower of dirty dishes another second and washed everything I'd used. Still had a batch of oatmeal raisin cookies and leaf-shaped sugar cookies to make. A check of the dough assured me it was ready to roll. I liked these to be a little on the thick side, so I carefully rolled without kneading the dough too much. Didn't want to make them tough.

And so it went for three more hours. Though the production stage was intense, so was my satisfaction at seeing everything checked off my to-do list. I walked home, showered, and dressed in a Holloway Catering polo and nice pants. I wanted Pete's staff to have a good impression of me.

A little after eleven, I loaded the van, my black cat Major glaring at me with accusing eyes. "Sorry, no cats allowed in the van. You had breakfast already, and we'll have cuddle time after this delivery."

I drove to the service entrance of the Creamery, and Pete came out to help me with the cart. I kept both hands on the ice cream cake pedestal stand. It looked so delicious, that's what I wanted for lunch.

Two of Pete's ice cream scoopers met us in the tiny kitchen, and each one picked up a batch of cookies. They slotted each cookie on edge in gleaming trays lined with lacy paper. "Nice trays," I said.

"Wait'll you see the new display case," Jonas said, waving me forward. "It's awesome."

Pete signaled for me to wait. "A word, please."

"What's going on?" I asked.

"One more moment." He smoothed a stray hair behind my ears. "Congratulations on your first successful gig at the Creamery."

"You're that sure?"

Pete nodded and ushered me forward, hand at my back, so that when I stepped through the swinging doors, I couldn't retreat as cameras flashed and people clapped.

I blinked in surprise. "What's all this?"

"The local deejay agreed to do a remote broadcast from here on the condition that he get the first slice of ice cream cake. Everyone else turned out to support you and buy cookies."

"Wow." I kept moving toward the counter, thanking the heavens I'd showered and dressed nicely. I recognized Radio Steve, though I'd never met him before. He held a microphone on the other side of the counter and spoke to the crowd. Then he faced us.

"I get the first piece," Radio Steve crowed. "I can't remember when I last had homemade ice cream cake. I think my grandmother made it for my sixth birthday party. Will you do the honors, River Holloway?"

I beamed. "Sure."

A man with a serious camera snapped photos of me

cutting the cake and serving it to the announcer.

Steve ate a bite of the Cookies and Cream Cake and his eyes rolled up in bliss. "This is so awesome, y'all. I'm telling you right now, better come to Island Creamery before this ice cream cake is gone. This is amazing. I adore it."

People formed a line through the shop and outside its open doors. Pete guided me from behind the counter so he and Jonas could handle the rush of orders and giggly Francine could ring up the purchases.

I spoke to people I knew, and several strangers asked for my business card, which I immediately supplied. It felt like a dream, as if I were living someone else's life. Then Radio Steve waved me over.

"I've cut to an ad spot," he said. "Would you talk with me on-air?"

Caught up in the glow of success I said yes. His sound guy hooked me up with a portable microphone. As we got settled behind a cozy café table, Francine snapped a cell phone pic and Pete directed her to post it to all the shop's social media accounts.

Radio Steve, to his credit, opened with questions about my new collaboration with Island Creamery and asked another question about Holloway Catering. I did a great job since I knew the answers. I kept the smiles going and the guy with the big camera snapped a few more photos.

"As a lifelong resident, are you alarmed by the wave of crime on Shell Island?" Radio Steve asked.

Blindsided, I sidestepped the question. "I'm unaware of any crime wave."

"Surely you heard about the Jasmine Garr homicide. It was in the paper."

"I read about it, same as everybody else."

Radio Steve gave me a fake smile. I'm sure he thought it was encouraging. It frightened the heck out of me. Whatever was coming next would not be good.

"Those of us in the know are aware of your crime consulting in Estelle Bolz and Curtis Marlin's untimely deaths."

Stunned, I said the first thing that came to mind. "We're here today to talk about the Holloway Catering cookies and cakes now available at Island Creamery."

He went on as if I hadn't spoken. "They kept your name out of the papers, but I'm sure you were behind that crooked deputy going down."

I rose. "This is really inappropriate."

He put a hand on my arm. "Are you investigating Jasmine's death?"

I shook it off and glared at the man. "The police are investigating her death. I'm a caterer."

Pete rushed over. "Is there a problem?"

I tugged off the mike. "Yeah. There's a problem, and his name is Backstabbing Steve."

"Don't leave," Pete said. "Please wait for me in the back while I handle this."

I nodded and hurried behind the counter and through the swinging doors. I wanted to throttle Radio Steve. He'd hit me with off-topic questions about an active police investigation. Deputy Franklin would be as upset as I was.

"What do you think you're doing?" Pete said, his booming voice carrying all the way to the back room. "You're here to promote the Holloway Catering desserts now available on Fridays at Island Creamery."

"You wanted publicity, and I handed it to you on a

silver platter," Radio Steve said, matching his volume. "River bakes like a dream, but we need her on the case. People are worried because we've had three homicides this year. What are the cops doing to protect us?"

"That's not for me to say," Pete said. "Show's over. Pack up and leave. If you're not out of here in five minutes, I'm calling the cops."

Radio Steve snickered. "Good luck with that."

Pete joined me in the back room. "Sorry about that. I had no idea he would promote anything but your delicious cakes and cookies."

I'd had a few minutes to calm down as I paced the floor. "I never thought my talent for finding things would lead to homicide investigations. I never asked for that. All I've ever tried to do is to help people. That man ambushed me and made it sound like I was smarter than the cops. It isn't true. I respect them. I'm not a trained investigator."

"Deputy Franklin knows that, though we're still stuck with Sheriff Vargas until the election is over."

"Do you think they'll hear about the show?"

"Most definitely."

Chapter Eight

"I need a lift to the funeral," Cora said when she called Saturday morning.

"Okay," I replied, stepping into black heels to finish dressing. "Happy to do it. What time?"

"Soon's you can get here. My biddies already had a good walkabout, and I can slip away without them following if you come before they catch a second wind. If I crank the truck, every chicken will go ballistic."

"See you in ten minutes."

Mom's old Buick would be a more comfortable ride for my senior passenger. When I went outside, Major stood on the hood of the Buick, confirming my choice of transportation.

"How do you know when I'm taking this car?" I opened the door and rolled down the windows. Major jumped into the backseat and stared straight ahead.

"All right, I get it." I drove through the congested part of the island and then out toward the old church. I turned on Emmeline Drive where the Chicken Lady lived. Major sniffed the air, and I swear he nodded his approval. Named for an old steamer boat that plied

49

these waters a hundred years ago, this landlocked road only served two residences.

Cora waited at her mailbox in a dark burgundy dress that hit below her knees and dark pumps. I nearly dropped my teeth at her hair being pinned up tidy and neat.

I pulled up beside her and said, "I'll catch the door for you."

"Thank you kindly, young lady." She sat beside me in a cloud of lavender fragrance and glanced in the back. "Mighty fine kitty you got there. Thought anymore about getting Jasmine's cat out of lockup?"

"I keep forgetting to talk to Pete about it. We've been busy with the launch of my cookies and cakes at the ice cream shop yesterday."

"That's good news about your business, but, just so you know, I've got a second sense about animals. You're the person Ivy needs. And your kitty is lonely."

"How can you tell what Major needs?"

"He's riding around in a car with you instead of catting around with a girlfriend. It's obvious once you think about it."

So obvious I hadn't considered it. Was that what Major's car rides had been about? Desperation to stave off feline loneliness? Guilt clawed at me. "I'll think about adopting Ivy."

~*~

I dropped Cora at the door and parked. This was my third non-family funeral this year, and they all seemed much too close in time to Mom's funeral ten months ago. It was hard to say goodbye but I finally felt better about Mom's eternal rest and how my brother and I pulled together afterward.

I hurried inside to join Cora. She sat across the aisle and several rows back from the family. Ash Braswell wept openly in the second row. Jasmine's cousin Iris O'Brien sat on the front row with real estate broker Milton Wainwright, his arm around her shoulders. A sneeze wouldn't have passed between them.

My curiosity sparked. Not a week ago, at the awards banquet, Milton fawned the same way over Jasmine, whose ashes rested in a patterned red and black urn on the dais. Now Milton appeared to be glued to Iris. If his motives were romantic, then he was impossibly fickle. If his motives were mercenary, he was the lowest snake on the planet.

I scanned the crowded sanctuary for Jasmine's vet friend, Linette Nelson. She wasn't here. "Must be working," I mumbled to myself.

"What's that?" Cora asked in a distracted voice.

"I thought Linette Nelson was Jasmine's friend, but I don't see her. I assumed she'd be here."

The sets of stained glass windows throughout the church yielded light rays in bold shades of red and blue, while overhead pendant lights added a soft glow. Golden tapestries provided the altar backdrop, and red carpet lined the tiled aisle and muted the sound of footsteps. Hauntingly poignant music poured from the organ, and I allowed the notes to fill me.

A man leaned in behind me and spoke softly, disturbing my peaceful reverie. "I need to talk to you after the funeral," he said.

Uh-oh. Deputy Franklin. I managed a half-smile. "Sure."

I once more tried to Zen-out to the flowing music, but the Chicken Lady's fidgeting disturbed me. "What's wrong?" I whispered.

"Don't know exactly, but I sure hope it isn't my chickens. I didn't feel antsy before. Only hit me just now."

I wasn't expecting that answer. "Do you get feelings like this often?"

She didn't answer as she visually scanned the room, so I repeated the question, leaning closer to her ear to speak.

"More often than I like," she said, twisting further around in her seat. "There it is. That white-haired man in the back with a yellow tie. Soon as he walked in here the air roiled. Who is he?"

Trying to be less obvious than Cora's twisting and turning, I glanced over my shoulder, thankful for the neck stretches I did every now and then. The only white-haired man with a yellow tie was a shark of a lawyer. I turned back around to confide in Cora. "That's Robert Crider, the lead attorney in Crider, Malloy, and Quaid."

The Chicken Lady nodded. "Heard of him. Too pricey for my blood. You reckon he's the estate lawyer?"

"Could be."

"Jasmine wasn't rich. Wonder how come she got such a big gun to read her cousin the riot act."

"You think the will reading won't go well?"

"I guarantee you it won't. Iris and Jasmine were oil and vinegar."

The music swelled, and we were invited to stand and sing. Mumble was more like it, but I tried to sing the familiar hymn. The priest's homily about a life well spent made me hope that someday someone would say that about me.

Afterward, we headed to the Parish House. On the covered walkway connecting the two buildings, I felt a tap on my shoulder. I glanced over to see Deputy Franklin. "You go on ahead, Cora. I'll join you in a minute."

Deputy Franklin drew me off on a gravel path toward a meditation area. "I see you're still consorting with my suspects."

The peaceful setting did nothing to slow my racing heart. "Cora called me this morning and asked for a ride. It wasn't my idea, honest."

"And yet, here you are."

"Here I am." I lifted my palms in an open gesture. "What can I do for you today, deputy?"

"Sheriff Vargas blew his top over the Radio Steve interview."

My hands came down, and my voice cracked. "Me too. That man ambushed me. He tried to get me to say bad things about the Sheriff's Office. I did not. Then he tried to get me to commit to investigating Jasmine's murder."

After a prickly pause, Franklin added, "Naturally, you declined."

"Naturally, I walked away from him before I lost my temper on the air. Pete threw him out of the Island Creamery. The whole thing surprised me. Pete set up the live radio spot to promote our new cookies and cakes collaboration."

"Whatever the reason, the interview made the department look bad. Public confidence in our ability to do our job tanked."

Not fair. Alarms sounded in my head. "You can't blame me for that. The current sheriff—"

"Stop. I don't want to hear a criticism of my boss because I'm under orders to report such information to him. I don't know how I got talked into running against him, but he's said I can pack my bags after he wins the election next month."

Of all the hare-brained things for Sheriff Vargas to say. Not once had I considered that running for sheriff might cost Franklin his job. He was a good guy who deserved better. He was also a friend in need of reassurance.

"You won't lose." My voice rang with conviction. "Islanders think your time has come. You're a good cop because you have an open mind and listen to what people say."

"It isn't that easy. We get whack-jobs telling us aliens live at the pier. The UFO kind, not the illegal ones. Some people call and complain about cops elsewhere; other people spit on us. It isn't easy being a cop. That's why I spend some patrol time talking to people. Influencers, like yourself."

I felt like tugging on my ears. "You pulled me out of a funeral reception to ask me for my vote?"

"Yes. No. Sort of. I heard the radio show. You said exactly the right thing, but I have to ask, do you mean it? Are you staying out of this ongoing investigation?"

"I don't always seek information. It finds me."

"Because you happen to know the suspects."

"I live on an island and have for my entire life. It's hard not to run into people."

Franklin looked around furtively. "What have you found out?"

"You go first."

"Can't do that, but we're not making much headway."

Hmm. Should I confide in him? I wanted to. Oh, what the hay. "Jasmine's search for that rare shrub took her to out of the way places, and it's possible she trespassed on private property. She has a podcast channel that I plan to view to see if I recognize where she went. Cora said there were dog prints circling the body. She thought it might be a medium-size dog. Since there were no reports of any loose dogs, I'm thinking it could've been a hunting dog, since they sometimes get lost in the woods. Except the shot to Jasmine's back seems very unsportsmanlike.

"And consider the two men who sat with Jasmine at the award ceremony last week. I've heard Ash wanted to date Jasmine, Iris wanted to date Ash, and Jasmine didn't want to date anyone. I thought she might've been sweet on Milton but if so, he's a snake in the grass because he's all over Iris today. I'd like to visit her house and yard to look around, but I guess the place belongs to Iris now." I paused. "My brother saw her buying new locks in the hardware store and she said she would inherit their family place."

Franklin shook his head. "We don't know who inherits that property. Robert Crider is the estate lawyer. He's supposed to read the will his afternoon."

"Sounds mysterious. Why doesn't he just give Iris a copy of the will?"

"Not so simple. He requested a police presence for the event."

"Sounds like trouble all right. Tell you what. I would not want to get between Iris O'Brien and anything she wanted."

~*~

On the way home from the funeral, Cora directed me

to stop at the Happy Paws Vet Clinic so she could see Ivy. To my delight, my friend Patsy manned the reception desk. Since losing her job at the wine bar to the owner's new girlfriend, she'd been looking for work. I wished I could afford her full-time, but anything I offered her would be as variable as my catering contracts.

"You got the job!" I exclaimed.

"I did, and don't you two ladies look fine," Patsy said.

"We just came from Jasmine's funeral." I added. "Cora wanted to check on Ivy, seeing as they'd been neighbors."

"Thanks for the recommendation at the clinic. It's only twenty hours a week, so I still have plenty of time to help you with catering jobs."

"Even better for me, and I can give you more hours soon since I'm expanding my business. Say, is it possible to visit Ivy, Jasmine Garr's former cat?"

Patsy grinned. "Linette has your name on the cage."

"Wishful thinking on her part. I already have a cat."

"What's one more? Anyway, you better take that monster home soon." My friend showed me her scratched hand. "I tried to feed Ivy, but it didn't go so well."

"Ivy's an outside cat," Cora said.

Sympathy for the orphaned cat tugged at my heart. I countered the emotion with common sense. "Ivy must hate being confined. I don't know if my cat will get along with Ivy, so that's why I didn't commit to her the other day."

"Your cat's outside in the Buick," Cora said. "Put Ivy in a carrier thingamabob and see if they like each other."

"That is an excellent idea," Patsy said, "only I can't leave the front desk now. Dr. Nelson is in surgery right now, and I can't risk the phones ringing and disturbing her. She's very particular about that."

Logic sailed out the window. The cat needed a home, and it liked me. I should step up. "If you'll loan us a pet carrier, I'll return it. And, fair warning, I might bring it right back with Ivy in it. Cora and I can transfer the kitty to the carrier."

The cat arched and hissed as we trooped her way, but she settled once I stood next to the cage for a few minutes. We arranged it so she could exit her kennel by entering the crate, which she did as if she knew it were her ticket to freedom.

"Now you let that cat outside soon's you get home," Cora said. "She's like me and don't want people all up in her business."

That seemed irresponsible. "I should release her in my house first, so that she knows this is her new home. Once she's used to the smells of our place, I'll let her run free."

"Do whatever you think is right, but Ivy's like your other cat. She needs to make the decision to stay."

"I'll think about it."

She hissed at Major, but my cat sat outside the cage and watched her all the way home, not even flicking so much as an ear when we dropped Cora off. At home, the decision got made for me. Major tripped the latch, and both cats dashed into the woods without a single glance at me.

I set out two bowls of cat food and water on the deck and called the cats. Neither one responded, which didn't bode well. Maybe Cora had been right about turning Ivy loose. In any event, it was a moot point.

Ivy and Major were off in the woods doing cat things. Major seemed keenly interested in the small female, and maybe he'd be more of an anchor for the kitty than I was. I hoped Ivy stayed because I would worry about her.

Now all I had to do was tell Pete we might or might not have two cats.

Chapter Nine

"You got another cat?" Pete set his fork down with precision. "What about the guard dog idea?"

"Maybe. Both cats bolted as soon as I opened the car door." I winced. "When it was just us, I was okay with the concept of a guard dog, but our extended family situation changed. Doug and Viv's small kids are in and out of the house now and their behavior is unpredictable. I don't want the hassle of keeping the dog and kids apart."

"I see," Pete looked away for a long moment. "I didn't think about the kids being here, but once we find the right dog, we'll train him or her to accept the kids. I've been looking for a retired police dog, but we can look for something smaller if you don't want a police dog."

I scrubbed my face with my hands, knowing I had to make this right. I expected him to discuss things with me before he acted, and now I'd been the rash one. "A smaller dog might be less intimidating for the children, and if you don't mind, let's revisit the guard dog conversation later." I paused to gather my thoughts. "I should've discussed the cat adoption with you, but I got swept up in the moment. Cora and I stopped by Happy Paws for her to visit Jasmine's cat after the funeral. She convinced me Ivy hated being locked up at the clinic. I couldn't leave the cat there. Major, who'd come along for the ride, seemed fine with the little calico, so I brought her home."

Pete's eyes twinkled. "Major calls the shots in our household?"

"Nothing like that," I stammered as I leaped to my feet. "A few days ago I used the excuse of the cats possibly not getting along as my reason for not seriously considering Ivy as an addition to our family. When the cats got along today and Cora said Ivy liked me, I caved. It was a snap decision. I can't give you months of research, analysis, and data to back up my decision. My heart went out to this kitty who'd lost her person. I wanted to help her. I was selfish. If you don't want Ivy here, I'll take her back to the vet."

Pete came to me, drawing me into his arms and stroking my hair. "No need to get flustered, hon. I understand how it happened and know your big heart wouldn't allow you to leave the kitty there. I have no objection to Major having a friend, assuming Ivy hasn't run off already."

"Really? You're okay with it?"

"Yes, but that opens the door for my guard dog, wouldn't you say?"

"As long as it gets along with Major and Ivy."

"Done."

I caressed his face. "Will we get a pony-sized dog named Brutus who patrols our yard with military efficiency?"

Pete chuckled. "For your information, I've passed on

four dogs like that. I'll know the right dog when I see it."

"Sort of like how I felt about Ivy?"

"Exactly."

~*~

Ivy didn't show her face the next morning and by afternoon I was concerned. Pete and I and Major rode to Jasmine's property to see if Ivy lit out for home.

"I see why you love this car, over and above the sentimental reasons," Pete said as he navigated through an aerial tunnel of intergrown oak branches. This wasn't the section of the island called Avenue of the Oaks, but it had the same feeling of a vaulted cathedral. "It handles great, rides smooth, and has a spacious trunk."

I stroked the wood-grained console. "This car is worth more than the monetary value of three grand. It's always been reliable. Mom got regular maintenance and put few miles on it, even though she drove it for ten years. I have so many memories linked to this car."

"Did Doug want the Buick?"

"Oh, heavens no. He was mortified at the thought of driving an old lady's clunker, as he dubbed this car. He got a good deal on that used pickup. Suits his handyman business better than a car does."

"I'm glad you kept it. My truck is a safe vehicle, but this is a good backup for hauling kids and pets around."

We motored through a traffic circle and the commercial district until we reached the midway point of the island. Major started pacing the backseat as we neared Jasmine's house.

"I know, buddy," I said in a soothing voice. "We'll find Ivy and bring her home."

But when we parked at Jasmine's house, two things caught my attention. First, the crime scene tape was gone. Second, Iris, Jasmine's cousin, stood at the front door.

Soon as we stopped, Major leapt out the car and sniffed the bushes. Pete followed the cat around the house while I mounted the steps. "Hi, Iris. It's been a while. I'm River Holloway."

Iris stopped jiggling her key in the lock and spared me a glance. "The catering woman."

"Yes, I adopted Jasmine's cat from Happy Paws Vet Clinic yesterday, and she vanished. Thought I'd see if she were here. Do you mind if my husband and I search the yard for the cat?"

"Yes, I mind, but go ahead. I don't need any cats hanging around here, and I want nothing to do with Jasmine's friends. You did the food the night she won that award, didn't you?"

"I catered the meal," I said, testing the roiling waters. Why was she so angry? "We were busy that night, but you would have been so proud of Jasmine. She got a standing ovation."

"Should've been my award for the work I did the bookbag project. Instead, Jasmine snatched the award right out of my hands, and she won it for doing her job and a few free vet clinics to spay and neuter pets." Iris sniffed copiously. "Ash accompanied her, didn't he?"

"He sat at her table. So did Milton and Linette and a few others."

"Ever since his adoptive parents died, I've wanted to be The One for him. No one should be all alone in this world."

I'd heard rumors about Ash's adoption in school, but

I'd thought kids were making it up because he'd always been more interested in critters than people. With the hindsight of age, I should've paid more attention, should've reached out to him, but I'd had my own issues with my mom beginning to get sick. I hadn't kept up with Ash over the years so I wasn't current on his family situation. Perhaps I could learn more from Iris.

I cleared my throat and gentled my voice. "I've been so busy with my family and business in the last ten years, I hadn't thought about him being alone. I can't imagine what that's like."

Shaking her hair back from her face with a practiced toss, Iris moaned. "It's no fun at all. My mom's gone, Jasmine's gone, and if not for my kids, I'd be alone too. I've always liked Ash despite his adoptive status. He's been polite to me, but that's as far as it ever went."

I imagined Iris was too high maintenance for a man that spent so much time in nature trapping wild animals. On the other hand, Jasmine's outdoorsy lifestyle seemed ideally suited to his lifestyle. Had they tried the couple thing?

Keeping my thoughts private, I said, "I see."

An anguished expression crossed Iris's face, and she closed her eyes momentarily. "Jasmine stole Ash and my award."

"What about Milton?" I asked, needing to know where Jasmine's affections lay. "He presented her award and seemed much more attentive to her than Ash."

"Milton is a charming leech if you have something he wants. He escorted me to her funeral and abandoned me at the reception an hour later. I knew he did people that way, but I never thought he'd dis me since we have some history. He was friends with my ex years ago so he came to our house for dinner several times."

Her words fired out bullet-fast, and I literally felt her pain. "I'm sorry he upset you, particularly when you counted on him for moral support."

"Milton's karma will catch up with him someday, but enough about him. I have to protect my property. I don't want you here, so look for the cat and leave." She paused to try the key again. "My key should fit this lock. Jasmine gave me this key last year, and now it doesn't work."

My brain whirred with possibilities about the key. Jasmine might have accidentally given Iris the wrong key. Jasmine might have rekeyed her locks recently. Or someone else might have changed the locks. But who and why?

Pete charged around the corner and waved me over. "River, you've gotta see this."

Chapter Ten

"Excuse me," I said to Iris and hurried down the steps. "Did you find Ivy?"

Pete laced his fingers through mine and guided me around the house. "No calico cat in sight but Major made a discovery. There's a set of prints you won't believe."

"Cora mentioned seeing dog tracks near the body."

He pointed to the ground beside a raised-bed wildflower garden. Our cat sat nearby, staring at the spot. "This track of prints definitely wasn't made by a dog."

I stepped with care in the soft ground as I didn't want to erase anything with my footprints. "You're right. I'm not certain but that looks like gator tracks, only why would an alligator be here? There's no freshwater pond nearby, no food source. I don't understand, but it's such an outlier of information it might be relevant. I'm calling Deputy Franklin."

Franklin answered on the first ring. After his greeting, I plunged into the reason for my call. "Funny you should call," he said. "I just got an earful from Iris

O'Brien. She claims you're trespassing on her property."

"How odd. Moments ago, she gave us permission to come onto the property and search for Jasmine's cat. We'll leave, no worries there. Anyway, it makes no sense for a gator track to be in Jasmine's yard."

"Is it near where the body was found?"

"I don't know that location."

"Take a few photos with your cell phone camera and send them to me. Get a crisp image of the animal track, then pan out for a few more so I can see where they are in relation to her yard."

"Will do."

I was sending the photos when Iris barreled around the house. "I called the cops," Iris said.

"So did I." I pointed to the alligator tracks. "You got any idea why a gator walked though this yard?"

"What? You can't be serious."

"I'm very serious. I don't see the cat, but Deputy Franklin has photos of the gator tracks now."

Iris glanced around like an alligator might plunge out of the trees and swallow her whole. "There were never gators here when I was a kid."

"Unless I'm mistaken, you have one now. Could be a traveling gator passing through, or there may be a new wallow nearby. In any event, people with small pets and children should be wary."

Iris scooted closer to me. "You think this gator ate Ivy?"

A shudder ripped down my spine. "I hope not. Maybe he heard the neighbor's chickens. Maybe it was a fluke that it was here. Your guess is as good as mine."

"Eep," Iris squeaked, inching next to me. "I can't

move here with my little Yorkie and my kids. Wonder how much it would cost to fence this yard?"

Pete cleared his throat. "I recently priced a split rail fence section for dog tie-ups in front of Island Creamery." He quoted her a price per foot. "And you'd probably want something sturdier, which would likely cost more."

"It'd be worth the cost if my dog was safe."

"Relatively safe," Pete said. "Some gators can climb fences."

Her eyes rounded. "No-o-o."

I caught Pete's gaze and nodded toward the Buick. "We shouldn't take up more of your time. Ivy's not here, so we'll search for her elsewhere. If she turns up, please let us know."

"Wait. I'm afraid to be here alone. Please, River, stay as I try my key on the back door."

"Iris, you just called the cops on us. I'd rather not stay where I'm not welcome."

"I apologize. Seems like I've waited all my life to own this property, and now I'm protective of it. I didn't want to be alone out here with you and your husband because you outnumber me. I should've said that instead of losing my nerve and calling the cops. Other things in my life have me in a pressure cooker situation, and I've been trying out a new medication. I'm a hot mess these days. Again, I should have stopped to think before I made that rash decision. You and Pete have no competing interest in the property. You're trying to find a lost pet. I'd do anything to find my Yorkie if he ran off."

An awkward silence followed. I glanced at Pete, who nodded slightly toward the truck. I wasn't ready to go, and after hearing her explanation, I felt sorry for Iris. "It's okay. Apology accepted."

"Good, because I am afraid to be outside alone back here. There are so many plantings close to the house. Snakes could be lying in wait for me."

"I didn't bring snake repellant, but you should be safe after all the noise we've made." I trailed her up the wooden steps, while Pete waited at the foot of the stairs. Iris swore aloud when her key didn't work in the back door lock either. We circled to the front of the house together.

"How'd the will reading go?" I asked for lack of anything better to say.

She shook her head. "It's another thing I don't understand. The reading got postponed until this afternoon. That lawyer gave off a hinky vibe so I wanted to inventory the house before the reading to make sure my grandmother's things were still inside. I wouldn't steal anything, but I don't understand why we couldn't dispense with the formalities Saturday after the funeral."

I silently agreed that the delay seemed suspicious, but the beauty of this property commanded my attention now that I wasn't staring at the sandy ground. It was a visual delight of greens and yellows and oranges. The air smelled just right, clean, fresh, and woodsy. "It's peaceful here, especially with the natural gardens Jasmine established. How large a parcel is this?"

"About two acres, last I knew."

"I don't know what your plans for this place are, but the grounds alone might be a big hit as another destination site for weddings, showers, corporate dinners, that sort of thing. The top places on the island are booked out at least six months in advance."

"If I go that route, I'll let you know. It would be good cross-promotion to have an affiliation with one of the island's top catering companies."

I glowed from her praise. Pete tensed beside me, and I saw the reason upon my next step. I said, "Deputy Franklin, hello."

"Show me the gator tracks, River, and then I've been ordered to escort everyone off the property."

"This is my property," Iris said. "You can't do that."

"Let me rephrase the message. The firm of Crider, Malloy, and Quaid requests all parties vacate the property until Jasmine Garr's will is read. If you don't comply, I have been authorized by the sheriff to use whatever means necessary to remove you."

"That's ridiculous," Iris said. "You and the sheriff just lost my vote in the election."

"This property is the estate of Jasmine Garr, and her executor Robert Crider instructed me to arrest any and all parties on sight. Since he doesn't have 'No Trespassing' signs posted, I reminded him of that deficiency."

"Well, I never," Iris said. "That lawyer is too big for his britches. I'm telling everyone in my tennis club how rude he is."

Deputy Franklin turned to me. "Gator tracks."

We retraced our steps, finding Major still perched on the raised bed. The deputy edged around the distinct tracks in the sand. "Looks like he's on a northwesterly course. Also appears to be a single gator from the spacing of the tracks and the tail drag marks. The back footprint is smaller than my shoe, so I estimate it's an older juvenile or a smaller adult."

"What's it doing on my property?" Iris demanded. "Can't you catch and relocate it?"

"Nuisance alligators are referred to either Department of Natural Resources or a guy out of Savannah, Trapper Joe, who catches gators for a fee. However, we don't know if it's a nuisance gator or not. All we know is it crossed this yard in the last few days."

"Will you follow the tracks?" I asked.

"I might give it a go once y'all leave, but only to see if I could follow them. I have no specialized training in animal tracking, and I've just shared the sum of my gator knowledge, other than the facts that gator hunting season closed a week ago and mating season was in the summer."

"Is this incident related to Jasmine's death?" I asked.

"Good question," the deputy said. "We're still in the gathering information stage, and this is another data point."

A cloud covered the sun, and the humid air felt heavy. Like my place, this property had privacy. There was so much we didn't know about Jasmine's life that made this a difficult case to solve. But I couldn't let that stop me from trying to get her justice.

Franklin gestured to the path around the house. "Time to leave."

I didn't budge. I wanted to ask Deputy Franklin a question in private. However, when Iris saw I wasn't turning around, she said, "I'm not leaving if she's not leaving."

"I have another question, deputy," I said, deciding to ask anyway. "Is it true that alligators only eat meat?"

"Everyone knows they eat meat, going after smaller

sizes of prey. Why do you ask?"

I jerked a thumb over my shoulder. "I've always thought gators were opportunistic feeders. Jasmine has several satsuma orange trees, and the fruit is ripe. If alligators feed on fruit or vegetables, the fruity scent might've been an irresistible lure."

Iris sniffed appreciably. "Those trees are coming down as soon as I get my hands on the deed."

"Or maybe it was something in her compost pile." I added. "I'm sure she has one."

"Doesn't matter what brought the alligator to the yard," Deputy Franklin said. "It's gone now and you three have to leave."

Chapter Eleven

Pete drove us home with his usual finesse. The Buick suited him as much as it did Major who purred in my lap. I enjoyed the open windows and fresh air.

"About the cookie order for this coming week," Pete said. "Can you double it?"

Counting prep work, I'd spent two days filling last week's order. "I know we sold out on Friday of last week, but I thought that sales bonanza stemmed from novelty and publicity."

"I doubt it. We had a 25 percent increase in ice cream sales, and you'll get a hefty payment for your baked goods when I write checks this week."

He quoted me a figure, and I gasped at the amount. I hadn't really thought about the proceeds. Pete took his share off the top, and I got all the rest. My expenses were a fraction of the income earned. And if I doubled the amount provided, I'd end up with twice the profits. That new income stream might be enough cookie money to see me through the year without taking on any side jobs.

Sweet deal.

A grin sneaked out. "Did the cookies sell better than the cakes?"

"Cookies went with ice cream the best. However, the ice cream cake was gone in half an hour. The yummy chocolate cake was the last to go, but three customers already requested it."

Light alternated with shadow on the road and in my thoughts. "I hoped to make different cookies and cakes each week."

"Here's a word to the wise. Don't vary too much from what sells. If you make a different cookie or cake that doesn't sell through, we can discount leftovers on Saturday. That'd be a smaller payout for you, but you'd earn back your ingredient cost with a little extra."

"I'm willing to double the order, and I'm fine with discounting my items late on Saturday. I should hire Patsy for Friday mornings or bake ahead of time and freeze the baked goods."

"Figure out what's best for you. As a business owner, I'd prefer everything freshly made, but in truth I can't distinguish your just-made cookies from the ones you defrosted."

I processed this as my thoughts raced ahead to what I wanted to prepare. I'd make the same ice cream cake and perhaps a red velvet cake. People who liked my Death by Chocolate Cake would try the red velvet cake. "What about an apple pie?"

"We won't know what works until it doesn't. I'm requesting six batches of cookies and four cakes or pies."

"Can do."

~*~

On Sunday afternoon, I parked near the mainland

offices of Crider, Malloy, and Quaid to witness people's reactions as they exited the building after Jasmine's will reading. I noted a sheriff's car parked out front and a nearby TV van from Savannah. Guess Robert Crider, esquire, had reason to believe things might get dicey and be newsworthy. What could be so controversial about Jasmine's will?

I'd gotten sucked into social media posts on my phone when Iris stormed out, red in the face. She threw her purse at her car, and the bag burst open, spilling contents everywhere. Iris covered her face and sobbed.

TV reporters and cameramen leapt from their vans and converged on Iris. Appalled at how they cornered a defenseless woman, I hastened to her side.

"Back off," I stated firmly. "Come with me, Iris."

"I can't. My stuff is everywhere."

"I'll return for it. Come sit in my catering van and gather yourself."

She followed me across the street, and I got her settled in the passenger seat. The TV reporter asked me for a comment. "No comment," I said. Then I gathered everything from Iris's bag, placed the items in her purse, and returned it.

"Thank you," she said, dashing at her tears. "I don't deserve your kindness after being so capricious yesterday. I thought any friend of Jasmine's wouldn't be friends with me."

"Truthfully, I knew Jasmine professionally. We became acquaintances when she hired me to cook meals for her mother, but we didn't keep in touch after that. Our interests converged at catered meals for her mom, so that was the extent of it." I paused, feeling guilty for having an ulterior motive for being here. "I take it things didn't go well in the lawyer's office."

Iris shook her head and then pointed to the front of the building where the TV crew and the newspaper guy clustered around real estate broker Milton Wainwright. "That man swindled me and my cousin."

If it rained shrimp, I wouldn't have been more surprised. "What?"

"Apparently Jasmine donated the house and property to the Nature Coalition to be used as a teaching center. Further, the contents of the house will be auctioned off to fund free pet vaccinations at Happy Paws Vet Clinic. Milton Wainwright is the property manager and the auctioneer. I get nothing. Zilch. Nada. Not even the family heirlooms that were handed down for generations. In what world is that right?"

"Oh, Iris," I exclaimed. "This is not what you expected. How odd you weren't named in the will. Didn't Jasmine know you cherished those family items?"

Her eyes brimmed with tears. "She knew, but I said terrible things to her the last time we spoke. You've seen firsthand how my moods swing out of control. I shouldn't have blasted her for hoarding everything after her mother died. I'm sure she excluded me out of spite. She hated me, hated that I had more friends than she did, hated the air I breathed."

I'd only seen Jasmine acting considerate around her mother, but spiteful? Obviously, I didn't know her very well. "Hate is such a strong word." Inspiration flared like a sheet lightning. "Perhaps it wasn't personal at all. Perhaps she desired to leave a helping legacy.

"She got everything when Gram died. I didn't get the first sterling silver baby spoon or the delicate floral-patterned china set—Jasmine had no use for the fancy stuff. She never entertained. All these years she's lorded that stuff over my head and I let her. I finally snapped and told her exactly what I thought of her."

Oh, dear. Zinnia Drummond hadn't shared equally among her grandchildren. That seemed so uncaring. "Why did your Gram will her estate to Jasmine?"

"As a kid and young adult, my cousin visited here all the time to stay with Gram. They were forever poking about in the yard and doing stuff with plants. Jasmine was a real suck-up. She must've poisoned Gram against me."

Whether Jasmine's will had intentionally omitted Iris didn't matter because Iris was taking it personally. "Would you have kept the property if you inherited it?" I asked.

"No. I planned to sell it once I removed the family heirlooms I wanted. I thought my pending windfall was why Milton acted so friendly at the funeral. Nope he just made sure I knew he'd stolen everything I wanted." She sniffed for a few moments. "I asked nicely in there if I could gather up family papers and heirlooms, specifically asking for the oil painting of Gram. Crider flat out refused. He said I could buy what I wanted from the estate sale. The nerve of that man, making me buy Gram's portrait."

This inheritance matter didn't square up for me. There must be a reason Iris had been frozen out, but I couldn't think of one. Her plight moved me. "Can he do that? Is it legal for him to withhold family records from a living family member?"

"Robert Crider made it sound legal. Leastways now I know why my key didn't work in Jasmine's locks. Once the police cleared the place as a crime scene, the lawyer rekeyed the locks. He handed the new keys to Milton a few minutes ago. I am devastated."

She broke down in tears again, and I patted her back. When she calmed, I said, "Have you considered challenging Jasmine's will? It's a reasonable response in your situation. The downside is you may not win, and you'd be out a lawyer fee. Did Zinnia Drummond's original will designate certain items to remain in the family? If so, you'd have leverage."

Iris dashed the moisture from her face. "I never saw Gram's will."

I felt a spark of hope for her, and the satisfaction of lending aid. "In that case, you might ask your lawyer to obtain a copy of it."

Chapter Twelve

I flipped through my recipe book on Monday morning, trying to decide what to bake for my Friday delivery to Island Creamery. Pete suggested I keep most items the same and only vary one cookie type and one cake type. That guaranteed repeat sales as customers returned for their favorites.

Suddenly, the idea of maple shortbread cookies popped into my head and wouldn't go away. I could cut them in maple leaf shapes since it was October. I reached up to the top shelf for my bag of cookie cutters and rooted through the collection until I found the perfect leaf shape.

Soon I was happily mixing ingredients. While the dough refrigerated, I dashed over to the house and ran a load of laundry and considered making chicken for dinner. I had a hankering for chicken pot pie, so I simmered chicken thighs in bone broth, along with onion, carrots, and celery.

On the way back to my commercial kitchen, I saw a streak of white in the woods. "Ivy?" I glanced again, not sure of what I saw. "Here, kitty, kitty. Come on, Ivy."

Given that Major had black fur, I was certain it was Ivy, so I moved her food and water bowl from the deck to the woods. I put it near the bush where I'd seen her face and hoped she'd eat.

Still praying the cat was nearby, I rolled out my shortbread dough to a ¼ inch thickness, cut out maple leaf shapes, transferred each cookie to parchment-lined sheet pans, and baked them. For the cookie glaze of maple syrup and confectioner's sugar, I experimented with food color until I got the orange and gold colors perfect. I was glazing the last batch when Deputy Franklin knocked on the door.

I unlocked the door, another safety lesson learned from an earlier case, and waved him inside. "To what do I owe this pleasure?"

"Smells like pancakes and maple syrup in here." He gazed hopefully at the frosted cookies.

"You can be my tester." I handed him a golden leaf-shaped cookie. "I'm trying out a maple shortbread recipe for my Friday selection at Island Creamery."

He bit into it and after a few slow chews he stopped and made a contented sound. I smiled inside at that. These would be big hits, for sure.

Deputy Franklin didn't say a word until he ate the whole thing. "I'm pretty sure those will work, but I'll be happy to test another cookie, to be more certain."

I chuckled and handed him a plate of two more cookies and a glass of water. "Help yourself. Hope this doesn't ruin your lunch."

"Lunch can darn well take care of itself. At times like this, I'm glad you meddle in my cases because I enjoy sampling your creations. These cookies are flat-out delicious. I may buy the whole batch Friday morning.

Seriously."

I couldn't remember any meddling. Just a few questions here and there. Didn't seem right he'd hold that against me. "How'd I meddle in your case this time?"

"First thing this morning, Iris O'Brien's attorney filed suit against her cousin's estate and halted the transfer of assets."

Oh, that. I released the breath I'd been holding. "Iris said there were family papers and such that'd been handed down for generations that should be hers as she's the last surviving family member."

"In her opinion. I got a furious call twenty minutes ago from Milton Wainwright who'd gone to the bank to itemize Miss Garr's safety deposit box but was denied access."

I didn't like the way his face tightened into an angry mask. Milton Wainwright didn't own this island, and he didn't make the rules either. "Iris has the right to challenge the will. A judge might see things differently, especially if the family heritage items were entailed in a prior will as family property."

"The Coalition wants to stop a hotel corporation from building in a dune meadow and needs those estate proceeds immediately to hire a legal team. Wainwright thinks I can pressure Iris to drop the suit."

"You? Why would you be involved? She hasn't broken any laws by filing suit. If my brother cut me out of family property and possessions in his will, I would challenge the will. I don't know what a judge will say, but it feels wrong that Iris got the shaft."

"I see." His gaze narrowed. "You told Iris to file a suit."

"I might have mentioned that's what I would do in her situation, but she would've come around to it on her own. This way, Milton doesn't have time to hawk her heritage to strangers."

"He's unhappy."

"She didn't do things his way, so his displeasure is expected." I drummed my fingers on the table. "You know what? I considered Milton a suspect in Jasmine's murder because of the love triangle aspect. But given Jasmine's will being made public, his motive to kill her is stronger. He profits immensely from her death."

Franklin's last cookie halted midway to his mouth. "As the Coalition's representative. Not personally."

I rose and began tidying the counter. "You don't think his standing in the organization and the community increases because of this? He'll be in newspapers for donating that money to the vet clinic, likely a photo and an article. He'll lead the publicity campaign for the teaching activities at the new nature center. He'll land business opportunities because of this. In my book, he's a prime suspect for her murder."

"I checked him out. He has no registered guns, no concealed carry permits, no recent gun purchases. Further, his name doesn't appear in the gun range's log and he's never had crime-related run-ins with the law."

Turning from the stack of bowls and pans in my sink, I leaned against the counter. "Sorry, not buying that bill of goods. There are other ways to acquire a weapon. I bet you don't have a listing of the guns I inherited with my house either. Think about it. Who better to case houses and have unlimited access to a person's possessions than a real estate agent or broker?"

"He has an alibi."

"Which means you have a specific time of death?"

"I do."

"Then what was the mighty Milton Wainwright doing at that time? Is it ironclad?"

"He visited clients on the mainland." He paused until I met his gaze. "I checked."

Drat. That fact made my argument weaker, but I wasn't ready to yield my point. I grabbed the sanitizer bottle and sprayed my clean countertops. "Even so, he might have influenced Jasmine to make that will. It feels out of character for Jasmine to intentionally cut her cousin out of family property."

"Iris and Jasmine did not get along. Why would she leave anything to her cousin?"

"Jasmine had a strong sense of family, as shown by her spending time with her grandmother and later by caring for her mother during her illness. Jasmine wasn't a money-grubbing person because she ended up with a flexible career path when she easily could've made more money with her veterinary degree. I bet Milton seduced her with the promise that her property would always remain a haven for naturalists in the event something happened to her. You know, now that I think about it, a speaker traveled around the island last year encouraging will writing and charitable bequests. I wonder if that person gave a presentation at the Nature Coalition and then Milton persuaded people to mention the Coalition in their wills so their legacy of good works would continue when they were gone."

"That's conjecture. We deal in facts."

"Now, deputy. You're more openminded than that. If you don't think Milton's guilty, who are you looking at?"

"Someone who doesn't have an alibi for the time of death and who had a strong motive to kill her."

"Jasmine was well liked. That can't be a large pool of suspects."

"This is an ongoing investigation."

He couldn't intimidate me with those cop eyes. "If I were in your shoes, I'd be looking at Iris who thought she stood to inherit, Milton who gains in prestige from her death, Ash for romantic reasons, and the Chicken Lady because she found the body. Oh, and Dr. Linette Nelson who profited from the death by having her clinic designated as a beneficiary."

A muscle twitched in his cheek. "They all checked out."

I pretended not to notice he'd revealed any investigative results as I slid the cookie platter closer to the deputy. "Then we're missing something. I wish I knew what it was."

He eagerly took another cookie. "The will challenge brings up interesting possibilities. If Iris makes a strong case that Milton unduly influenced Jasmine to write her current will, her suit could be successful. If so, inheritance would hinge on whatever the judge decides, as in voiding the entire will or only a portion of it. And if Iris is mentioned in a prior will, winning the case would paint an even bigger motive target on her back. No way Iris comes out of this unscathed."

"We're assuming there's an earlier will." I took a cookie and ate a bite. Yum. Simultaneously, an idea sparked in my head. "What if Jasmine had a change of heart about her will and wrote a new will that supersedes the one the lawyer had? It could be in her lockbox or her house."

That sounded like a strong possibility. I stared at my gripped hands for a moment before I caught the deputy's eye again. "Seems like it would be prudent to check with area lawyers or on Jasmine's computer for mention of another will."

He shook his head. "I don't recall a computer in her possessions or a paper calendar of appointments on her wall."

"That's strange. A woman who has a variable schedule would keep track of her variable workdays. Maybe she coordinated everything through her cell phone or other electronic devices. What about the topo map she used for her plant excursions?"

He huffed out a breath. "We didn't see any of those items."

"The killer covered his or her tracks, but I have faith you'll find them. I hope you're seeking permission to view her phone records, computer, and cloud content. It's possible Jasmine could've done an online will if she didn't want to pay another lawyer for a will."

"Sure you weren't a cop in a former life? You think like one."

"I'll take that as a compliment. I possess abundant curiosity and approach challenges in a stepwise fashion. I also think sideways, and often do so when it comes to recipes."

"Those qualities help you to ask the right questions."

"From what you haven't said, I assume the investigation stalled. The gator tracks and the will challenge are your only leads."

"And keeping an eye out for suspicious behavior among her family and friends."

"You never said if we shared the same list of

suspects."

"Hopefully, the answer to that question and your Island Creamery production rush will keep you busy for a few days."

"You think it'll come to a head that quickly?"

He swiped two more cookies on his way out. "I always hope so."

Chapter Thirteen

Rain. Not my favorite thing, though it'd been so dry lately that we needed a good soaking, so I shouldn't complain about a socked-in Tuesday drizzle.

Rosemarie called first thing. "My customer rental on Rude Dog Lane paid extra to stay until two o'clock today. I know you have tutoring at the elementary school this afternoon, but can you come over afterward to help?"

I had a catering gig tomorrow, but I could start the prep after helping my friend. "Sure, I'll come straight from tutoring."

"Great. See you then."

I pocketed my phone and took out my checklist for tomorrow's Ladies Invitational Bridge Tournament for twenty-four people. They contracted for fancy finger sandwiches, Greek pasta salad, Waldorf salad, broccoli salad, lemon squares, brownies, and raspberry iced tea. No reason why I couldn't start the prep work of veggie chopping for the salads right now. My pasta salad tasted better the next day too, so I should make that first.

To the patter of constant rainfall, I boiled the pasta

and chopped cherry tomatoes, cucumber, onion, red and green bell pepper, and black olives. To those, I added feta cheese and a light dressing. After stirring, I mixed in the cooled pasta. Since I'd made a double batch to have a surplus, I harvested a cup to split with Rosemarie after our cleaning session on Rude Dog Lane.

I still had a couple of hours before tutoring, so I mixed up a sheet pan of lemon squares. While they were baking, I made my specialty brownies. Soon as the first oven emptied, I oven-roasted a pound of bacon for the broccoli salad. I also brewed up three gallons of raspberry tea and another gallon of unsweet tea in case someone didn't like the raspberry tea.

I'd baked four loaves of white bread yesterday so I was covered there. Tonight, I'd bake the turkey and roast beef and slice them thinly so they'd be ready for assembly tomorrow, and I'd toast walnuts and chop celery for the Waldorf salad.

Time to get ready for tutoring and housecleaning. I tidied the kitchen, zipped to the house, and snarfed down a peanut butter sandwich. Thinking ahead, I stuck two small portions of pasta salad in a cooler with ice packs and spoons.

When I changed into my house-cleaning jeans, the zipper wouldn't close. Yikes, I better cut back on sampling those cookies. In minutes, I switched to a pair of stretchy pants with a longer top.

Much to my surprise, both Major and Ivy were sitting side by side on the roof of the Buick under the carport. I didn't notice them there earlier, but I was glad they'd sought refuge from the rain, even gladder that Ivy hadn't disappeared.

Tutoring went well. One child I worked with

struggled with reading comprehension, but we were making progress. After that, I motored over to the Rude Dog Lane rental under overcast skies, though the rain had stopped. As usual, Rosemarie beat me there, and the washing machine was already spinning with bedding inside.

Whitney Houston belted out how she would always love you from the great room television. I greeted my friend, who was in the back scrubbing the shower, and got to work. Some people thought housecleaning was a lousy career path because it lacked upward mobility. But I enjoyed the work, loved seeing how nice everything looked afterward, and felt proud that the next people to see it would be pleased.

As well they should be. Rosemarie had a double case of OCD when it came to cleaning. She'd gone through over twenty helpers who didn't rise to her level of cleaning. I wasn't sure how I made the cut, but I liked to think it was related to my sanitation practices for catering. Cleanliness was a mainstay in my business too.

Sinead O'Connor was singing how nothing compares to you by the time we knocked off at a little past four. With the steps too damp to sit on, I passed around the food I'd brought as we stood in our usual spot. "I know we're later than usual, but I brought us a treat, nonetheless. It's Greek pasta salad. Hope you like it."

Rosemarie reached for the plastic cup of salad with both hands. "I want." She tasted it and hummed with delight. "You could sell this. I'd buy a quart of this a week, maybe two. Yum."

I dug into my portion as well, savoring the flavors. "The problem in selling food products is that some items don't sell, and I would have to toss that food due to expiration dates. That amounts to lost income. I prefer to create just what I need for each event. Better cost-benefit ratio."

"Yeah, yeah, you always have a reason why you can't do something like this, but I noticed your cookies and cakes were a big hit at Island Creamery last week."

My entire face smiled. "It was awesome, well, except for backstabbing Radio Steve who I did not like. He stated on the radio that I solved the murders of Curtis Marlin and Estelle Bolz, neither of which is true. I helped solve them. There's a big difference."

"Um-hmm."

"You don't agree?"

"Don't sell yourself short, River." Rosemarie set her empty dish on the landing's rail cap and fixed me with an encouraging look. "We all know you're a finder. Discovering clues in an investigation is a natural extension of that talent. I'm proud of you. You've got the career you always wanted, you married the man you love, and now you've got this great sleuthing hobby. Say, did you hear that Louise Jubie over in Marsh View called Trapper Joe yesterday? A five-foot gator made himself at home in her carport. Trapper Joe and his helper caught and removed the gator in less than twenty minutes."

"Really? I was just talking with Deputy Franklin about Trapper Joe the other day. My cat found gator tracks out at Jasmine's house, and I wondered if the gator was related to her death."

"Not too many gun-toting gators," Rosemarie said drolly.

Body heat steamed up my collar. "Of course not, but it's unusual for a gator to be anywhere near her yard.

Her property is landlocked and there's no freshwater pond nearby. Everything I know about gators indicates they conserve energy. They don't wander randomly about."

"Maybe the gator smelled her spilled blood. They have a keen sense of smell. Right now those gator tracks are an outlier of data."

"Possibly, but if that's true today's rain should've removed that enticement. If the gator returns, it could be relevant to the case."

Rosemarie massaged her hands for a moment. "Could someone have a pet alligator that followed him or her around?"

"Doesn't seem prudent. Think about it. Would you want an alligator following you on a hike through woods and swamps? If he struck and you somehow survived the attack, who'd find you before you bled out?"

My friend snorted. "I see your point. Never turn your back on a predator that would eat you, no matter how tame it seems."

"Darn straight. Smart people don't become gator bait." Even as I said this, the wheels in my brain turned. Could someone have released a gator in Jasmine's yard to lure her outside?

Chapter Fourteen

On my way home, I stopped at Happy Paws Vet Clinic to ask about Ivy's cat food preference. The unlocked door opened to a deserted lobby. "Hello?" I called out. "Is anyone here?"

The door to the clinic's staff area cracked open. "We're closed," Dr. Linette Nelson said. "Oh, it's you, River. Is everything all right with Ivy?"

I crossed the room, noting the strain in her face. She looked like she'd worked around the clock. "Ivy is okay. She hid from me for the first few days, but now she and my black cat Major are friends. What's going on with you? Looks like you've had a long day."

"Today is surgery day. We booked surgeries for two vets weeks ago, and I didn't want to let anybody down, so I did both sets." Linette covered a yawn. "Is there something you need?"

"Yes, but it's a small thing. Ivy is a picky eater. Did she normally eat the food you sell here? I'd like to make sure she's getting enough to eat."

"Now that I think about it, Jasmine bought her cat's food here. What size bag do you want?"

"Let's try the small bag first. If that makes her happy, then I'll come back for a bigger bag. If there's no change in her behavior, I'll stick to the canned stuff. My cat prefers that."

Linette strode toward the stack of pet food in the lobby. "Tell you what. Since you helped me out the other day, I'll comp you the medium bag for the small bag price. It's hard to tell anything from a few meals for cats. Something else can put them off their food for a day or so and you might consider that real data."

"Thanks. I appreciate the extra pet food and the advice. Say, I didn't notice you at the funeral or Jasmine's will reading. I thought beneficiaries had to attend the reading."

"I sent my regrets. Yes, I was invited to the reading of her will, but I've got a vet clinic to run and only one set of hands to do it. We had a full kennel of pets with medical needs. I couldn't blow off a few hours of the day, not when animals depend on me. Also, I make it a policy never to attend funerals."

My eyes widened as I gave her my credit card. "You don't go to funerals?"

She swiped the card and completed the transaction. "Too much drama, and I have enough of that here. Every pet owner thinks their dog or cat is royalty."

While spending a single afternoon here, I witnessed demanding pet owners firsthand. "I heard your clinic is in line to receive a donation from the sale of Jasmine's belongings and that the money is earmarked for pet vaccinations."

Linette nodded. "It will be nice to have that enticement to acquire more customers, but that helps a limited set of animals. If their owners can't afford the vaccines, they are unlikely to patronize the clinic. It's a do-gooder move. Doesn't matter though. I'll be lucky if any of that money comes to the clinic."

"Why?"

She handed my credit card back along with a receipt. "Iris O'Brien is challenging the will. That woman is like a bulldog when she sinks her teeth into something. She'll fight the will all the way to the Supreme Court."

I'd never thought of Iris in that light before, and it tickled me. I kept my amusement to myself though. "I hope there's a way everyone benefits." I gathered my cat food to my chest. "One more thing. Did Jasmine ever mention having a gator problem at her place?"

Linette startled and stepped back from the reception counter. "Why do you ask?"

Her voice sounded a little throaty, as if the query provoked a fear response. What was going on?

I took a moment to push a few strands of hair behind my ears, allowing time for her nostrils to stop flaring. "We saw gator tracks in her yard on Sunday. That seemed strange. I wondered if it had happened before."

Linette's hands found each other and held on tight. She cleared her throat a few times before speaking, and her voice sounded stronger than before. "Jasmine never mentioned gators in her yard to me. Now if you'll excuse me, I need to finish up in the back."

As she whirled and fled, suspicions played havoc with my peace of mind. Sure seemed like Linette just lied to me. The question begged to be asked. Why?

Chapter Fifteen

Wednesday blew in like a nor'easter, blustery and raw. I arrived in plenty of time to stage the buffet luncheon for the Ladies Invitational Duplicate Tournament at the fire hall. The food came out perfect, but I couldn't shake a bone-deep sense of unease. It felt like I had five minutes to empty four clotheslines full of clothes before the sky opened.

Despite the weighty sensation, I donned a professional expression and made sure everyone was served. The duplicate crowd included two guys. Both men wore dark colored dress shirts, resembling crows in a simpering flock of pastel parakeets. Despite the serious game play, the mostly senior crowd kept a steady stream of table talk going at each of the six tables.

The ladies made a beeline for the raspberry tea as soon as I opened the drink station. I kept busy for a few minutes putting ice in the small party cups and filling them with the tea.

Ola Mae sauntered over when most everyone had tried it. "Hit me," she said, holding out an empty hand.

I put a cup of raspberry tea in her hand. "Where's your sister? I thought she loved duplicate bridge."

She sipped her tea. "Valerie's a bit under the weather today. Said she feels like the sky is about to break."

"I had a similar thought a few minutes ago, as if my body is picking up a danger message from a distant channel. I can't rationalize that unease, but it certainly looks stormy today."

Both of us glanced out the French door entryway to the muted daylight on the lawn. I noted that every handicapped parking slot was full with two more sedans parked on the grass. "I wouldn't have mentioned it if you hadn't broached the topic. Do you feel it, Ola Mae?"

Ola Mae guzzled the rest of her tea and held the cup out for a refill. "Heck, no. I feel great, and I'm on track to have a winning score today."

I emptied the first pitcher in her cup. One gallon down, two to go. "Glad you're doing well. Back to Valerie. Is there anything else bothering her? Seems like she's been out of sorts for months."

"She's slowed a mite, but she's got plenty of starch left. She'll come around."

A few months ago I learned these ladies hadn't been to any doctors as adults. It boggled my mind that they didn't know their cholesterol level, their blood pressure level, or any underlying chronic health issues. The ladies had to be pushing ninety, and they'd outlived most of their friends.

Still, something nagged at me. I prodded one more time. "Nothing else bothering Valerie?"

"She's not too keen on alligators taking walkabouts on the island. Says it's a sign the island is reverting back to nature. That soon the gators will take over and people won't live on Shell Island."

"I've only heard about the gator that Louise Jubie found in her carport. Have you and Valerie heard of more gators roaming island neighborhoods?"

"Have you ever just seen one rat or cockroach? Stands to reason if an alligator's wandering around, more will follow." Ola Mae nodded at the dwindling buffet fare. "I better get my treat before it's all gone."

Soon, only a few desserts remained. I placed the remnants on a paper plate and began loading my empty containers in the van, thankful the wind had calmed, and the rain had stopped.

Lizzie Collins, president of the bridge club followed me out of the fire hall to the van. "Nice job on the luncheon. All the ladies are pleased, and take it from me, that's darn hard to do."

"Thanks."

"How's the investigation going? You figure out who killed Jasmine Garr yet?"

The feel-good vibe from concluding an event faded. Foreboding pulsed from the gunmetal clouds overhead, and the air felt too still, too close, and too thick. Must be nearly 100 percent humidity.

Realizing I'd drifted off mentally, I rewound the conversation. Lizzie had asked about the case. "Her death makes no sense to me, so I've asked a few questions, though I wouldn't call that an investigation."

"Come now, River. Everyone knows better than that. Radio Steve put it out all over the county that you are hot stuff when it comes to solving murders."

I laughed out loud at that. "I've never been hot stuff in my life, but I thank you for that visual." I glanced down at my plus-sized curves and considered my slightly below average height. "I've been called short stuff before."

Lizzie Collins patted my back. "Nonsense, dear. You always make a great impression and don't you forget it. We're counting on you to keep our streets safe until we get Gil Franklin elected as sheriff."

Boy was I glad the topic changed. "You're part of his election committee?"

"We all are. Ola Mae told us we had to do it for our own safety, and she's right. There've been three murders this year. On Shell Island. That's unthinkable."

"I hope Deputy Franklin wins the election too. We need a sheriff who doesn't rush to judgment and who will keep asking questions."

"Well said, dear."

As Lizzie turned to join her friends, I tapped her shoulder. "I have a question about Valerie. She's been feeling poorly for months. Can you encourage Ola Mae to take her to a doctor?"

"Not likely. Those two let health matters take their natural progression."

I should back off, but I had to ask the other question burning in my thoughts. "Ms. Lizzie, are you afraid of alligators wandering the island?"

"I went over to Louise's place to see the gator in her carport. That fat-cat gator wasn't scared of people. In fact, once Trapper Joe snared the head, the gator marched up the truck bed ramp like it had done it a million times before."

"Is that usual?"

She shrugged. "Trapper Joe didn't know what to make of it either. He stood there scratching his head while his helper raised the tailgate and covered the truck bed."

Lizzie left me alone with my questions. I had two to consider. Why did the gator act like it had been handled before? Where did it come from?

Chapter Sixteen

Before I left the parking lot, I placed a call to Pete from my van. When he didn't answer, I left a message that I planned to pick up shrimp for dinner. Movement out the corner of my eye had me turning to see who was coming my way. A girl couldn't be too careful these days.

I recognized the dark-haired man on sight—Ash Braswell. He stopped moving to gesture with his arm as he spoke loudly on the phone. I listened hard to hear what he was saying.

Bits of his conversation reached my ear. Something about golf carts. Oh. He was complaining about golf carts on the roads.

Good luck with that. Everybody and their brother owned a golf cart on the north end of the island, which hadn't posed a traffic problem due to the area's relative isolation. Those social neighbors didn't impede traffic on the through road because all the activities and amenities were in the neighborhood.

However, golf carts had become more prevalent in a less tony neighborhood closer to the island hub of traffic. Those residents used their golf carts to zip to the grocery store or the liquor store or a popular restaurant, and to do that, they brought traffic to a crawl on the main route.

Ash saw me and stopped mid-sentence in his tirade. "I have to call you back." He pocketed his phone and stopped beside my open window. "Ms. Holloway, or should I say Mrs. Merrick? Could I have a minute?"

People often got confused about my last name now that Pete was my husband. I'd kept Holloway because of my established business but my legal name was River Holloway Merrick. "Either is fine, though I'd rather you call me River. How are you, Ash?"

"Good." He frowned for a moment. "I'm sorry you overheard me ranting on the phone. Those golf carts are a hazard on the road. Bad enough they slow traffic down and turn with no signals. One was veering all over the road this morning. I reported it, but of course by the time a deputy got to where the golf cart had been, it was gone. It's my pet peeve."

"It's a hot button topic for sure. With people so passionate on both sides of the issue, we may be deadlocked."

"Deadlocked is how I feel, and frustrated, but enough about that." He glanced at the fire hall. "Have you been catering another function?"

"Served lunch to the bridge ladies. They had a tournament today."

"I noticed all the cars in the parking lot." He regarded me steadily. "They must've loved your cooking. That pork tenderloin you made the other night for the Coalition was to-die-for."

His cheeks flushed as his brain went to the same place

mine went. "Sorry," he said with a rueful expression. "That was tactless in light of Jasmine's subsequent death."

"It's okay. I understood what you meant and thank you for the compliment."

"If not for Pete Merrick, I'd be pursuing you hard, gal. He gets to eat like that every day?"

"Well, yes." His question surprised me. I knew of Ash Braswell, but we weren't friends per se. "And I'm a very happily married woman."

His hands shot up reflexively. "Message received. I'm relatively new on the dating scene and finding it a maze. After my divorce finalized, I dated Jasmine for a while, but it became apparent she'd rather be tromping through the woods than hanging out with me. When she invited me to sit at her table for that fancy dinner, I hoped she'd changed her mind. Instead that sleazy Wainwright was all over her, and she didn't even notice. Her indifference to how close that guy was standing and how he kept touching her made me wonder if I'd misinterpreted those dates we had. Like I said, dating is hard second time around."

My gaze caught on some nasty scratches on his hand. "I understand. Say those scratches on your hands look red and swollen. What happened?"

"Got tangled up with raccoons who fancied themselves as trash pirates. They didn't take kindly to being trapped or relocated."

"Dealing with wild animals sounds dangerous. What did you do with those raccoons? I've often wondered where you take nuisance animals."

"Usually I transport them to an underpopulated area, such as a wildlife preserve or a conservation area. Also, some property owners who value native plants and animals are happy to have an occasional influx of critters. Keeps the ecosystem in check."

"Was Jasmine one of your refuge providers?"

"As a matter of fact, she was. She had a critter problem in her garden and needed a natural way to keep the insects and lizards in check out there. That's how we connected, actually. I took her a couple of oak snakes that kept terrorizing users of the amenity center over at Sea Pines. Those folks should've realized that lighting that place up all night meant they'd attract insects and insect-eaters. Anyway, they were glad to be rid of the two oak snakes I caught, and Jasmine was equally glad to take them."

Snakes. I was okay with them as long as they left me alone. "I guess you heard there was a gator caught on the island in the last few days."

"I did. I can relocate small gators but Trapper Joe is a pro all the way. I'm glad the matter resolved quickly. We can't have gators free-ranging all over Shell Island. People might get hurt."

He seemed about to go on but he shook his head instead. "What?" I asked.

"They were here first. If this island weren't colonized, these gators would have the run of the place. All the hardwood swamps that got filled for housing would be chock full of gators. They're natural predators in the food chain. People are the interlopers."

Ash was the second person to voice this sentiment to me this afternoon, and it wasn't something I'd ever considered. "So we're keeping them out of their home?"

"Something like that."

I got ready to end the conversation, but another idea

popped into my head. "Did the cops question you about Jasmine's death?"

"Boy howdy, did they," he huffed. "I was there for hours and the questions kept coming. I finally told them if they wanted to arrest me, fine, but I was supposed to be helping put up a fence and I had to go. They haven't so much as called me since."

"Did they ask you about guns?"

"They did, which told me she'd been shot. I own a gun but so what? Wainwright has a handgun too. I've seen him at target practice at the mainland range several times over the last year or so. He may have been shooting longer than that. Six months ago I got my life back and started doing things I like to do. I love my career trapping animals. My ex never got that, and he left the island the minute the papers went through. Good riddance, I say."

I grimaced at his callous attitude. "It's a terrible feeling when a relationship is broken. Pete and I had a rough patch when he moved to California for a year."

"But you two figured it out. Way I see it, Pete Merrick will end up owning half the island one day."

"He has his hands full with Island Creamery right now."

"I heard your desserts are there on Thursdays."

"Fridays. I take in cookies and cakes, and they're available from noon Friday until they're gone."

"I'll make a note of it."

We said goodbye, and I drove over to Neptune's Harvest to pick up shrimp for dinner. I kept rerunning my conversation with Ash in my head. I wanted to like him, as a friend, of course, but there was something about him that made me hesitate. He'd pursued Jasmine for months, thought she liked him, then found out his feelings weren't reciprocated. By his own admission, he owned a gun. And those scratches on his hand, were those really from nuisance raccoons?

A chill swept down my spine.

Chapter Seventeen

Armed with a big stock pot of chicken soup, I knocked on Ola Mae and Valerie's front door later that afternoon. Valerie's flagging health concerned me. Sure, both sisters were spry for early nineties, but still, Valerie hadn't shown her usual pep in weeks.

Ola Mae beamed when she saw the big pot in my hands. "Is that for us?"

"Yes. I made chicken soup for you and Valerie."

"Come on in, dear. Valerie's on the sunporch. Thank you so much. I'll transfer the soup so you can carry your pot home with you. Oh, I'm looking forward to eating this."

I made my way through the marble-topped antiques, floral upholstery, and brocaded curtains to the sunny room.

Valerie sat ensconced in a thick blanket on a lounger, an open book on her lap. She looked up at my arrival. "Hey, River."

Her speech sounded different, less precise. Was she in that much pain? Did she have a mini-stroke? I perched on a wingback chair near where she lay ensconced with blankets. "I hope I'm not intruding. I brought you some soup. I'm sorry you're still under the weather."

She nodded, leaving the open book in place. "It's good to see you, dear. Everything right as rain out in the world?"

"More or less. How are you feeling, Valerie?"

"About the same. Just too tired to do much of anything. It takes the starch out of me to sit here."

"I'll run you to a doctor if you like. This could be something serious. You've not felt well for a couple of months."

She shook her head, a slight movement that telegraphed her disapproval of the idea. "No, thank you. Ola Mae and I don't believe in doctors. They're all practicing, you know."

I bit back a smile. "Even so, there are tests they can do to find out what's wrong."

"It's not our way. I'll be fine, unless I'm not, and then that will take matters out of my hands."

"How did you two develop such a distrust of doctors?"

"Always felt that way. Our mother, God rest her soul, birthed us at home because she couldn't abide doctors either. Maybe she instilled that certainty from the cradle. We were blessed with healthy constitutions and neither of us has ever called upon a doctor."

"What about vaccinations for school?"

"Home-schooled. Mother taught us everything."

"Not your father?"

"He died not long after we were born."

Her mother was widowed early too. "What a remarkable woman," I said. "She did a great job of raising two fine women."

Valerie just barely covered a yawn. "My apologies. I take a lot of catnaps these days."

"I won't keep you. Is there anything else I can do for you?"

She shrugged. "I've got all I need right here. Ola Mae makes sure of that."

I rose and gently patted her shoulder. "Take care. I'll get out of here so you can get your rest."

I made it to the hall before Ola Mae intercepted me with my soup pot. I tucked the pot under my arm. "Thanks."

Ola Mae walked me to the door. "You figure out who killed Jasmine Garr yet?"

"Not a clue, but the cops haven't made much progress either."

"There's no husband and it isn't clear if she had a boyfriend. Looks to me like she played Ash and Milton against each other. Maybe those rumors of unrequited love are true. I'd check them out."

"I'll do that, but I don't understand why someone shot Jasmine in the back. If I knew the reason she was targeted, I'd have a better idea of who to question."

"Well," Ola Mae said, both hands propped on her hips. "If it isn't the animal trapper or the real estate broker, your best bet is to look closer at the person who reported the incident."

"Thanks for the tip," I said, though I'd already spoken to the Chicken Lady. Even as that thought occurred, I was glad I'd thawed out vegetable soup and cookies for Cora. It wouldn't hurt to talk to her again about finding Jasmine. Sometimes people's stories changed.

Ola Mae's expression was deadpan serious as she

opened the door. "Anytime, and thanks for the soup. It smells divine."

"You're welcome." I sailed out of there and cranked the van. Might as well try to connect with Cora right now. I sent her a text message saying I was on the way. Though I waited for a few minutes, she didn't reply.

As I drove to her place, my nerves tingled. Cora wasn't the type to be married to her phone, but we'd all become so accustomed to responding to the various phone beeps and chirps, that it was unusual she didn't reply in the ten minutes it took me to drive to her place.

When I arrived, chickens were in the yard, on the porch, and inside the open doorway. I clutched the cold soup container to my belly, cookies balanced on top, and called out, "Cora?"

The chickens gathered around me, nosily clucking and herding me into the house. This place had weathered several decades of hurricanes. The single-story concrete block structure was furnished with utilitarian pieces as sturdy as the house itself. The only thing that perked up the unrelenting drabness were the colorful ornamental chickens everywhere.

No one in the living room or the kitchen. The only rooms left were the bathroom and bedroom. "Cora? It's River. I brought you some vegetable soup and cookies."

I found her on the floor beside her bed, a bloody gash on the back of her head. I felt for a pulse, half afraid there wouldn't be one, but it was steady. I called her name again but she didn't awaken.

As I dialed the emergency number, I had a chilling thought. Jasmine and Cora were neighbors. Both had been struck from behind. What was going on out here?

Chapter Eighteen

By the time I heard sirens blaring, Cora awakened and rolled onto her back. "Sit tight," I said. "Help is here."

She blinked at me and tried to sit, then groaned and grabbed her head. "Who? I mean, what? I mean, River. What happened?"

"You're at home. There's a bloody knot on your head. Stay put."

"You can't make me go to the hospital."

What was it with this older generation and their distrust of the medical profession? "It's not my call. Let's get an evaluation of your health status."

Heavy footsteps rang out on the steps and pounded inside. Chickens squawked and lit atop lamps, the mattress, bedside tables, and the open closet door. In the flurry of wings, several chicken figurines on the shelf and tables wobbled and fell with spinetingling crashes on the wooden floor.

In the same instant, Deputy Gil Franklin charged through the bedroom door, gun drawn and eyes quartering the room.

"We're down here, deputy," I said from the floor where I sat beside the fallen senior. "I called for help when I found Cora unconscious on the floor."

Franklin nodded to Deputy Zillo. "Stay with them while I clear the house."

Zillo gave me a wry smile. "You turn up in the strangest places."

I pointed to the plastic containers beside me. "I brought soup and cookies out to Cora. When I couldn't rouse her, I called 911."

"You're getting a reputation with the dispatch staff. Every time you call someone is hurt or dead."

"I see many people in my business," I countered.

"Stick to cooking," Zillo said. "It's safer."

Nothing good would come of my snippy retort, so I said nothing.

Deputy Franklin returned, his gun holstered. Zillo put her gun away and went outside to escort the EMTs inside. Franklin squatted next to the prone woman. "House is clear. Cora, what happened?"

Her eyes blinked repeatedly. "I-I-I don't rightly know. I'd just returned from a ramble with my chickens and was thinking about making dinner then the next thing I know I wake up with River beside me."

The EMTs arrived, and Franklin and I were in the way, so we stepped outside under a hazy sky. For some reason, I'd grabbed my bag of cookies. "That's a nasty gash on her head," he said.

"She must've fallen and hit her head on the edge of the bedside table."

"How was she positioned when you found her?"

"Face down." I thought for a moment. "Oh, it's probably not the table then."

"No. From the shape of the lump, something struck her from behind."

The way his cop eyes narrowed concerned me. "I didn't hit her, I swear."

"I don't think you harmed her, but I have to ask you a few questions. Where were you earlier today?"

I recounted my day, ending with my visit to Valerie Reed. "Then I came here and found the door open and her on the floor."

One of the EMTs, a sturdy woman with a rolling gait, came out and told the deputy, "She's asking for River Holloway."

I raised my hand. "That would be me." I turned to the deputy. "May I see what she wants?"

"I'll come with you. We need to get to the bottom of this."

Turned out there was no need to go anywhere. They had Cora belted onto a gurney and rolled her out to us in the living room.

Cora strained to sit up, but the other EMT, a kindly man with a graying beard, gently kept her from lifting her head. "Concussion," he whispered to the deputy, but I understood the word just fine.

I moved to the gurney and took her cold hand. "What can I do for you?"

"You are such a good finder, dear. Mrs. Wiggles is missing. Please look for her."

Since she didn't have dogs or cats, I assumed it was a chicken. This would be a first. I'd never looked for a chicken before. "What does she look like?"

"She's a gorgeous barred Plymouth Rock, about ten pounds worth, who never misses a meal. I've had her for years and she's my favorite with her black and white speckled look and gentle disposition. You've got to find her and quick. I fear for her life."

"When did you see her last?"

"I, uh, can't remember."

Deputy Franklin stepped forward. "Cora, do you remember who struck you?"

Her face paled. "I planned to take a nap after a long hike with my chicks. The next thing I know I'm on the floor, and River is talking to me."

"We need to get her stabilized at the hospital," the male EMT said. "She's dehydrated, and we need to do further testing."

"I can't go to the hospital," Cora said. "I've got chickens to feed."

"I'll come check on them tomorrow and for as long as you need," I offered. "You take it easy and get better."

Her fingers tightened around the bag. "Thank you, dear. I so admire your strength and compassion. You've set my mind at ease."

The gurney rumbled out, and the deputies and I stood on the porch. "What happened here?" Franklin asked. "Who would strike an elderly woman in her home?"

"Is anything missing?" Deputy Zillo asked me.

"I'm not that familiar with her property. Far as I know, the only thing she values is her chickens, and one is missing."

"Does she have any enemies?" Franklin asked.

"Sorry. I don't know."

"Did she take her chickens where they weren't wanted?" Zillo asked.

I was still a bit miffed at Zillo for her earlier crack about the chicken lady. "These are questions you should ask her."

"Here's one you can answer," Franklin said. "Why did you come here today?"

My spine stiffened at his harsh tone. Didn't he know that I was looking into Jasmine's murder? "She's an older woman who lives alone. I take food to people all the time. I told you I'd taken soup to Valerie Reed earlier today. I also brought soup to Cora. Older people often don't eat enough. Far as I know, Cora is all alone in the world. I don't know what happened to her, but if I hadn't visited her, she might have had serious repercussions from being coshed on the head. Maybe whoever did it heard me coming and left before he or she harmed her further."

Franklin shook his head. "Do-gooders. You can't save everyone."

I thought this man was my friend. Now I hated him a little. My lips pressed together.

He drew me aside and spoke confidentially. "You aren't fooling me with your innocent act. I know you're talking to people on my suspect list. You'll get yourself killed one day."

Words tumbled out, fast and furious. "I am a human being who cares for other human beings. I'm also a busy person. Soon as I remove the chickens from the house, I'll close up the place so nothing else wanders inside. I'll make sure the chickens have food and water outdoors, and then I'll leave, unless you and Deputy Zillo prefer to be on chicken patrol."

Zillo's eyes widened, and she made for her vehicle. "Not me. I've got work to do."

Franklin glared at me. "I'll help because I want to see you safely gone from this neighborhood. If Cora didn't run into trouble from today's rambles, this may be a result of what she saw the day Jasmine Garr was killed. I won't leave you in a potentially dangerous situation."

"Suit yourself." I turned on my heel, went back to her bedroom, and scooped up my container of soup. No chickens in that room, so I closed the door. Opening the door of the refrigerator, I saw several cartons of eggs and not much else, so there was plenty of room for a quart of soup and a bag of cookies, both of which I left for her. I made a mental note to keep this woman on my food rotation list.

Deputy Franklin turned out to be an asset. "Where'd you learn how to catch a chicken?" I asked as he systematically caught one chicken after the other.

He grinned. "My grandparents had chickens on their farm. When we visited, it was my job to collect the eggs."

I followed his lead of securing the chickens and soon we had the house cleared and the windows closed. The air felt tight and fetid in the small house. "I see why she kept the house open," I said, trying not to inhale too deeply. "I'd like to lock the door, but I don't know that she has a key with her."

"I doubt she ever locks the door," Franklin said.

I wandered around to the shed, found a sack of grain. "What do I do with this? I don't see a pan to put it in."

Franklin came up behind me. "You sure get yourself in pickles. Here. Let me show you." He sprinkled the grain on the ground and called the chickens. To my surprise, they darted over.

"You're a chicken whisperer," I said as I filled the empty water trough.

He chuckled. "Believe what you like."

We walked back to the vehicles, and I glanced over at

Jasmine's place. "I wonder if Mrs. Wiggles wandered over there."

He groaned. "You're headed next door to look for the lost chicken?"

"I am."

"You know there's nobody in shouting distance if something happens."

"Now deputy, you know I'm not looking for trouble."

"And yet it finds you so often."

He insisted on following me over there. I searched around the house while he waited by his patrol SUV. Jasmine's place had a sad and neglected look, as if it knew its owner died. Even the beautyberry blooms and the swamp flowers around her house seemed less vibrant.

I made the same "Here chicky-chicky-chicky" noises that Deputy Franklin had used to call the flock of chickens to the grain. I heard a faint noise that seemed to come from inside the house. I stood on tiptoes to see in the window, but I wasn't quite tall enough. Oh, to be two inches taller!

Hurrying, I joined the deputy in front of the house. "No sign of the chicken out here, but I hear a noise inside the house."

"This is private property and its ownership is under dispute. You can't go in there."

I challenged him with a knowing gaze. "But you can." When he hesitated, I added, "For a welfare check."

"Not sure that applies to chickens."

"Something is wrong if Mrs. Wiggles is in that house."

He groaned and mounted the steps. "If I don't look, I have a feeling you'll come back and try to get inside."

I followed him. "A helpless animal could be trapped

inside."

"The door should be locked."

But it wasn't. He cracked the door open and called "Police."

The air stirred. Then I heard a sliding sound. It didn't sound like a chicken.

"Stand back," Franklin said, moving from the center of the doorway. "Something or someone is inside."

He took a moment to announce his intention to go inside on his police radio. Deputy Zillo promised she'd circle back.

Franklin pointed to the side of the porch. "Over here. Stay outside." He palmed his gun in both hands and pushed the door wide open. He called the chicken, and we heard the sliding sound again and a squawking chicken.

I held my breath as he advanced in the house, peering around the doorway every now and then. Items in the house were upended and, in the case of pillows and upholstery, some were shredded. I ducked behind the door as I heard heavy footsteps coming my way.

Franklin emerged, Mrs. Wiggles under his arm, and he handed the black and white hen to me. "Somebody locked a gator in Jasmine's bedroom with the chicken. My guess is the chicken sought shelter atop the bed. The gator climbed up and wedged its head in the wrought iron frame."

I gulped, securing Mrs. Wiggles to my side. "There's a gator inside?"

"Yep. I called Animal Control, and they called Trapper Joe."

Deputy Zillo slid to a halt in the drive, lights flashing with no siren. "What's the situation?"

Franklin filled her in. Zillo's gaze tracked from the chicken clutched firmly in my hands to the open door. She peered through the doorway at the chaos. "I have to see this."

Both officers entered the house. I stood there for a moment and then followed them inside. Mrs. Wiggles made clucking noises.

With a sharp eye out for hungry reptiles, I kept the deputies in sight. All at once Mrs. Wiggles went bonkers in my arms with a terrible squawking, and I lost my grip on her. Soon as she was free, she left the building.

I heard that sliding sound again, only now it sounded more like thump-slide, thump-slide. I peered between the gap in the deputies shoulders. Sure enough an alligator was trapped with his head through the footboard rails of an iron-framed bed. The quilt, pillows, and mattress had been shredded by the reptile's claws, and there was a strong, fetid odor.

"What's that smell?" I asked.

Zillo laughed, but she still kept her weapon trained on the gator. "Looks like this experience scared the crap out of the gator."

Embarrassed that I hadn't thought of that, I felt heat steam up my blouse. "Oh."

"You shouldn't be in here," Franklin said.

"Neither should the chicken and the gator. Did someone try to murder Mrs. Wiggles?"

"If they did, they underestimated the chicken."

"How'd the gator get on the bed?"

"I've seen one climb a fence on social media. I'm sure he climbed up there to get his dinner."

I shuddered. "I'm glad the chicken outsmarted him."

"I'll say," Zillo said. "Puts a new spin on all the

chicken jokes in the world."

"Speaking of the chicken, where is it?" Franklin asked.

"She got away from me, but she's no longer inside the house."

Deputy Franklin shut the door and ushered us outside. "Let's hope she knows her way home."

"I'll return to Cora's place to make sure she's there." I paused in the living room to take in the destruction. An antique cabinet must've splintered when it overturned. Bits of china were everywhere. "Iris will be so disappointed her family keepsakes were destroyed."

"No telling what Ms. O'Brien thinks about this place now that she found out it's loaded with debt," Franklin said.

My head bobbed at this astonishing news. "Debt? This place should've been debt-free for as long as it's been in her family."

"It's mortgaged to the hilt. The Nature Coalition is trying to find out how to break the will before it breaks them."

Chapter Nineteen

After all the chicken and gator chaos, I observed that Mrs. Wiggles clucked with her fellow chickens, so I drove home and savored a glass of tea on my back deck, the sun barely cresting the westerly treetops. Birds trilled in the woods, reminding me I was no closer to getting justice for Jasmine Garr. Her debt-laden estate made no sense to me.

Was that why she willed her property to the Coalition? She didn't want to saddle her cousin with debt? I couldn't make heads or tails of the information.

I wished the cops had better luck with their investigation. The problem seemed to be spreading from Jasmine to her neighbor. Someone attacked Cora in her home and targeted her chicken for extinction. What was it about Emmeline Drive?

The facts were that a killer shot Jasmine in the back. Jasmine left her cousin Iris out of her will, but Iris challenged the will, halting the estate closure. Said estate had a hidden cloud of debt, making it less desirable.

Was this case about money instead of the Ash

Braswell-Jasmine-Milton Wainwright alleged love triangle? Passion proved a strong motive but on the other hand, so did greed. All this time I'd assumed Jasmine was a straight shooter, but the debt angle clouded the waters.

The more I thought about it, Jasmine's situation seemed ideal for some slight-of-hand maneuvers. Her freelance career gave her autonomy and freedom to do as she liked. She made a big deal about searching for that rare shrub. It occurred to me that she could've been doing something else with all of that free time, something that cost a lot of money. How could I find out if that theory were true?

Twilight thickened around me. What about those infected scratches on Ash's hands? I assumed he'd told me the truth about their cause, but perhaps he'd gotten them from going after Cora, kidnapping a chicken, and herding a gator into Jasmine's house. Any of those activities might have resulted in hand scratches.

Gators were an unusual element in this case. There'd been a possibly unrelated incident of a gator in someone's carport, gator tracks at Jasmine's house, and then a gator inside her home. We had lots of wild alligators in the rivers but not so many nuisance alligators. I shuddered at the thought of tangling with an alligator. I wondered if by now they'd freed the one trapped on Jasmine's bed and where Trapper Joe took him.

Usually I had a handle on the suspects and a clear way to proceed. I had nothing, except a burning need to see to Cora.

~*~

Cora called just past breakfast on Thursday morning.

"I'm ready to come home, River, and since you're the reason I'm here you can darn well come get me."

"Yes, ma'am, I'll be there as soon as I can."

"Come quick. These people keep taking my blood, and nobody will tell me what they're pumping into my veins."

"Did the doctor give you permission to leave the hospital?"

"I don't need nobody's permission. I'm going home in the next hour. If you can't get here that quick, say so."

"I'll do my best."

She hung up on me. I pocketed my phone and jumped into action. I'd already been thinking about visiting her, so her call dovetailed nicely into that plan. Moving quickly, I filled a medium size cooler with several meal items I had on hand and detoured to the market for bread, milk, and fruit.

Traffic flowed briskly over the causeway. I drove the Buick, with Major and Ivy in the backseat. I was tickled that the cats got along so well, but I sure hoped they didn't run off while I was picking up Cora.

Turned out, she was waiting for me at the curb in a wheelchair, a lanky attendant standing at the ready. I pulled up beside them. "I wasn't expecting you to be outside."

Cora rose from her perch on shaky legs. "Couldn't take no more of that shut-up air and fake light. God didn't intend for people to be hemmed in like that. Felt like I couldn't stretch my wings or scratch in the dirt."

The attendant scowled. "I should hope not. Our hospital is very clean."

Before I could blink, Cora sat in the passenger seat. "Stomp on it," she said.

"A moment, please," the attendant said. "Ms. Holloway, may I have a word with you?"

"Okay."

He gestured for me to get out of the car. I cut the motor and joined him, not trusting Cora to wait for me.

He pulled a roll of papers from his back pocket. "Cora refused treatment, but she has medical issues that require treatment."

"I'm a friend," I said lamely. "She doesn't have any family."

He shoved the papers my way. "Please make sure she follows up with her doctor for treatment as soon as possible. Also, she's gonna have quite a bruise on her hand from where she yanked the IV line out."

Cora sounded like a noncompliant patient. "Is she endangering herself by leaving now?"

"I don't know, ma'am. I'm the transport person. All I can tell you is the head nurse was steaming mad."

I grabbed the papers. "Got it. I'll take her off your hands."

His lips curled into a sneer. "Does she really haul a flock of chickens around Shell Island in her truck?"

Suddenly I'd had a bit too much mainland as well. "Yes, she does."

I stuffed the papers in my purse, cranked the car, and headed back to the island. To my surprise, Ivy had nestled in Cora's lap. "Looks like you've got a friend."

"By my count, I've exactly two friends. Ivy and you. I hate goldarn hospitals. That hatchet-faced woman in there tried to tell me I've got sugar. That ain't right."

Sugar. It was an older term country folk used for diabetes, one I hadn't heard in years. "That can be serious, Cora. If you don't manage it the right way, you could die."

"Nobody would care one way or the other. I'm just the Chicken Lady to everyone on the island."

"I'd care," I said, "and we need to figure out what's going on with your health. Us strong women need to stick together. Did you remember what happened before you fell?"

Her hand stilled from petting the cat and she stared out the passenger window at the marsh flats bordering the road. "No."

"Deputy Franklin will come by later to ask you about it again."

"Nothing to tell him," she muttered.

"You haven't asked about Mrs. Wiggles."

"You found her?"

"I did."

"Where?"

"That's the strange part. The really strange part." I recounted the tale of the trapped gator and chicken.

The woman shrank in her seat, most of her eyes showing. "Holy feathers. She's lucky to be alive."

"I can't imagine how an alligator and your chicken got locked in Jasmine's house."

Cora tsked. "What's this world coming to?"

I was still pondering that question we reached her home. She wouldn't let me read the medical papers but she accepted the groceries, seeing as how she'd been ailing. We opened every door and window in her house, and she perked right up.

"Should I stay with you for a while?"

"Nope. I need a quiet day with my chickens after all that commotion."

She was in good spirits and happy to be home with

her flock, so I left, planning to check on her by phone later today and in person tomorrow after I dropped off my cookies at the ice cream shop. I headed home with both cats, as Cora insisted Ivy belonged to me.

My phone rang as soon as I pulled into the carport. "River Holloway?" a deep voice rumbled after I'd answered with my standard Holloway Catering greeting.

"Yes."

"LaShaundra Delight."

Chapter Twenty

I grinned at the name LaShaundra Delight. Ever since I'd run across this former Savannah drag queen entertainer who'd returned home to Shell Island, she'd called me for various meals. Even though she was biologically a male, she identified by her stage name and gender. No telling what she wanted today. "What can I do for you today, ma'am?"

"Some friends rented a house for the week, and I invited them for a meal. Our schedule is wide open, though we'd prefer your meal this coming Saturday or Sunday."

I thumbed the phone to speaker and flipped over to my calendar. "Give me an idea of how many people and what kind of meal you want so that I can better gauge the time I need."

"I want a seafood buffet for twelve adults. All big eaters like me. Only thing is we don't want anything fried. It needs to be grilled or broiled. Any chance of oysters?"

"Still a bit early for local oysters. Give that choice another month. So we're talking grilled shrimp, blackened fish, and broiled crab cakes?"

"Yes, yes, and yes."

I hurriedly made notes in my phone. "What sides? I can do asparagus, slaw, green beans, broccoli, squash, stewed okra and tomatoes—well just about any vegetable that's available this time of year."

"I want that sweet potato dish everyone makes for Thanksgiving, the one with pecans and melted marshmallows."

"Noted. What else? You may select three sides and bread. What about a salad?"

"Need slaw for the fish. Then something green that isn't beans."

"I'll include a broccoli side, and I assume you prefer cornbread over rolls?"

"You got that right."

"All that's left is dessert. What's your pleasure?"

"I missed out on the ice cream cake at the Creamery last week. I want an ice cream cake, any flavor, and something naughty with booze in it."

"Like a bourbon-laced pecan pie or a rum cake?"

"Rum cake! Land sakes, I haven't thought about that treat in twenty years. Mama used to make that for New Year's. Yes. I want two of those and a batch of oatmeal raisin cookies because one of these gals is on a health kick."

"This will be pricey."

"Not a problem. I want blue corn chips with salsa and guacamole for an appetizer."

I immediately envisioned the blue chips on my yellow platter with bowls of both colorful condiments. My mouth watered. "Sounds yummy and delightful. All right. You know the drill about beverages. I'll serve iced tea, coffee, and water. You'll provide and serve whatever booze you prefer."

"What day?"

"Let me see if I can line things up for Sunday. Saturday is cutting it close for me, but for Sunday, I'll be able to order from my wholesale supplier and keep some costs down. Let me check my seafood suppliers for availability and get you a price before you invite your guests. I'll call you back in a few hours with something definite, and then I need a deposit to hold the date."

"Don't let anyone else steal my date."

"You have first dibs on my weekend, trust me."

"You figure out who shot that veterinarian in the back?"

"It isn't straightforward. Right now I'm trying to discover who wanted her dead."

LaShaundra sniffed copiously. "She always was a bit of a suck-up and a buzzkill. Not many people liked her in our class."

"You went to school with her?"

"Briefly."

"This is my lucky day. I'll be over at three this afternoon with the contract."

~*~

Contract and macadamia nut cookies in hand, I knocked on the gorgeous estate home where LaShaundra and Johnsy Hubbard lived. She met me at the door, made up to the nines, wearing a tight and sultry sequined number and sparkling high heels. An elaborate blonde wig crowned her mahogany head.

"Oh, my! You look like you're headed onstage," I said, a bit starstruck as I followed her to the den.

She smiled coquettishly over her shoulder. "Just

trying on a few gowns to see what'll do for my soiree. I'm asking everyone to dress for dinner so we can reminisce about the good old days."

"Are your guests also former entertainers?"

"Most are. Let me see that contract."

I handed it to her, and she pulled out a pair of rhinestone-studded reading glasses and studied it carefully. "The red drum fish are a little pricey but you'll be happy with them," I said when I saw her scowl. "I allowed four pounds of crab meat for your group. Comparatively, the shrimp are a bargain."

LaShaundra signed with a flourish. "My friends are gonna love your food. Bring your calendar when you come Sunday at six because I'm sure they'll want more deliciousness later in their beach week."

"Never fear, I'll arrive Sunday at four thirty to set up, and I will have a calendar to book more meals." I ran through my spiel of requiring a deposit and she handed me a card to charge the entire meal in advance. Luckily, I had an app on my phone for this sort of thing. Business completed, LaShaundra tore into the cookies.

"Thank you for bringing the cookies. I swear everything I eat of yours is better than the last. How do you do it?"

"I love to cook."

"You must be stirring love into everything you make."

"Speaking of loving things," I began confidently, "I was surprised by your assessment of Jasmine Garr. I had the impression everyone loved her."

LaShaundra took another cookie. "Not hardly. That gal was plumb turned wrong. She used good manners when it suited her, but her true self was an ugly sight."

"I'm usually a good judge of character. That's why I'm stumped. Was she a bully?"

"She left that role for cousin Iris. Jas would smile to your face and stab you in the back. Get this. One kid wanted to be on the debate team, and the Queen Bee said no. This was after we had to beg people to do it. I tried to reason with her, but she said absolutely not when it came to that kid. I never knew what she had against him but she wasn't the kind to forgive and forget."

Another slighted person from her past? "Who was the kid?"

"Oh, just some short-timer. Esme something. Heard she died up Macon-way, head-on collision with a drunk driver."

So much for that possible lead. I reviewed what LaShaundra said and came up with another question. "What would Jasmine need to forgive?"

"Anyone and everyone who ever slighted her. That was a pretty long list, especially if you asked her for a favor. She preferred her own company, and left a sad trail of broken hearts in her wake. Sure she dated, but she was never into having a committed relationship with anyone. She spent her passion on plants, animals, and the search for the *Franklinia alatamaha*. Though she was blessed with looks and brains, she missed out on heart."

"I had no idea. What's your take on why she was killed? As near as I can figure, it could have been a relationship that went sideways, a dissatisfied veterinary customer, her plant search rambles, or whatever she mortgaged her house for."

LaShaundra made a disapproving sound. "Takes a

cold person to shoot another human being in the back."

"True, but a spurned lover would be cold, as would someone whose adored pet died from inferior treatment. By the same token, she could've stumbled into an illegal operation in the woods somewhere, and they couldn't take a chance she'd keep what she saw a secret."

"What was that about a mortgage?"

"Apparently the property is underwater in debt. Jasmine borrowed against it and didn't repay the loan."

"Ooh. This sounds racy. How'd she spend the money? Vegas, dog track, ponies, plastic surgery?"

"Last I heard the cops were sifting through her finances trying to solve that mystery."

"You follow that money, River. My gut says that's how you'll figure who got screwed bad enough to kill her."

Chapter Twenty-One

From LaShaundra's I drove to my favorite seafood mart, Neptune's Bounty, and waited in line at the seafood counter. The proprietor, Jerry Allen, beamed and showed off his new baby pictures to each customer as they passed through the line. Jerry and Dasia named their son Arlian. I was curious how they chose that name. It wasn't one I'd heard before, and Pete and Dasia didn't seem the literary type to plan the alliteration of Arlian Allen, though it had a definite ring to it.

My heart panged at their joy. Pete and I had been trying for months to conceive, and we'd both been tested for fertility and passed. I'd miscarried an early pregnancy months ago and that had been as far as I'd gotten in the world of babies. The doctor said to relax, that these things happened in their own time, but age thirty was already in my rearview mirror. Not too many more years and I'd be out of time.

Behind me, the dangling bells on the door clanged. Everyone in line turned to see who'd entered. Much to my surprise, Iris O'Brien filed in behind me.

"Hey, River," she said, thrusting her sunglasses in her hair and her keys in her double-wide purse. "Glad I caught you. I've been meaning to call."

Mentally crossing my fingers, I hoped she needed a caterer. "What can I do for you?"

"I am in a big mess about my cousin's," she paused to whisper the last word behind her hand, "murder."

"I'm sorry for your difficulties," I said. No way was I breaking the news to her that a gator and a chicken had ruined the furnishings in Jasmine's house. Talking with Iris was like tiptoeing through a field of sleeping rattlesnakes. You didn't want to misstep and set her off.

"It's all wrong," Iris wailed, wringing her hands. "I need your help to find out why she died, and I don't deserve it. I've been rude and ugly, and there was no call to be mean. I was raised better. Only I got so out of sorts by Jasmine winning my award and living in my house with my family things that I couldn't see my nose to spite my face. I thought I was better than everybody else, but now I'm gonna be lucky to stay out of the poor house."

I nodded, hoping she'd continue. "It's okay. Deaths and inheritances often cause division in families."

"The odd thing is, now that people know Jasmine drained her estate, that sucky Milton Wainwright is trying harder than I was to break the will. He called me and said even if the will holds, he'll relinquish the rights to me, the legitimate heir."

She sniffed as we moved a step closer to the sales counter, and Jerry helped the next customer in line. "If we pull it off, I'll get everything I ever wanted with the house, family papers, personal property, and real estate, only I'll have to sell the property to cancel the debt load."

As I recalled, she originally planned to sell the property once she emptied the house. Now there'd be no profit in it. Oh, how things had changed in the span of a few days. "Maybe the bank will work with you in these unusual circumstances," I offered.

"Fat chance of that. I humiliated the Island Land Trust president's wife three months ago at a garden club meeting when she just kept raving about these flowers she used to grow in Maine that are totally unsuitable for our climate. I mean, really? Why would Maine lupines survive the year round heat of coastal Georgia? Any gardener who's ever laid eyes on a hardiness map would know we're zone nine and Maine is a two or three depending on how far you are from the coast."

I shared Iris's frustration. Retirees from elsewhere went through an adjustment phase after they got here. In addition to learning the routes, shopping areas, and doctors, they had to face a sometimes hostile climate, greedy gnats and mosquitoes, hair-trigger natives like Iris, and a Southern culture that varied by neighborhood. My pet peeve was when they mispronounced local road names like Demere, and kept saying it wrong after they were told it rhymed with emery.

"She'll come around." I said.

Iris cut her eyes at me and barked out a laugh. "But she'll never get back the money she spent shipping all those northern plants down here. She should've known there was a reason she couldn't find them at the local nursery."

Seems strange to discuss plants with Iris, but at least

she acted friendly. "They might survive the winter, though it won't be nearly as cold as they're used to, but those plants will certainly burn up next summer."

"It's a crime against nature to commit plant homicide like that." We moved up another place in line. "You'll help me?"

"I don't have any answers, and the Sheriff's Office is investigating the death. They aren't forthcoming with their findings."

"Because they have nothing." Iris vibrated with tension. "They don't know this place or the islanders like you do."

"You're on the suspect list," I countered, tired of the cat-and-mouse game we were playing. "You quarreled publicly with Jasmine ,and you were assumed to be her heir."

"I don't know why I wasn't her heir. Milton Wainwright must've seduced her into changing her will. That's the only thing that makes sense to me. She knew I wanted the china and silver. I've asked her for them many times over the years. She wasn't even using them."

Finally it was my turn at the counter. I ordered my shrimp and read off the list of what else I wanted to pick up on Saturday morning for LaShaundra's party, cooed over the baby picture, and turned to leave.

Iris touched my arm. "You'll do it, right?"

I understood her distress, but this woman had a temper. I didn't want a closer relationship with her. Time to be blunt. "Iris, I have to focus on my business, and it's taking off right now,"

"But you solved the two other homicides that occurred on the island this year. You're a natural at this. Please help me."

I closed my eyes, momentarily hopeless to resist her plea for help, knowing I would cave. True, I was already nosing around but that was for my own reasons. Not for Iris. She had to recognize that I didn't—and wouldn't—answer to her.

"I can't promise anything," I said. "And if I do learn something pertinent, I'll notify the deputies first."

"Sure, sure. We want them to catch the bad people."

Iris followed me outside into the bright sunlight. I pulled my shades down from the top of my head to cover my eyes. "Jasmine had secrets. Are you sure you want her dirty laundry to be public knowledge?"

She copied my sunglasses move. "Not like I can stop the cops from lifting rocks. At least I know you're discreet."

"I can't investigate full-time. As you heard when I placed my seafood order, I have an event this weekend, plus I'm baking a double batch of cookies and cakes for Island Creamery by noon tomorrow."

"Everyone's talking about those cakes and cookies. I missed them last week, but I hope to swing by there on Friday before they sell out." She gave a Miss America wave with her hand. "Toodles."

Patsy Wilson came over that afternoon and, after reviewing the health code regs we had to follow, such as using the hand sink for washing our hands and keeping our hair covered, we baked all the cookies and made the cake layers for the ice cream cake. With the two of us working, we knocked that out and cleaned up in under four hours.

Despite standing on her feet for so long, Patsy

beamed the entire time. "This is a great setup. I see why you love to cook in this kitchen. I'll help you anytime I'm not working at the clinic."

I stuck the mixing bowls in the dishwasher as she dried cookie sheets. "Appreciate it. How's that job going? Dr. Nelson has her own way of doing things."

"I got that vibe from Linette in the first five minutes. It helped that I was familiar with the clinic's software. Trouble is that job won't ever be full-time until they add another vet. She can't pay for more than twenty to twenty-five hours a week, and she promised me thirty."

"My business is picking up now." I started the dishwasher and turned to face her. "I'd like to book you for four hours every Thursday afternoon, and I could use your help serving at the event I'm catering on Sunday, about three hours there."

"Great on both counts." Patsy beamed. "I'm free Sunday afternoon."

"I'll text you the time and address later this week. Pete can help me load the van, so I'll only need you with the serving."

"Whatever you need."

Chapter Twenty Two

After an early morning of baking two cakes and assembling the ice cream cake, I was on time for my Friday high noon delivery. To my surprise, a line of people stood outside the shop.

When I knocked on the back door, Pete and crew burst outside to help me carry the sweets inside. "They're chomping at the bit today," he said, directing his staffers to carry everything.

After I handed everything out the van and closed the door, I asked, "That radio guy from last week isn't here again, is he?"

"Nope. Your treats went viral. These people missed out last week, and they've been waiting nearly an hour for your cookies."

Joy welled up and blossomed into the biggest, splashiest flower. I tried to speak, but my voice sounded like trembly laughter. "Wow."

Pete spun us in a tight circle. "Double wow. We're both making a killing right now. I knew these product lines would sync, and I'm so glad you said yes. Say, on another note, did you see the paper yet? The gators from the golf course ponds disappeared."

Took me a second to switch gears, but I felt so giddy I couldn't focus. "Like they went for a swim in the ocean?"

"Nope. According to reports, they've been missing for a few days."

"That's strange. Who would steal an animal that would eat you?"

"Don't know. The reporter interviewed Sheriff Vargas, and he assured the public there was no cause for concern. His department has everything under control."

I scoffed. "That man wouldn't recognize 'under control' if it swam up and bit his big toe."

"Be that as it may, he's handing out interviews like Halloween candy to Jacksonville and Savannah TV networks who want an official quote."

"Seems odd that gators are in the news again so soon. First we noticed the gator tracks at Jasmine's house, a nuisance gator appeared in a carport, and then the gator and chicken tango occurred in Jasmine's bedroom. Maybe the missing golf course gators are part of this somehow."

"I don't see how it could possibly connect," Pete said. "However, it is unusual that gators are so newsworthy in the last week. They live in the wild year round, but we almost never think or hear about them."

"It is unusual. Since two of the disturbances were on Jasmine's property, I believe gators are relevant to her case. We don't have all the pieces yet, but we're inching closer to the truth."

After finishing at Island Creamery, I swung by the post office to pick up my mail. Both Ola Mae and her sister Valerie were present, with Ola Mae keeping a group of postal patrons entertained. It surprised me to see Valerie there, but I waved to the sisters and rounded the corner to collect my mail from the next section of mailboxes.

Behind me, I heard a faint cry, clothing rustling, and then Ola Mae called loudly, "Val. Oh my God. Valerie. Somebody, help!"

I hurried around the corner to find Valerie on the floor. "Call an ambulance," I shouted.

For the first time, Ola Mae seemed stumped. She stood frozen in place, pale as an ice carving, and stared down at her unconscious sister. I muscled through the small crowd, knelt, and checked to see if Valerie was breathing.

She was.

Relief rolled through me like ocean breakers in a nor'easter. It wasn't too late. I heard Lizzie Collins talking to the 911 operator and felt a second wave of relief. EMTs were coming. I sandwiched Valerie's hand between mine and sat on my heels. "You hang on, Valerie. Help is on the way. I'm here and so's your sister. You're not alone."

Ola Mae moaned in anguish and sank down beside her sister. "Valerie, hon, you can't go. It's not your time, you hear me. You still have many good works to do on this earth. Please hang in there. I can't do this without you."

I glanced up at the crowd. "Where's the ambulance?"

Luther Thompson limped over from the door. "Blue lights coming. Looks like the deputy."

"Y'all make way for him to get in here," I said, hoping it would be Deputy Franklin. "He may know something else we can do for Valerie."

The crowd parted as Deputy Franklin strode in, allowing him access to our party of three on the floor. He knelt beside me. "What happened?"

"Valerie was standing when I came for my mail," I said. "When I was at my mailbox around the corner, she gasped and fell to the floor. She's been unconscious ever since." I glanced down at Valerie. "She's alive, but she needs medical attention."

"Gonna be a long wait. Both ambulance crews just made runs over to the hospital. They have to discharge their patients and drive back to the island. I can take her in my patrol SUV if that's all right with Ms. Ola Mae. Probably get her there fifteen to twenty minutes faster. If it's her heart, every minute counts."

I checked my watch. How was it possible only a few minutes had passed? "By my estimation, she fell five minutes ago. She looked fine before that, even waved at me as I came in."

"Please, take her now," Ola Mae said. "I can't bear to see her like this."

"I don't have a body board in the SUV. We'll have to carry her out of here." He glanced at the seniors hovering over us before his gaze landed on me. "Can you help lift her?"

I nodded. "I lift heavy trays of food all the time."

With him at Valerie's head and me at her feet, we made short work of transporting her to his vehicle parked at the front door and seat-belted her. "River, ride with me to watch her and make sure she doesn't stop breathing. Luther, would you bring Ms. Ola Mae over with Ms. Valerie's insurance cards and IDs."

Ola Mae trailed us outside. "She doesn't have

insurance."

"Surely she has a Medicare card," I said. "Bring that and her driver's license."

Luther gently tugged Ola Mae away from the vehicle. "We'll be right behind you."

Deputy Franklin turned on his siren and his lights and sped across the causeway. I kept glancing over my shoulder to make sure Valerie's chest rose and fell. After each check, I encouraged her to keep going. "You're doing fine, Valerie. Keep breathing. It won't be long now."

My eyes strayed to the speedometer. "I've never been this fast in a vehicle before."

He didn't glance away from the road, where vehicles lined the shoulder allowing a straight shot for us. "We're making good time. We'll be there in two minutes."

I checked on Valerie again, only this time I wasn't sure if she was breathing and had to stare extra-long. Finally her chest rose and fell. Deputy Franklin turned a corner as I glanced over my shoulder, and the world blurred for a few moments. I gripped the armrest and stared toward the horizon. Soon, everything righted itself, and I drew in a shallow breath.

When we arrived at the hospital, E.R. personnel rolled Valerie inside. Deputy Franklin followed the gurney into the triage bay, while I stepped to the nurse's station to fill out her paperwork. Name and phone number were easy. With a start, I realized I didn't know her post office box number. Nor did I know what happened to my mail. I must've dropped it when I saw Valerie on the floor.

Franklin strode toward me in the noisy waiting room.

"Good thing we didn't wait for an ambulance. They're taking her for heart surgery immediately."

I rose, taking in the pallor of his face. "What's wrong?"

"Her heart isn't moving enough blood."

My fingernails dug into my palms. "She's been failing for a while. I urged Valerie to go to a doctor, but neither she nor Ola Mae have ever been to a doctor."

He shook his head. "If she'd had consistent physicals, this crisis could've been prevented. They'll do what they can for her."

His grim tone scared me. "I hope she makes it."

~*~

Franklin directed me to the surgical waiting room, where I helped myself to coffee and a sweet roll. The coffee tasted acrid, and the sweet rolls were sawdust dry. Still, it gave me something to do.

Soon Ola Mae joined me, and her wan face matched the gray sheet-tile flooring. "Luther dropped me off and went home. This is awful, and it's my fault. When she didn't bounce back health-wise, I should've insisted she see a doctor weeks ago but neither of us likes doctors or hospitals. Reminds us of when our husbands died. That was a bad time."

"It's okay, Ola Mae. Best not to dwell on the past right now. The important thing is your sister gets the care she needs."

"I hope it isn't too late." Ola Mae perched on a molded plastic chair, her shoulders nearly touching her ears. "We nearly made an irreversible mistake because of our stubbornness. I won't let that happen again. I'm proof you can teach new tricks to an old dog."

"Be strong, for yourself and Valerie. The doctor said

her condition is very serious."

Pete picked me up at the hospital several hours later when Valerie was in recovery. I'd been so consumed with keeping Ola Mae company and lifting her spirits that I lost track of time and day. I was relieved to see the stack of today's mail on his console.

"Everything all right?" he asked as I sank into my seat.

"It will be. Valerie needed major heart surgery, and now she has a good chance of recovery, according to her surgeon."

"I'm glad you were there to help out, hon. You must be exhausted from baking all morning and falling right into this situation."

"I had a busy day, that's for sure." A few miles rolled by. I realized I hadn't thought about lunch or the case once. Further, I didn't ask Pete about the cookie and cake sales. A yawn slipped out. "How'd we do at the shop?"

His grin stretched from ear to ear. "We sold out in an hour and a half. It was a feeding frenzy in the shop, and then we turned away customers the rest of the afternoon."

The incredible sales seemed surreal after my long stint at the hospital. "Awesome. Sounds like you need more cookies."

"I do, but you're in no shape to do anything tonight."

"I can bake a few batches in the morning, but I've got a catering gig for LaShaundra Delight on Sunday that I need to start prepping for."

"I'll take whatever you can spare. When we have time next week, let's talk strategy."

As we drove over the tallest bridge, another yawn slipped out. "Why's that?"

"We can drive demand for the cookies and cakes by limiting when they're available, or we can keep adding them to the menu to find out what the true demand is. It could be that we could sell cookies every day."

His sales strategy tutorial went in one ear and out the other. "I don't want to bake cookies every day. That'd make me a bakery instead of a catering company."

"We'll figure it out. In any event, high demand is a good thing to have."

"Patsy needs a few more hours of work a week to earn a living wage. Maybe she can help me bake on Monday evenings. We got most of the heavy lifting for today's batch knocked out in four hours yesterday evening. If she's available to help, you could have fresh goodies on Tuesday and Friday. I can't promise more."

Chapter Twenty-Three

In a blink, Saturday's catering prep rolled into Sunday's catering job. Pete said he wouldn't miss any opportunity to see LaShaundra in action, so I cancelled Patsy for the seafood buffet and booked her for Tuesday. Pete and I arrived at four thirty as scheduled and began setting up in the kitchen.

Johnsy Hubbard entered the kitchen wearing a sparkly, spangly amber colored gown. He gestured to the gown and the dyed-to-match pumps. "Is this too much? LaShaundra said I was stressing over nothing, but I don't want to blind anyone."

His attire definitely caught the light, but, knowing Johnsy. that was the point. Further, from what I'd seen of LaShaundra's practice outfit a few days ago, sequins and sparkles would be the theme tonight. "You look great. That color flatters your skin tone."

He smiled, and it was transformative. This Johnsy was someone I'd never seen before, a friendly happy person. "LaShaundra did that for me. She's good with colors and such." He reached down and tugged off the shoes. "I love the dress, but I'm still learning how to love women's shoes. I admire them on others, but barefooted is my preference."

"You'll figure it out."

Barefoot and with shoes in hand, he gave a knowing nod, turned to leave, then halted at the threshold. "Say, LaShaundra mentioned you were working Jasmine's case."

Alarm flared throughout my body as I washed broccoli florets. "I'm not working the case. Unofficially I'm asking some questions to help determine why Jasmine got killed. Someone shot her in the back, for goodness sake."

"She had an effect on people. She either charmed folks because they had something she wanted, or she went after fools standing in her way."

"LaShaundra mentioned she had a mean streak, but I never saw her go after anyone. It puzzles me why she would be so aggressive."

"Trust me, Jasmine only cared about herself," Johnsy said, waggling a finger.

"She cared about her mother too."

"She loved the property her mother owned."

I stared blankly at him. "Oh. I thought she moved Mrs. Garr in to live with her."

"She did. Her mother allowed Jas to live rent-free in the family home, while she lived the high life in a beach condo."

I wrestled with the new facts. "I thought Jasmine inherited the land from her grandmother. Makes sense it passed to her mother first. But, still, all of the landscaping Jasmine did out there must've taken years. Why'd she invest so much of herself if the land wasn't her property?"

"Can't say and don't care." Johnsy examined his bluntly cut fingernails. "LaShaundra asked her to do our gardens. Jasmine turned us down cold. Said her gardens weren't some rich person's frou-frou hobby. LaShaundra nearly blew a gasket. Me too, but you probably expected that. Shea had to physically keep me from punching your friend."

I rolled the name Shea around in my thoughts until I remembered that was Johnsy's nickname for LaShaundra. "Jasmine was friendly to me, and I'm glad you didn't attack her. From what you've said, she wouldn't have fought fair."

His eyes shuttered. "Karma caught up with her, for darn sure."

Pete started the grill for the sea bass. I put the fully cooked sweet potato casserole on the warmer and began roasting the broccoli. My broccoli recipe called for four pounds, and I'd doubled the recipe. It took two big roasting trays to hold everything. The double ovens in LaShaundra's kitchen made my task easier. The slaw and tea stayed in my coolers for now, and the two rum cakes sat side by side on matching crystal cake stands. I set out lovely painted bowls of sea life for the blue corn chips and decided the salsa and guacamole could chill a bit longer in the cooler.

I checked the dining room to be sure the water in the buffet warmer heated as it was supposed to. Looked good. Twelve place settings of stunning red china, sparkling crystal, and silver graced her table. Curious, I picked up a spoon and studied the back. The number 925 was there. Definitely sterling silver. I replaced the spoon and took a moment to rejoice in the quiet and study the beautiful gardens beyond the bank of windows.

Johnsy's allegations against Jasmine sounded harsh but they rang true. Just because I hadn't witnessed someone doing the wrong thing didn't mean they weren't capable of wrongdoing. In my short stint of working on murder cases, I'd been fooled by the social masks people wore.

A door opened loudly overhead. Singing floated down the stairs. I listened intently and recognized the feel-good tune of "Cheek to Cheek." Unable to resist, I stepped out into the hallway to watch LaShaundra's grand entrance. She was resplendent in a violet gown with a slit up to her left thigh.

Pete and Johnsy joined me, and at the sight of an audience, LaShaundra amped up the volume and attitude. As she descended, Johnsy added in a baritone that complemented LaShaundra perfectly. He stepped forward to take her hand and then they danced the length of the hallway. It was spectacular.

Pete and I swayed to their music. It felt magical. Wow. What would it be like to live like this? When they stopped, LaShaundra clapped her hands with glee. "All right. It's definitely an Ella Fitzgerald night. Johnsy, you set up the tunes, I want to check out the food."

She oohed and aahed over every dish, insisting on tasting my sweet potatoes. Her eyes rolled in bliss at the mouthful, so I was happy my version of this casserole met her expectations. "I need you to move in here and cook for me full-time," LaShaundra cooed. "Girl, you can cook."

Feeling saucy, I copied her pose of hand on hip. "Girl, you can sing."

"We goin' make beautiful music together, me and you. Wait and see," the chanteuse said.

Faint sounds of music reached the kitchen, punctuated by three blasts of the doorbell. LaShaundra whooped. "They're here!"

After she charged out, Pete and I shared a smile. "Wow," I said. "This is happening. We know someone famous."

Pete gave me a kiss. "LaShaundra hit the jackpot with your cooking. She can entertain to her heart's delight now. You're just the right fit for her."

I cocked my head. "How so?"

"No judgements. Pleasant. Professional. And of course, your cooking speaks for itself."

Quickly Pete and I moved the appetizers into the den, living room, and dining room. "I'm all about repeat business, as long as it's not mobsters."

Pete chuckled as we retreated to the kitchen. "I don't think Dylan Barresi will be back on Shell Island. Once his rival was arrested, he had a clear shot at what he wanted."

Dylan Barresi was a mysterious fellow from an earlier case. He'd tasted my food at poker night and hired me for a meeting of his "team." I hadn't heard from him since then, which was good. I hardly knew what to think of a man who took all his meetings in a moving limo and paid cash.

The musical stylings of Louis Armstrong's "Isn't it a Lovely Day" filtered into the kitchen as I pulled out a pan of garlic roasted broccoli and turned the florets. "Glad we helped that bad element move along."

The boisterous crowd, all sparkly and sequined for the big to-do, ate everything, and I mean everything. A blonde guest in sky blue looked sad-eyed at the last empty cake stand as I went to remove it. "That was the best cake I've ever eaten," she said. "Cook for us every night?"

"I make it look easy, but I need time to pull something like this off. The soonest I can do this again is Tuesday or Wednesday, but not both. After that, my next opening is Friday."

"Tuesday," Sky Blue said. "My treat, as long as LaShaundra hosts us here again."

I glanced over at the hostess, and she nodded, so I turned to Sky Blue. "Shall we meet in the kitchen? I need to discuss the menu before I can give you a price quote."

"I trust your judgment. Nothing fried. Same amount of food, different seafood dishes and veggies, and something decadently chocolate for dessert."

LaShaundra pulled her guest aside, then Sky Blue turned to me, credit card in hand. "Same price as this meal, paid in full in advance."

"Deal." I quickly processed the payment and returned the card.

Sky Blue, whose name on the card was Chris Greenlaw, waved me over to sit beside her. "Tell us about the case."

I sighed in exasperation toward Johnsy. "First, I'm not part of the official police investigation. I'm an amateur sleuth trying to find out why a local woman was shot. Not a lot to tell at this point. So far motives include greed, passion, and revenge, as I've been made aware that this veterinarian wasn't always a nice person." I paused. "There are also a few oddities."

Chris' eyes gleamed. "Do tell."

"The Nature Coalition has a claim to her family estate, the estate has money issues, gators are on the move, and a rare plant search was re-ignited."

Chris nodded. "The *Franklinia alatamaha*."

"You know it?"

"I hoped to spend time looking for it on our trip here, but I need different gear to tromp through the woods. Definitely didn't pack that."

"It's probably for the best right now, since we don't know why this woman was murdered. You're better off enjoying the seashore and the company of old friends."

She winked at me. "New friends, too."

Chapter Twenty-Four

Monday morning brought paperwork, money deposited in the bank, and helping Rosemarie at the rental.

We rocked out to nineties music, and it was good to stay busy, my mind never far from Valerie Reed's situation. She was recovering and in a rehab center for now. With no insurance, I didn't know how she'd pay her hospital or rehab bill.

After we finished cleaning, we sat on the porch and ate chicken salad on dinner rolls and drank sweet tea. Rosemarie asked, "What's up? You're less chatty than usual."

"Thinking about Valerie Reed. She's been hospitalized since Friday when she had emergency heart surgery. She has no insurance. How will she pay her bills?"

"She should have Medicare at her age," Rosemarie said. "That should cover part of it."

"When I mentioned that card to Ola Mae earlier, she said nothing. Those ladies claim they've never been to the doctor, and I don't know that either woman bothered to get their Medicare cards since they don't believe in doctors or treatments."

"I'm sure the hospital will work something out with her. They're in the habit of getting paid. Are Ola Mae and Valerie wealthy by any chance?"

"Not that I've seen. They pinch pennies same as the rest of us."

Rosemarie sighed. "Maybe that Angel Donor that's been helping others will take care of her medical bills."

"Sounds nice, but we can't count on that. A group of us could rent a place and hold a fundraiser dinner. I'd charge for the food supplies but not for my time."

"That's sweet of you. We should keep that in mind. First though, let's see how things settle. Doesn't help to worry about things we can't control."

"My heart goes out to them. Ola Mae is hit just as hard as her sister with all of this. I can't imagine going to the post office without the sisters there spreading the local news." Death weighed on my thoughts. "In the last year, I've buried Mama and Estelle Bolz. I'd just as soon not have to bury any more of our senior citizens for a while."

"It'll work out, River," Rosemarie said.

I shot her a sideways glance. "How can you be so sure? Are you the Angel Donor?"

She laughed so heartily I couldn't help but join in. "There, now," Rosemarie said. "I feel better and so should you. Nothing beats laughter for lifting one's spirits."

Rosemarie didn't act like someone who gave away thousands of dollars at a time. If she had money to burn, she wouldn't be cleaning houses six days a week.

"You're right, I do feel better."

"Good. Now update me on the case."

I shared what I knew about the reading of Jasmine's will, her cousin's will challenge, the gator sightings, and the kidnapped chicken. It was the last bit of news that Rosemarie focused on.

"A kidnapped chicken?" Rosemarie shook her head and ate another bite of her chicken salad roll. "Why would anyone put a chicken and a gator in a house? Every predator on the planet eats chickens, so whoever did it, must've wanted to hurt our Chicken Lady."

"You're right about Cora Radley being a target. She recently lost another chicken. Somebody has it in for her. I wonder why. And with her being Jasmine's neighbor, I believe these attacks to undermine Cora might be relevant to the case."

"Are you any closer to figuring out why Jasmine was shot?"

"Nope. It's frustrating. Here are the various suspects I'm considering. Jasmine didn't return Ash's interest in deepening their professional relationship, and Iris wanted Ash for herself. So there's a possible romantic angle. Speaking of Iris, for years she's been upset with Jasmine for hoarding all the family heirlooms, and maybe something pushed her into removing Jasmine so she'd inherit. Also, Jasmine's plant-hunting rambles might've put her in the wrong place at the wrong time with an unknown suspect. I learned Jasmine's property is heavily mortgaged, and I wonder why she was so broke."

"That's a lot to chew on," Rosemarie said.

"You're funny. I am so busy cooking I barely have time to focus on this. Jasmine needs justice. She was so attentive to her mother, and I thought I knew her as a kind and generous person." Johnsy and LaShaundra's warnings about Jasmine echoed in my head. They'd known her best ten years ago. People could change. I couldn't bring myself to consider Jasmine wasn't the person I thought she was.

Rosemarie brushed the crumbs from her face. "She didn't get shot for nothing. Somebody wanted her out of the picture."

~*~

Rosemarie's words stuck with me while Patsy and I baked cookies and cakes that evening. Since it looked like Patsy would be a regular helper with cooking, I made arrangements for her Food Handler Card. I also booked Patsy to help with preps for the second catering gig with LaShaundra's friends tomorrow afternoon. Having another set of capable hands in the kitchen suited me just fine.

"You sure this isn't too much for you?" I asked Patsy as we cleaned up. "You can stand on your feet and cook for four hours after helping at the vet clinic all day?"

"The vet job is relatively easy, and Linette doesn't need my help on surgery days for more than two hours. Her assistant feeds the animals most of the time too. I love being here and feeling like I'm doing something productive. Much better than pouring wine at the Wine Bar and watching others mellow out while I got stressed from dealing with drunks."

"Thanks for your help. I couldn't meet this baking demand by myself. If your former job came open again, would you go back?"

"Heck no. I'm making better money and don't have to put up with Reggie's sour moods. Besides, working with women is nice. Feeling like I'm making a difference by helping animals and feeding people is even nicer. I was drifting through life before, caught in a young person's lifestyle and not seeing a different way forward. I was unhappy."

"You are making a difference here and at the vet clinic, never doubt that. Who knows? This may be a steppingstone to Patsy Version 3.0."

She waggled a marble rolling pin at me. "I'm not thinking about leaving either job. Don't you go tempting fate."

"While we're talking about the clinic," I said, "and I understand if you don't want to answer this, but I'm trying to figure out who killed Jasmine. I recently learned her property was heavily mortgaged and she had a mountain of debt. Are there any undercurrents at the clinic about Jasmine leaving them shorthanded?"

"Not that I know of. Linette would like to have another vet join the practice, but she isn't looking. If someone called for an interview or sent a resume, I would've noticed."

I spritzed the clean counter with sanitizer. "Any money problems at Happy Paws?"

"Not that I've seen. My checks cash just fine. Also, they have an electronic system for writing checks. Linette approves the bill payment amount when bills arrive, and I print out the checks that day."

"Good to know."

"I hate to mention this, but it is information, even if it is gossip."

"Gossip often has a foundation. What is it?"

Patsy opened a cabinet by the door and removed her purse. "Something from my Wine Bar days. Some of the guys at the bar one night started talking about dating prospects and Jasmine's name was mentioned."

"Nothing unusual about that. From all appearances, she seemed to be a successful single woman."

"Another guy told them not to waste their time. Said he'd asked her out lots of times and she said she wasn't interested. Because he was such a stud, he assumed she was a lesbian."

"That's hardly a killing offense, if it's true, but that's news to me. She seemed friendly to men and women, but she didn't date in the months I took food to her mom. I think she was just a driven female."

Patsy grinned and headed for the door. "Takes one to know one."

I bustled around the kitchen doing a few more small tasks for tomorrow. I was driven. What of it? Didn't mean that I didn't have time for Pete. The same would've been true for Jasmine. If she wanted companionship, she would've sought it.

Unless she kept that part of her life secret.

Chapter Twenty-Five

Right at noon the next day, I arrived at Island Creamery with four batches of cookies and an ice cream cake. To my surprise, a line of ten people waited in the shop for my cookies and cake.

"How is this possible?" I asked as I unloaded the van. "You said you didn't buy ads or radio promo spots for adding baked goods to the Tuesday lineup."

"I didn't, hon, but your items are that good," Pete said, handing each batch of baked goods to an assembly line of helpers. "I mentioned earlier that you'd gone viral."

"So you did, but I wish there was another word for when something takes off, business-wise."

"You want viral for product sales. It's the best form of advertising there is."

"If you say so. I thought bringing these cookies in would lead to more catering gigs. So far, no new business opportunities off those cookies."

"It'll come. You're operating on a wider platform now. Plus you have the cookie income, which should be making a difference in your company's bottom line."

My bank account had never been so flush with money. For tax simplicity, we'd decided to keep the income from our businesses separate, though we each contributed through owner draws to our joint account. "It does. Thanks for thinking of this."

"You sure you're all right with Patsy helping this evening? I have two trainees working today, and I didn't want to stick them with a potentially busy event on their first week of work."

"I'm fine with Patsy. And truthfully, it will be fine with LaShaundra's friends. Patsy and I work well together."

~*~

LaShaundra's guests fell on my food like piranhas. The Boom Boom shrimp and celery stalks went as soon as I put the serving dishes down. I was afraid people would fuss about the shrimp's battered exterior, but the oven-crisped, gluten-free casings were yummy, if I did say so myself. For the main course, we served broccoli slaw, baked apples, roasted catfish, Brussel sprouts, homemade tortillas, spicy sauce, and crab legs with butter.

The Death by Chocolate layer cakes were huge hits, as expected. With twelve guests, once one person wanted seconds, they all wanted them. Over the hostess's brandy and my coffee, LaShaundra asked me to come sit with her patrons. Tonight they'd all dressed as if going to a Jimmy Buffet concert, so I felt overdressed in my white blouse and black trousers.

"What's this about alligators running wild on the island?" Chris Greenlaw asked. Instead of blue sequins, tonight she sported a Margaritaville tee, tied above the belly, Daisy Duke shorts, hot pink nail polish on her toes, and platform lime green flipflops.

"They were here first and we only think it's our island. They're dangerous. Steer clear of any gators you see, same as you would any other threat down here."

Everyone had more questions, including Dena who asked if the gator guy was cute. Another guest, Avon, asked if it was safe for them to walk on the beach.

I fielded all the questions with common sense answers, ending with, "It is safe to walk around public places on Shell Island. Otherwise, there'd be alerts of danger in the newspaper, on radio, and TV. If you see a gator where it shouldn't be, call the emergency number."

"Any progress on the case?" LaShaundra asked.

Every person in this room leaned in to hear my answer. In that moment of crystalline silence, I realized these people might enjoy my cooking but they loved hearing about The Case.

I turned my empty palms up in a theatrical gesture worthy of this crowd. "I've heard nothing new about the official investigation, other than the cops have asked a gator removal guy to be on standby. I'm still no closer to learning why Jasmine Garr died."

"She acted like a good person," Johnsy said, "but her heart only had room for herself. We've all known divas like that."

"And we've seen diva backlash in action," Chris said.

"Um hmm," Dena said. "Karma is a mean bitch."

The group laughed. "Seriously," LaShaundra said, "this woman wore a mask to the world. River's found some of what was behind the mask. Must be some other nasty business lurking around. Someone who puts themselves first repeatedly doesn't change. I bet she crossed the wrong person and paid with her life."

"Ooh," Avon said, "let's wager a hundred dollars in a betting pool. Winner buys the first round of Holloway Catering dinners on our next visit to Shell Island."

"Great idea," Johnsy said. "I want in on this action. A hundred dollars on the brokenhearted man."

"A hundred on the real estate guy," Dena said. "Them fellas is slippery."

"My money is on the woman vet," said a dark-skinned and blonde-haired Norma Jean. "Two queen bees can't share the same hive. It's a fact of nature."

"Who's left?" said the tall, skinny woman whose name I couldn't remember.

"We got the Chicken Lady, the jealous cousin, and the unknown rare plant rival," LaShaundra said.

Tall and skinny opted for the unknown plant rival. Across the room, a woman with large thighs did a chicken dance and claimed the Chicken Lady. LaShaundra took the cousin.

"Nobody is left," a stunning redhead said.

"That's where it gets fun." LaShaundra grinned. "Use your imagination."

The room broke out in an uproar before the remaining five picked the butler, the island cop, the county extension agent, a mobster, and a post office lady. Johnsy noted each guess in a mason jar.

"Murder is no joke," I said.

"No one's joking here," LaShaundra said. "We're just having a little fun."

"Guess I should be glad none of y'all said the baker."

Chapter Twenty-Six

After a busy Tuesday, I needed to catch my breath on Wednesday. It was all well and good to make money, but between the twice a week baking frenzy for Island Creamery and cooking for LaShaundra and crew, I needed to recharge.

Pete and I had a low-key bacon and eggs breakfast, and then I retreated to my back deck, my nature sounds, and the rare treat of Ivy and Major frolicking in the yard. I closed my eyes to drowse in the morning sunshine, only sleep wouldn't come.

It irked me that I was no closer to finding out who killed Jasmine. She may not have been a totally nice person but she deserved justice, same as the next woman. Those podcasts of hers—I'd meant to start on them before now—those were next on my to-do list.

Just as I picked up my phone to search Jasmine's podcasts, a call came in. It was Iris and she skipped the hellos to say, "I've blocked the Coalition from moving anything out of the house. Not that everything is still in prime condition. That stupid gator made a mess in

Jasmine's house and will probably cost me several thousand dollars in sales to antique dealers."

"It's good you still have some say in the matter," I said politely.

"Looks like I might have a lot of say as me and my kids are Gram's only surviving descendants. My lawyer found Zinnia Drummond's will. She split everything equally between her two daughters, Holly and Marigold, my mom, with the codicil that the estate would not pass down per stirpes, and I had to look that up. Basically, whichever of Gram's daughters lived the longest, the property went to that side of the family. It stated Gram's intention that the property would remain in the family and remain one parcel."

"And if I'm remembering right, your mom died first?"

"She did, and I never knew any of this. Now it makes sense why Aunt Holly wanted an official copy of my mom's death certificate. She used it to get a clear title to the property. Aunt Holly owned the land until she died this summer. Jasmine was an only child, so the entire estate passed to her at that time."

"I see."

Iris exhaled a wobbly breath. "All that time I thought Jasmine hated me because she wouldn't let me have anything from Gram, but she didn't inherit Gram's estate. She never bothered to tell me. She let me stew in bitterness and jealousy for years. I hate her for doing that. Anyway, my lawyer will argue that Jasmine's will violates Gram's intent or something like that."

"At least you finally know the legal sequence of events. That must give you comfort."

"May not matter in the long run. I'm broke. I planned

to sell the property after inheriting it. I don't tell many people this, but Billy O'Brien stopped paying alimony and child support, and I can't afford to sue him. He'd hire a better lawyer anyway. He's all about his partner, and their life in San Francisco. The reason I didn't go to that awards dinner the other night was because I couldn't afford it."

"Iris." I clutched the phone tighter as her sobs became louder. Once she calmed, I said, "It's okay, Iris. You're healthy, and your kids are healthy. You'll get through this."

"How can you maintain such a positive outlook in such a dreary world? I thought Billy would be my forever Sugar Daddy but he flew under a false flag. I need to find someone else, but my desperation scares people off."

"This will be behind you soon enough. Say, to change the subject, I'm interested in knowing more about Dr. Linette Nelson. Since she's the only full-time vet on the island, I thought you might know her personally."

"I always requested Dr. Nelson when I set up my appointments at Happy Paws, but we only had a professional relationship. I didn't want Jasmine caring for my animals."

"Now who's being vindictive?"

"Jasmine fooled many people into thinking she was a brilliant ray of sunshine, except Jasmine's sunniness always felt fake to me."

"People saw what she wanted them to see," I said.

"You got that right. And another thing. With Jasmine gone the road is clear to Ash Braswell, but though I'm attracted to him, I need to marry someone with deep pockets. He's too poor for my taste."

"I thought he owned a pest removal company where he goes and removes small nuisance animals."

"How many wild animals you see running around Shell Island? With nothing to catch, he could be flat broke. His career is an anachronism from another era. Love would not keep us together. Hunger would drive us apart."

After Iris abruptly hung up, I glanced at the tall trees, listened to birdsong, and basked in the warm light until my thoughts cleared. Nothing I could do for Iris's property and financial woes, but I could get started on reviewing those podcasts. I used my phone to access the popular video channel and searched for Jasmine's name.

A list of videos appeared, each one showing a far-gazing image of Jasmine Garr on the cover photo. It felt strange to see her face, and then to see so many images of her. I started with the most recent recording, with Jasmine in a kayak, and the camera panning wide around the lush riverbank.

After a few minutes I learned that she kept track on a map of where she'd searched previously. Today she was accessing a small branch of the Altamaha River and planned to walk the banks when she reached a pre-determined GPS location. The video stopped and started a few times, showing butterflies on natural shrubs, revealing a narrow canal filled with cypress knees, both ghostly and majestic at the same time, and catching a nearby woodpecker hammering into a tree.

At each segment, Jasmine pointed out the different kinds of plants I'd always lumped together in the weed category. My brain had nearly glazed over before she pulled the kayak ashore and hopped out to wander the bank. According to Jasmine, the *Franklinia alatamaha* preferred a sandy loam soil that was well-drained and near a water source.

I saw several panoramas of riverbanks, each a little different than the last. She talked about the plant and referred listeners to her inaugural podcast about the plant for more information.

As the short video ended, Jasmine said, "Not successful today, but there's always tomorrow. Until then, I remain on the lookout for this rarest of plants in the wild."

I watched a dozen videos and couldn't make out a single house or recognizable landmark. However, Jasmine repeatedly referred to a map she used to record the area where she'd searched. What happened to that?

The scope of Jasmine's botanical knowledge impressed me. What a waste for such a brilliant woman's life to be cut short. She loved being outdoors, paddling on the river, and tromping through the woods.

Something was missing, though. In all the freshwater videos she'd posted, not one single alligator was videoed. What did that mean? I thought the rivers around here were chockfull of gators.

Another thought occurred to me. I didn't see a kayak anywhere on her property. Was it borrowed? If so, had someone gotten tired of her using his or her gear?

A couple of times her camera inadvertently panned the kayak. She traveled light with a small backpack and several water bottles. That was it. She dressed in the same style clothing each time, a dark green ball cap, a beige twill shirt, green twill pants, and hiking boots. Sometimes she "put in" at a roadside culvert. Other times she used a boat ramp at a public access point.

There were no photos of her cat, Ivy, and no shots at all with any dogs in them. In fact, the limited scenery shots must've been deliberately angled, so that viewers couldn't tell where she'd been. Guess she didn't want to give any competition a helping hand.

I scrolled through her channel listings and observed her posts averaged about 500 views each. Nothing I'd seen or heard gave me a fresh insight into her murder. I hoped Viv was having better luck scanning these vids from the beginning.

Another day loomed before me, and since I'd been so busy cooking lately, I needed to clean my house and lay in several meals for when Viv delivered that baby.

Sometimes keeping busy was my best sleuthing superpower. While my hands were occupied, random facts in my heard whirled and circled each other until they created new avenues of pursuit.

Chapter Twenty-Seven

I spent the afternoon happily making casseroles for my brother and Viv. For the creamy spinach and mushroom lasagna, I doubled the recipe and Pete and I ate that with a green salad for our supper. As I puttered around getting ready for bed, I looked forward to making my bakery items on Thursday evening to take to Pete's business on Friday.

Jasmine's murder investigation simmered in the back of my mind, but I had too much to do tomorrow morning to do any active sleuthing. It would have to wait until Friday afternoon.

The phone rang, and my immediate plans changed. Viv was in labor and on the way to the hospital. Pete and I raced across the causeway to be with Doug. Thankfully, he'd asked a neighbor to stay with their kids.

Moments after our arrival, Doug loped into the maternity waiting room to greet us. "I can't stay but a second. Thanks for coming. They say it'll be soon." He grinned. "I'm going to be a dad!"

"And we'll be an aunt and uncle, not that I don't already feel that way about Harry and Zoey."

"Me too. I'm not thinking clear right now." He jerked his thumb toward the birthing room. "I better get back to Viv."

Pete and I sat together on a loveseat as we waited. "This is exciting," I said. "We're welcoming a new family member today. I hope Viv is doing okay."

"She'll be fine. She's always been a capable sort of person."

"What does that mean?"

"It means she's strong, healthy, and determined. She'll come through this like so many women before her—a proud mama with a precious child."

The longing in his voice got to me. "You wish it was ours?"

"Sure, don't you?"

"I do, more than I should say, but I didn't want to be a sour grape. What kind of friend and sister does that make me?" I scrubbed my face with my hands. "Long before they got pregnant, we were trying for a baby and wanted one. They got pregnant without meaning to. In what world is that fair?"

"In our world, unfortunately for us." Pete hugged me, and I clung to him for a long moment. Tears blurred my vision. He lifted my chin and continued, "We've had the tests. Everything is okay. Our turn will come."

I dashed the moisture from my cheeks, so very thankful he didn't mention my miscarriage in March. "I wish our kids and theirs could grow up together and be friends. At this rate, it may be years before we have a baby."

"Though I'm not the most church-going of our

family, the saying 'to everything there's a season' applies here. Think about all the seasons we've already had. Remember when Freddie knocked you down on the playground?"

"Yes." A smile bubbled up and quenched my sadness. "You made him apologize."

"I did. I knew all the way back then you were my girl. I didn't want anyone to make you sad, and then I nearly blew it last year with all that trouble in California. Somehow your heart was big enough to forgive me, and I count myself as the luckiest of men every day. We want a baby, but we're together and that counts for something."

"It counts for a lot. Sorry I'm such a mess tonight."

"If you want to try clinical things to increase our chances of conception, I will do anything that makes you happy."

I pulled myself together as another group of people invaded the room. "Let's wait on that. I'm okay, really, and I'm sincerely happy for Doug and Viv."

"That's my girl. Besides, we get to practice parenting skills on their kids, so when ours come we'll be pros."

"Somehow I can't imagine you not knowing what to do."

His breath hitched. "You'd be surprised."

"What?"

"Your detecting hobby. It concerns me that you put yourself in jeopardy."

"I see." Suddenly I felt the ground shift beneath me. "You don't want me to do it?"

"I want to keep you in a bubble so that you stay safe. That's not feasible. You would hate it, you'd hate me, and I'd get dumped. So, no bubble."

"If it's any consolation, I am careful. Finding answers is a way I can balance the scales of justice, a small thing I can do for my fellow islanders, and I'm determined to help Jasmine Garr right now. If I weren't so busy, I'd be out there every minute of the day looking for her killer."

"I understand, but know this, River Holloway Merrick. You are my whole world. The businesses I turn-around, those hobbies fulfill me in the same way that detecting does for you. I can't imagine not being in business."

"That last job in California nearly killed us both."

"I won't do that again. You can take that promise to the bank."

~*~

About thirty minutes later, Doug joined us, beaming. "Our little girl is eight pounds four ounces. We're calling her Ginger Belle after our moms."

My eyes misted. "That's so sweet. Congratulations!" I nearly burst with happiness. This baby was such a blessing for our family, an assurance that the Holloway line would continue.

Not long after, Pete and I got to hold the baby and speak to Viv. She was beaming. We all beamed. The baby cuddled in my arms, and I glowed. Babies were such miracles. We laughed and talked until Viv dozed off. Pete and I took our cue to leave, and somehow it was two in the morning.

Thank goodness Pete drove, because I couldn't keep my eyes open. When we got home, he picked me up to carry me in, but I protested. "I can walk."

He set me down but kept a steadying arm around my waist as he propelled me forward. "Good, because we've both got full days tomorrow. I forgot to mention that your Tuesday delivery sold out in the first hour we were open on Wednesday. We need to renegotiate the cookie order."

I yawned and plodded inside. "I love that they're selling. But I can't think straight right now. Can we talk tomorrow?"

"Yes, but I've got an early staff meeting. Call me after your morning coffee."

It was all I could do to change for bed. What was going on with my cookies? Tomorrow, I mused in Scarlet O'Hara fashion. Tomorrow would bring cookies, a new baby, and a murder investigation, I hoped. Couldn't do much about anything right now. Auntie River needed her sleep.

~*~

Morning came, and I awakened to an empty bed and bright sunshine. A check of my watch confirmed that I'd slept late, much later than usual, but it wasn't every day my brother had a baby.

I made a breakfast casserole, the kind with everything in it. I'd need some tomorrow and I could sneak some in the hospital for Doug and Viv. Usually insurance companies mandated that they'd pay for a twenty-four hour hospital stay post-delivery, barring any complications.

While the casserole baked, I showered, dressed, and sipped my first cup of coffee. Cora Radley wasn't eating enough. Maybe she'd like a veggie omelet since the sausage and bacon in the casserole I was baking wouldn't suit her diet. I made her a spinach, mushroom, and Swiss cheese omelet, and then my casserole was ready.

Loading up a small tray, I carried my breakfast and coffee outside. I owed Pete a phone call, and I dreaded talking to him. I didn't understand the ever-swelling demand for my cookies and cakes. If this kept up, I'd be forced to make a choice to become a bakery or a catering company. No way could I bake cookies all morning, and then cater a larger banquet in the next twenty-four hours.

Currently my Friday delivery was for eight batches of cookies and two cakes. That usually sold out before noon on Saturday. I was making good money on the baked goods, but Pete must be raking it in on the ice cream.

I picked at my casserole, not wanting to finish. The cats ate and lay together, Major kept an eye on our surroundings. Little Ivy purred beside him, her belly round, and her coat sleek.

Finally, I could put it off no longer. I called Pete. "Is this a good time?"

"A good time would be you and me in my office with the door locked."

His sexy tone made me laugh. "Not a chance, Ice Cream Mogul. You wanted to talk cookies. And no innuendos about my cookies. Some things are sacred."

"Trust me. I hold your cookies in the highest regard. You are the sales magic this place needed."

"No magic at all. Just cookies from scratch."

"Delicious cookies that keep customers returning. I have no right to ask you this, but can you make more?"

"More?" My mind went to me and Patsy already baking for four to six hours on Thursday evening and me at it again in the morning hours on Friday before the noon delivery.

"Don't freak out. Next week, I want four batches of cookies delivered on Monday, four more on Wednesday, and four batches with three cakes on Friday."

The wires crossed in my head, but I didn't want to sound negative. "It should be doable. I'll check with Patsy. For how long?"

"Here's the thing with sales. You increase supply as long as the demand is high. Right now the demand for your cookies is incredible. Customers are disappointed when we've sold out, so disappointed they sometimes walk out of the shop without ice cream. I need cookies in the shop, and I'd rather have yours."

"I'll make our agreed-upon Friday delivery, and I'll figure out how to accomplish next week's order."

"Great. And, there's one more thing. The health department received a complaint. Unbeknownst to me, a customer asked for the ingredient list of your cookies. My employee didn't know and said so. Said customer complained. Danny the health inspector said he'd be here first thing tomorrow to see the information. I need it digitally and in print format in a three-ring binder as soon as possible."

"You don't ask for much."

"Ha! You love a challenge."

"My busy day just got busier. Remember you asked for this when I end up living in my commercial kitchen because you need so many cookies."

"Never fear," he said. "I'll find you, and we could always outsource your recipes to a co-packer. That'd give you your time back."

I glared at the phone. "Nope. My cookies. I make them."

"Message received."

I ended the call, texted my contact at the elementary school saying I would miss tutoring today, placed more orders with my supplier, and prepared the ingredient binder Pete had requested as well as a digital format.

With that done, I dropped both the binder and a flash drive at Island Creamery and set off to deliver Cora's omelet. She wasn't home, nor were her chickens. I placed the omelet on a refrigerator shelf, took my egg order from her fridge, and put the money owed in the orange chicken cannister.

I took my time walking out, looking to see if a handgun lay on top of a table or if there were any of Jasmine's things here. Nope. Nothing out of the ordinary.

Chastened, I headed over to the hospital to see Doug and Viv. To my surprise, Viv was checking out of the hospital later today.

The surprises kept coming. "Can you keep Zoey and Harry tonight?" my brother asked.

I drew in a quick breath. "Sorry. Under other circumstances, I'd love to do it. This is my big cookie baking night. I have a huge order of eight batches of cookies and three cakes due at noon tomorrow."

"Can't you make all that stuff now and take the kids tonight?" Doug asked.

"No, Doug," Viv said, from the bed where she reclined burping the baby. "She can't, and you shouldn't have asked her. We can do this. Moms and Dads have been doing this for centuries."

"I want you to take it easy," Doug said, red-faced.

"If I wanted easy, I wouldn't have a husband and three small kids."

"I can help with meals." I thrust the insulated cooler

bag toward Doug. "There's half of a breakfast casserole inside. It's iced down, so it will hold until you get home."

"I'm starving," Viv said. "Let's ask the nurse to nuke that sucker now."

"Good idea," Doug said, and he left with the cooler.

Viv smiled and patted the side of the bed. "He likes to hover. Always thought I'd like that, but it turns out I don't."

A bolt of unease arrowed through me. Would Viv give up on my brother? "Doug means well. This year brought so many changes for him. Generally, it takes him a while to adjust to a new situation. I hope you two can work through this issue."

"We'll certainly discuss it," Viv said with a yawn, "but whether he can give me space to breathe is another matter. He's not the only one with a new situation. I wonder how I'll shepherd three children through life. So many things can go wrong."

"You'll both do fine. Most things in life are common sense and teaching right from wrong. I'm not saying it'll be smooth sailing all the way. Bound to be rough waters at times because that's the nature of life. Pete and I will help as much as we can. Unfortunately, my time isn't always my own due to catering gigs. With Pete's help, I'm suddenly in the black. It's a strange feeling, and truthfully I'm cooking more of my waking hours than I've ever done before."

"You've needed to step outside your comfort zone for a long time. Pete is good for you, same as Doug is good for me." She paused to shift the stirring baby across her knees and pat her bottom. "Say, I haven't mentioned my podcast research. I watched two dozen vids, and they were real snoozes. Found out I don't have rare plant fever. Jasmine's quest to find that *Franklinia alatamaha* was her end-all, be-all. No wonder she didn't date. She was too passionate about those plants."

I couldn't help myself from reaching for the baby. To my delight, Viv allowed me a turn holding little Ginger Belle. She smelled baby fresh and snuggled close like last night. Didn't know if that meant I was a natural or not, but it sure felt that way. Joy filled me from top to bottom, from front to back.

"I watched the newest Jasmine videos," I said, returning to the investigation. "I couldn't find a single landmark to gauge where she was. You're right about her level of animation. She surely loved searching for that flowering tree."

"I didn't notice anything helpful either. Jasmine was so busy walking around and pointing out the plant names around her, it felt like botany class. At the risk of repeating myself, a real snooze for me."

"Her pacing behavior caught my eye. Was she hyper as a kid?"

"I don't recall," Viv said, reaching for her baby. I yielded the infant to her mother, but my arms felt empty afterward.

"Wait a minute," I said as a thought popped into my head. "I saw Jasmine's arms as she spoke. Both of them. No way could a stationary camera keep up with her movements. Someone accompanied her."

Viv's jaw dropped. "You're right. Who could it be?"

"That's a very good question."

Chapter Twenty-Eight

I called my cop friend on the ride back over the causeway. "Been thinking about the Jasmine Garr case. It might be useful to know where her last podcast was filmed. If by any chance she found that rare plant, that would be a gamechanger."

"I've got a connection for video analysis," Deputy Franklin said. "I'll ask them to pull the GPS location of Jasmine's last excursion from the image file."

"That would be a big help in the long run," I said tentatively, "because we don't know what she found there, or if she trespassed and got caught."

"The long run being *my* investigation?"

Though we were talking on the phone, I nodded. "Absolutely."

Franklin cleared his throat. "Moving on, did you read the paper today?"

"I've been too busy to do more than catch my breath. What happened?"

"A reporter did a deep dive on Milton Wainwright. If the young man's allegations are correct, Mr.

Wainwright may have a problem."

"*If* the allegations are true?" I managed a strangled laugh, delighting in playing the devil's advocate. "The story ran in the paper. There are standards for reporting."

"Ah, yes, but as with any system there are loopholes, like the word allegedly. Rest assured this department is looking into the real estate broker. With a surface glance so far, it appears the cub reporter's allegations have substance. Wainwright isn't the upstanding man he presents to the business community."

I crested the final causeway bridge and savored the invigorating island air. "What did you find?"

"That's all I'm prepared to say right now. I mentioned the matter so you wouldn't go off half-cocked to expose the guy as a fraud and maybe even a crook, though you didn't hear that last part from me. River, you risk a lot each time you nose around in our homicide cases. You've been lucky so far, but you've got a husband now, and from what I hear, a brand new niece. Your family relies on you. Do us all a favor and stay safe."

"Um-hmm," I managed as I turned the car toward Iris O'Brien's neighborhood.

"River."

"I hear you, Deputy Franklin. Gotta run."

He sputtered as I ended the call, and it served him right. The news about Wainwright meant something, and Iris had the most to gain if the man was rotten. I drove to a nice home in an upscale waterfront neighborhood. The "For Sale" sign in the yard caught my attention as I parked and strode across the steppingstones set in crushed shells and bordered by shrubs closely trimmed to calf-high.

Iris opened the door with her Yorkie in arms and ushered me inside. "We need to talk. I'm glad you're here. Come on back to the kitchen. My kids are napping upstairs so we need to speak softly."

Two formal rooms branched off the foyer. One looked to be an old-fashioned parlor. Even I wouldn't want to sit long on those rigid chairs. The other room held a gleaming table long enough to feed a dozen. What must it be like to live in such a formal home?

That thought vanished in the next heartbeat. It wouldn't work for me. I preferred a home I could live in, a home that wasn't overly perfumed with air freshener. "I can't stay long, but I just heard the news about Milton."

"That snake," Iris said, showing me into a much more lived-in kitchen stacked with dishes, clutter, and a brimful trash can. "He needed my inheritance for a land deal he put together. The man is unconscionable. Plus, he's running on fumes financially. All of his property holdings are for sale."

I took the chair she indicated. "How do you know all this, Iris?"

Iris sat across from me, placing her dog on the floor. "Researched the county property records under his name. It's publicly searchable. Anyone can log in there and find out what you own, how much it's worth, and how much you paid for it."

"Gotcha. Were you looking into his holdings after the newspaper story aired?"

"Prior." She looked away and cleared her throat. "I, er, may have sent an anonymous tip for that reporter to investigate."

It took a moment for that to soak in. Iris had turned

into an investigator. "So you've been checking him out for a while?"

"Only since Jasmine passed. At first, I vetted him because he seemed interested in me. I wondered about getting involved with him, so I researched his property records to help shape his financial picture. He has a lot of holdings, and I thought he was a man of means." She grabbed a rolled poster from the next chair. "Look at this map."

She pointed out Jasmine's parcel and I saw that the adjacent parcels were cross-hatched and the super parcel circled in red. "I don't understand what this means, but she willed her land to a non-profit."

"I looked up Milton's holdings and the Nature Coalition's. My guess is that Milton planned to do a deal with the Nature Coalition to create a large parcel. He makes most of his money from developments, so I believe he would've billed this as a neighborhood of homes in natural colors, landscaped with native vegetation."

As if on a seesaw, Iris's motive for killing her cousin dropped and Milton's motive increased exponentially. "You have any proof?"

"Nope. Just been calling around asking my builder friends if they'd heard of any new developments going in. Got a nibble from one of the larger construction companies, and it felt right."

"Wouldn't this be fraud?"

"We're talking about a land swindle. It would've been big."

My eyebrows raised. "You're speaking in past tense. Did your appeal succeed? Is Jasmine's property yours now?"

She scowled. "Still in limbo. With the property going to Aunt Holly when my mom passed, I don't have a strong enough claim to the house or land. My lawyer thinks I have a shot at family papers and such. Being excluded makes me feel awful. I may not have been the fair-haired grandchild, but my Gram loved me. She said it all the time."

I wished I remembered what her Gram was like. "That's interesting. Wonder if Zinnia Drummond had more than one will."

"Who knows? She died so long ago."

"Unless both wills were on file with the county. Is it possible Jasmine's mother pulled a fast one to get that property for her side of the family?"

A child's shrill cry came through a small device on the table. Iris rose. "My kids are awake, so we're done. Besides, I don't think I can challenge Gram's will. Must be a statute of limitations on estates. I'm counting on my lawyer to win the personal items case."

I stood too. "Given the huge debt the estate has, winning the case might bankrupt you."

"Doesn't matter, as long as I beat Milton Wainwright. That sucker finally knows what it's like when his world shatters."

Chapter Twenty-Nine

With such a large bakery order due tomorrow, I started early. Patsy would be over sometime in the next hour, but it felt good to have already finished one Death by Chocolate Cake. A knock at my door had me turning too fast. Guess I was at the stage in a case where sudden noises startled me. Hard to forget we had a killer running loose on Shell Island.

Luckily, I had nothing to fear from this visitor. I crossed the room to unlock my door and usher Deputy Gil Franklin inside. "To what do I owe the pleasure?" I asked.

He took two steps into the room and inhaled for all he was worth. Then he did it again. His eyes rolled in bliss. "If you could bottle that scent, you could make millions."

"Except I'm not in the fragrance industry. Cooking is my thing. I love to cook."

"I love to eat." His gaze rested on the empty frosting bowl, and he moved toward it. "What are you doing with this?"

"Washing the bowl. I've got eight batches of cookies and three more cakes to make before noon tomorrow. Contrary to popular belief cookies and cakes do not grow on trees."

"I could lick the bowl clean."

His determined manner worried me. "Move to the other side of the counter."

He retreated, his posture suddenly alert. "What?"

"Park yourself on a stool, and I'll see what I can do for you." When he complied, I scraped the remaining icing into a paper cup and handed it to him with a plastic spoon. "Knock yourself out."

"Thanks."

While he savored each bite of icing, I soaked the mixing bowl in the sink and boxed my cake. "Let's start again," I said. "Has something happened with the case? With Pete?"

"Pete's fine. I'm here because someone registered a complaint against you."

"Oh?" My thoughts shot to the binder of cookie and cake ingredients. Pete had them now so why the complaint?

"They said they wanted you off the case."

In that whiteout moment, I couldn't hear a thing, but I didn't want him to see me as weak. I chanced a small breath and sight and hearing returned, though my heart raced. "I don't know what to say."

"Further, they said us cops should feel embarrassed that an islander routinely outsmarts the entire police force. Vargas is livid. He ordered me to come over here and tell you to stick to cooking."

I spritzed sanitizer on the counter between us while I collected my thoughts. "You're ordering me to stop asking questions about Jasmine?"

"I can only suggest, but, yes, that's the official message."

Ah. Could there be a loophole? "What's the unofficial message?"

He waved a hand and shrugged. "I'm personally not afraid of getting showed up by anyone. Catching bad guys is what we do. If your questions get more response, so be it. At least justice is served."

With a clean cloth, I wiped the counters dry. "So, we're good?"

"For now, but stay out of Sheriff Vargas's way. He sees your success as our failure."

"No problem there. Who made the complaint?"

"Someone on a burner. Can't trace it."

Patsy would be here soon so I pulled out my cookie sheets and stacked them on the stove. "What about Jasmine's last podcast GPS location? Did you get it?"

"I have it, but Vargas says exploring it isn't a priority. I'll have time when I'm off-duty this weekend. You think she found that plant out there?"

My whisk. I needed that again, so I handwashed it. "I'm keeping an open mind about all the suspects. Cora seems fragile, and I'm especially worried about her."

"She got rattled by somebody coming after her chickens," Franklin said. "From what I've heard, she's a survivor."

"What do you mean?"

"She's fed and clothed herself all these years without holding down a steady job. She must sell chicken eggs by the barrel. That money and a small life insurance payout are all the income she has. She's got pluck."

Plucky and thrifty weren't the same thing, but I

agreed she was a survivor. I turned off the water and dried my hands on my apron. "I'm worried about her, but Milton Wainwright is a hot mess. Sounds like he's involved in shady real estate dealings that border on fraud."

"He's under investigation."

I leaned against the counter. "Such as?"

"Such as this is an active case, and Wainwright's financial juggling act most likely has no bearing on the murder."

His comment seemed shortsighted. "Milton stood to profit from Jasmine's death. So did Linette Nelson. And, Iris O'Brien is desperate to overturn the will so she can inherit. What's more, Ash Braswell's hands and arms are covered in scratches."

"Wainwright, Nelson, and O'Brien will be sorted out soon enough."

I tapped my foot. "You didn't mention Ash Braswell."

"Braswell has no dog in the property fight." Franklin's gaze drifted to my cake box. "Critter Control, where he works, specializes in small pest removal. He routinely handles squirrels, raccoons, armadillos, snakes, iguanas, and the like. It follows he got those scratches naturally in the course of removing nuisance wildlife."

I did a doubletake, then started again, cautiously. "You said 'where he works.' I thought he owned that business."

"Critter Control is a subsidiary of a larger extermination company that covers a multi-county coastal region. Ash is an entry-level employee."

Wow. Would Ash's employee status have mattered to Jasmine? Probably not, since they both had an interest in animals. Far as I knew, Ash wasn't after the rare plant. Or was he?

"Do you have a list of people who were searching for that lost plant?" I asked.

He laughed out loud. "It would be easier to make a list of who wasn't interested in the Franklin tree. Say, could I buy that chocolate cake from you? Now that I've tasted the icing, I want the entire cake, too."

My back teeth clenched, and I forcibly worked them apart. "That one's promised to Island Creamery. Better for your waistline to buy a slice of it there."

"The heck with my waistline. You have time to make another cake, and you have a paying customer right here. I'll even pay a premium."

Hmm, a bird-in-the-hand deal. I could make another cake after Patsy and I finished the cookie baking tonight. It'd be a long evening, but I'd be cementing my relationship with the potential next county sheriff.

I reached for the box. "Deal, but no premium price. Pay what you paid last time."

He placed his money on the counter and reverently cradled the box. "River, you've made my day."

Chapter Thirty

Patsy and I mixed, cooked, and laughed to our heart's content. We baked the cookies, made the chocolate cake layers again, and baked additional cake layers for two ice cream cakes. Early Friday morning, I finished the order. Since I planned to stop by Cora's place later, I tucked a frozen soup container in a cooler to offer her.

When I arrived at Island Creamery before noon on Friday, a line of customers once again stretched out of the shop and down the block. It amazed me that people would stand in line for my baking, but what the hey? I'd enjoy the ride while it lasted.

Pete's staff hustled out to help unload, big smiles all around despite the overcast day. I noted he'd added another worker to his Friday staff. Good for him. He knew this place could be more profitable and he'd made it happen. Best of all, he'd enticed me to be part of his success.

Next, I drove to Cora's place on Emmeline Drive. For my own peace of mind, I needed to see her to know she was safe. Her attack the other day baffled me, so I sincerely hoped Cora was feeling better, and her chickens were safe.

With today's mild temperatures, I had my windows down, loving the ocean-fresh island air, so I heard the racket before I rounded the final bend in the road. Squawking chickens perched on her porch rail and in the bushes. Some pecked noisily in the weedy yard. Others walked around emitting solitary loud clucks. No sign of her truck.

Even so, I grabbed my soup and hurried to her door. "Cora?" No answer to my knock. I called louder and then lapped the outside of her house, calling and looking for her. Nobody appeared to be home.

Heart in my throat, I opened her unlocked door and called her name. No live chickens in the house. No Cora either. The inside air smelled musty, and I felt guilty at intruding in her home without her permission. As quickly as possible, I put the frozen soup in her freezer and dashed off a note that I'd stopped by. I also fed and watered her chickens before I left.

I didn't know where the Chicken Lady was, but I might as well check Jasmine's property while I was out here. Cora might be at her former neighbor's place and in medical distress.

The clouds felt heavier and lower in the sky as I pulled into Jasmine's crushed shell driveway. With no yard maintenance happening now, her landscaping had that overripe look. Seed pods waved on the lawn, ragged new growth jutted out of shrubs. The house, with its dark windows, appeared abandoned and forbidding.

Those shiny new locks gleamed on the door, but I still walked up, knocked, and called Cora's name, all to no avail. No one was here, and with each passing breath my skin felt prickly. I recognized the spied-upon sensation, and from the front porch I scanned the property. With so much vegetation here, hiding places abounded, but I didn't see anyone.

"Hello?" I called out. "Anybody here?"

No answer. I returned to my van, locked the doors, and departed. Jasmine's place needed a family living here. It felt lonely, as if it missed human activity.

That ache I felt out here made me think of Jasmine Garr. What did she stumble into? Who did she get crossways with?

I spent the afternoon visiting my suspect list again. At the vet clinic, Linette Nelson assured me that Ash and Milton were Jasmine's only friends. I caught up with Iris at the playground. Her kids ran between the slide, jungle gym, and swings as we chatted.

"Jasmine had no friends," Iris insisted, her Yorkie on a leash at her feet. "She used people to get what she wanted out of life. She was the most selfish person to ever walk the planet."

"She took good care of her mom," I countered.

"Because that rep suited her, and she'd ultimately get the place she'd always craved."

Thunder rumbled, and the dog yelped. Iris waved her kids over. "Time to go."

Stymied, I returned to the van as big raindrops pelted the vehicle. Neither Milton Wainwright nor Ash Braswell answered their phones. I opted not to leave messages because I'd rather talk to them in person.

I reached behind the seat for the local phone directory, but only Milton was listed as having a landline and the home address was his business location. I drove to Wainwright Realty and noted the lights were off and the parking lot empty. That was interesting. I looked up the name of Ash's business, Critter Control, and the phone number was the same one I had for his mobile phone.

Rats. No more suspects to interview. Time to visit the island's font of information. I circled back by the house to get more soup out of my freezer. Major and Ivy sat atop the Buick, so I changed vehicles, and they joined me for a ride to Ola Mae's place. The rain had slowed to a light drizzle, and my windshield wipers creaked on every swipe.

Ola Mae waved me in, delighted to see me and my soup. "Come on in. Valerie will be so happy to see you."

Stepping into their house brimming with antiques and doilies felt like I'd time-traveled to another era. "I should've called first, but I wanted to make sure you ladies were okay."

"We're fine, and Valerie's getting better every day. Even taking her medicine."

"My goodness. That is wonderful news." We turned to their sunporch where Valerie sat on a recliner tricked out in extra pillows, a crossword puzzle book in hand.

Valerie set the book aside and grinned. "River Holloway! Or is it Merrick? I get confused about your last name now."

"My legal name is River Holloway Merrick, but I go by River Holloway because of my catering business. It took years to build up that name recognition."

"Married life suits ya," Valerie said. "What's the news around the island?"

I laughed as I took a seat. "That's why I'm here, to find out what you ladies have heard. My investigation of

Jasmine Garr's death is going nowhere, fast. Wondered what tidbits of information you two knew about her."

"Haven't been to the Post Office in days," Ola Mae said settling in the wheelchair in the corner. "We don't know the latest scuttlebutt."

"I'm not seeking the latest information. Rather, I'm looking for anything you two know about Jasmine Garr. Anything at all."

"You mean like she was arrested for selling babies, she secretly tap-danced with dentists, and she abhorred polka dots?" Ola Mae said, her face deadpan serious.

Stunned, I could only spit out a one-word answer. "What?" How could these ladies withhold this information? "Why are you just telling me this now?"

Valerie chuckled and then cradled her ribs as if laughter was painful. "Oh, don't mind Ola Mae. She was having a bit of fun. You said 'anything at all' and so that's what she told you."

The starch left my spine. She'd spun a tale, and I'd believed it. "Ola Mae, you made that up?"

She grinned from ear to ear. "I did, and it's the most fun I've had all week. You should have seen your face. Just trying to keep it light." She fixed me with a stern look. "Islanders count on you to keep us safe. We have no answers to Jasmine's death here."

Was she sending me a message to leave? I stood. "Sorry to have bothered you. I know getting Valerie back to a hundred percent is your priority."

"Now, now, now," Valerie said with a stern look at her sister. "No need to dash out of here like your tail's on fire. Ola Mae's a free-range chicken. Being cooped up here with me is making her squawk a bit. She meant no harm, and she doesn't come-by caretaking easily like some folks in this room. Please visit with us a spell. Tell us about that brand new baby in your family."

How could I resist? I showed both ladies photos of little Ginger Belle on my phone and explained how cuddly she was, though I didn't sit again.

Valerie nodded. "She's a hand-baby."

I stared at her in a new light. "I've never heard that expression. What does it mean?"

Valerie's smile broadened. "It means Viv needs a baby sling because Ginger Belle will want to cuddle for as long as she can."

"It's an expression our mother used," Ola Mae said. "For goodness sake, Valerie. Speak in plain English." She made a tsking sound. "If Nathan could hear you now."

My ears pricked with interest. I glanced from one woman to another. "Who's Nathan?"

Valerie shot her sister a near-lethal glance. "Somebody from our past who doesn't matter anymore." She cleared her throat. "Now, getting back to the case at hand. It occurs to me that Jasmine had Daddy issues."

Didn't expect that and I wanted to hear more. "How so?"

"In the way of females who either idolized their fathers or those who missed having a dad so much that they only dated men his age. You know, the postmodernism shift due to the change in societal mores."

"Quit showing off, Valerie," Ola Mae groused. "My eyes are glazing over, and River is too polite to complain."

Valerie gave a hint of a shrug. "Suit yourself. All that

hiking in the woods seems clear to this amateur psychologist. Jasmine searched for that rare plant because it assuaged her father hunger. It also suited her narcissist tendencies, and her unceasing quest for parental approval and peer group approval."

I translated her assessment to plain English in my thoughts. "I didn't study psychology but that makes sense. Jasmine bent over backward to help her mom, and she had no close friends. The people who knew her were acquaintances, not friends. She never confided in any of them."

"Because they weren't her father," Valerie said.

"What happened to her dad?" I asked. "I don't remember him."

"Good question. We got to know Holly Garr briefly when she joined the bridge group. She lasted about a minute. It wasn't for her. Anyway, Holly never talked about her husband. Far as I know he wasn't in the picture."

"Dead, divorced, or deadbeat dad?" I wondered aloud.

Ola Mae rose to her feet. "Well, now. Guess we did have a lead for you. So glad you could drop by."

It was a dismissal, and I said goodbye. Out in the Buick with the cats' supervision, I searched online to see what popped up for my dad, who'd been gone nearly twenty-five years. Mostly what I found were genealogy sites where I could pay to access to those government records.

Another idea occurred to me as the sun came out from behind a cloud. To act on it, I drove to the public library and headed for the reference section. Our county's cemetery book released to much local fanfare about eight years ago. My father's death record should be in here, as should Mr. Garr's. I thumbed to the index. Yes, Douglas Allen Holloway was listed. Under Garr, I found one Desmond Ennis Garr, who seemed the right age to be Jasmine's dad, only he wasn't in the same cemetery as Holly Garr. "That's odd," I muttered as I copied the record.

Back in the car, the cats barely opened their eyes from drowsing in the sunny backseat. I recited my findings for them anyway, but it didn't rate even the first meow. However, Major's head turned as if he wanted to hear better.

No matter what tidbits I discovered, Iris, Ash, Milton, and the Chicken Lady remained on the suspect list.

Only one thing would fix my headache and frustration—a comfort food dinner. I'd start with macaroni and cheese.

Chapter Thirty-One

First thing Saturday morning, I took the cats and headed to the Chicken Lady's house. No truck, no Cora Radley. Hmm. I checked inside. The food I'd brought earlier, and the note on the counter were in the same places.

Was she truly missing? I tried her phone. The call rang and rang in my ear but not in the house.

I pondered her absence as I fed and watered her chickens. They seemed flighty and riled up. Odd, but I was no learned student of chicken behavior. Major and Ivy had watched me from the hood of the Buick. As I approached they, leapt down and trotted around the house. Nothing to do but follow the cats because I wasn't leaving them here. Major paused midstride and turned his head just a smidge to catch my eye before dashing into the underbrush.

I called both cats, but they kept striding ahead. Though I wasn't doused with bug spray for hiking, I figured it must be important if both cats were on the same trek. I ducked under a branch and picked my way down the faint animal trail. The further away I traveled from Cora's flock, the louder the clucking of a single chicken became. Briar scratches and tick bites fled from my mind as I zeroed in on the sound.

After stepping over a bramble of weeds and thorns, I saw Major and Ivy sniffing a metal cage. Inside was a plump chicken, a Rhode Island Red, by my estimation. I opened the trap door and stepped away. The hen marched out and trotted home to Cora's place, clucking for all she was worth, ignoring me and the cats. I closed the trap door again and turned the cage on its side so no other chicken could get trapped.

Maybe Deputy Franklin needed to see this. I righted the cage, snapped a pic, and sent it his way. He called immediately.

"What's going on?" he asked.

"Good morning to you, too," I said. "I'm out at Cora Radley's place. She's not been home for at least 24 hours, maybe more. I fed and watered her chickens a little after noon yesterday when she wasn't home, so I checked over here again this morning when I was out running errands. Still no Cora or her truck. I cared for her chickens, then my cats took off through the woods and led me to an animal trap with a chicken in it."

"Same Plymouth Rock that the gator was after?"

I walked through the woods, leaves underfoot giving a satisfying crunch. Virginia Creeper vines brightened the woods with their scarlet and golden fall colors. I hadn't noticed the pretty colors as I followed the cats out here. What else had I missed?

"Nope," I said. "A reddish brown one, Rhode Island Red, I believe."

He chuckled. "We'll make a chicken woman of you

yet. What do you want me to do about the animal cage?"

"I tried to remove it so it wouldn't catch another chicken but it was too heavy to carry. I left it in place and sent you that photo. I am very concerned about Cora."

"She's an adult, and an adult that leads an off-the-grid lifestyle. She may not appreciate you poking around in her life."

"Cora may be hurt somewhere, or be held at gunpoint, or already dead. She doesn't deserve any of those fates."

A strained silence followed. I could almost feel the gears in his head whirling as he weighed and considered different plans of action. "I'll stop by to verify she's not at home and put out a BOLO for her truck. She's not the type to vanish or abandon her flock."

It wasn't much, but probably more than I had a right to expect.

"River?"

Deputy Franklin's voice lanced my musings. "Yes."

"You have news about the case?"

I ducked under a thorny vine. "An amateur psychologist suggested Jasmine had narcissistic tendencies and daddy issues. Further, she thought the impossible search for the rare plant translated into a search for her father's approval."

He snorted into the phone. "First, and don't take this the wrong way, most women have daddy issues and yet very few of them become outdoor adventurers. Second, also generic, and not meant to inflame your feelings, many women and men are self-centered and what they want matters most. That amateur psychologist didn't reveal anything new."

"It was new to me. I spent time with Jasmine and Holly Garr this summer. Holly's her mom. It certainly appeared that Jasmine cared for her mother."

"Doesn't mean there wasn't a conflict. She sought her mother's approval by being her caretaker."

The cats waited for me atop the car, staring in that knowing way of all felines. "Well that's all fine and dandy but nobody better analyze me. If they do, the cookie train will stop.""Now that would be a crime."

Chapter Thirty-Two

"Thanks for seeing me," I said apologetically the next day, whisking through the door of the vet clinic and noting the just-mopped smell of the lobby. "I know you're not open on Sundays, but I need an animal expert."

Dr. Linette Nelson chuckled and locked the door behind me. "As long as it's small animals, I can help, but fair warning, I let you in to help me feed the cats and dogs."

"I'm happy to help. You have the best job to be around animals all day long."

"If you weren't so good at cooking, I'd twist your arm to work for me. Cats and dogs really respond to your energy."

My lips tugged into a smile. "Maybe it's the food aromas in my hair and clothing. A friend is fond of saying I smell like something Grandma baked."

"Whatever, I'm glad for another set of hands. I'll take the dogs and give you the cats. You know the drill."

I did, so I grabbed the cat food cart and rolled it

toward the cat area. Only a few felines here today. All looked sleepy and wary. I cooed and talked to them until they came over to investigate their food. The kitty at the end of the run of cages took the longest to coax from his corner, but he came eventually.

I talked to him as he ate, encouraging him, and he lay down beside the door of the cage, purring. I gave him an ear rub and turned to find Linette watching me.

"You got Mr. Pibb to eat," she said. "Amazing. He's been sulking since he arrived. Have you ever considered you went into the wrong field?"

"I'm sure cooking is what I'm meant to do, but it's nice to help animals. If Mr. Pibb won't eat for you, feel free to call me."

"Actually, I'm hoping you'll look at a German Shepherd that is a recovering surgery patient. Artie had a fatty tumor that impinged on his leg movement. The tumor is out, but he doesn't want to get moving again. Since the dog's surgery, his owner had complications from an emergency appendectomy and can't visit. Maybe you can cheer him up."

Poor thing. "I'll try. What do you have in the way of treats?"

"For a couple of days he'd eat the bone-shaped treats but not anymore, nor any kind of dog food. He misses his home."

We walked outside to the kennel where the Shepherd lay, his eyes rife with suspicion. "What should I do?" I asked as other dogs barked.

Linette spread a blanket on the ground and handed me a can of food, a bowl, and a spoon. "Put his food in this bowl. I'll open his run so he can join you in the yard."

"Sounds easy enough."

The vet surprised me by saying, "I'll slip inside to catch up on some records. Please be patient and get him to eat."

The other kenneled dogs settled once I sat on the ground. I spoke softly to Artie, who didn't move at all from his blanket. I glanced at him from time to time, and he looked away. So I took my time spooning half of the food into the bowl. Then I placed the bowl between me and the run.

The sunshine was so nice, in that warm-without-being-hot way, so I lay down on the blanket and hummed a few songs. I pretended not to notice when the dog limped forward, sniffed the food, then tasted it like it might be full of poison. I kept humming softly, slipping from tune to tune, enjoying this time with nature.

Artie crept forward, nuzzling my hand, and I petted him. He edged closer, leaning on me, sighing like he'd been through the biggest ordeal of his life. He stretched out full length beside me, and I realized he was a big dog with a tender heart. I told him how brave he was, and we both drowsed in the sun a bit.

"Hey," Linette called softly from the doorway. "I see River therapy worked for Artie."

The dog's ear twitched, but he didn't move from my side, even when I sat up. "He's definitely lonely."

"His owner can't take care of him right now, or he'd already be recovering at home. I just learned his owner is in a rehab center and has to stay there for some time. Any chance you could foster Artie for a couple of weeks?"

Artie had gotten a raw deal for sure. "He's a sweet

dog, but I can't make that kind of commitment without talking to Pete. Last time I visited here I came home with Jasmine's Ivy. Besides, we have little kids in and out of our place with Doug and Viv's family. Artie might not like boisterous youngsters."

"Artie needs you, River. He can't keep skipping meals, and he needs to move around to keep his leg limbered up."

I wanted to help this gentle canine. Maybe there was a way. "I can bake him some fresh dog treats. I'll commit to coming back tomorrow and doing this again, but that's as much as I'll let you twist my arm."

Linette looked skeptical.

I soon found out why. Artie wouldn't budge from the blanket. He stared at me with doleful eyes, and my heart cracked wide open. "Okay, okay. I'll take him home."

The vet beamed her approval, and Artie wagged his tail. "What did you want to speak to me about?" Linette asked when I sank back down on the blanket and Artie placed his head on my lap.

"Oh. Right. Cora left her chickens without making provisions for someone to care for them. I've gone by to feed and water them for a few days. They act very ill at ease and anxious. How can I help them?"

"Those chickens have a tight bond with her. They miss her as much as Artie misses his person. If the chickens aren't responding to your good energy, keep doing what you're doing. Are they eating?"

"Yes."

"Then they'll be okay. You'll eventually earn their trust through familiarity." Linette's brow creased with lines. "What possessed Cora to leave her chickens behind? She's very attached to them."

I gave a sigh of relief for the chickens. Now I needed to figure out what happened to Cora. "I thought so too, but no one's seen her or her truck in days. I reported her missing yesterday after going over there twice and not finding her. I also discovered one of her chickens penned in a trap in the woods. It's strange."

"Cora's a strange woman. Unusual behavior is the norm for her. Before Jasmine died, would you have known if Cora left the chickens to fend for themselves for a few days?"

"No, but someone should know where she went, and she would've made arrangements to care for her flock." I pondered a narrow, lacy cloud for a long moment, daring to voice a niggling suspicion. "Is her absence related to Jasmine's homicide?"

"I don't know, but I have mounds of laundry to wash and my weekly grocery shopping to do. Let's get you and Artie in your car."

Another thought darted into my head and onto my tongue. "Sure, but I have another question. Do you know if Jasmine owned a gun?"

"She had handguns and rifles. She repeatedly invited me to target shoot with her. I declined. I never want to shoot anything, and I will never own a gun. I became a vet because in my childhood someone shot a neighbor's dog that died in my yard."

How awful. "Goodness, that must've been traumatic."

"Very, more so because my mother wouldn't stop crying."

"I'm so sorry."

"Thanks, but I don't dwell on the past. People are best served by looking ahead. So let's get you two loaded up and on your way."

Fortunately, I was in the Buick. When I opened the driver's door to set my purse down, Artie lunged for the passenger seat, his mouth open in the equivalent of a doggie grin, his pink tongue lolling.

Linette laughed. "He's really taken with you."

Artie filled the entire passenger seat. "I hope he doesn't chase cats."

"He'll be fine. You let him know the cats are part of his pack, and this dog will accept that condition."

"I've never had a dog, but Pete has. He'll know how to train him."

"Pete can be his trainer, but I assure you, this dog has imprinted on you. He'll be your shadow."

~*~

Pete bounded home when he heard the news. "We got a dog?"

I gripped my hands tightly together, hoping like anything my husband would be okay with another impulsive decision. "A temporary dog. Artie wasn't thriving at the vet clinic, and his elderly owner had an emergency appendectomy and now requires physical therapy in a rehab facility. The dog had surgery on a fatty tumor behind his left leg, so we have to be careful of that as it heals."

Artie kept glancing at me as Pete approached. So I knelt down and made sure Artie was comfortable with Pete. "Linette sent home some canned food, but I might try making food for him."

Pete let the dog sniff his hand. It took a few moments until Artie relaxed on his blanket. "He seems to have a very gentle disposition," Pete said. "Any idea of his history?"

"Nope. I told you everything I know. I wasn't

planning to bring a dog home. It just happened." I gave him the story of the blanket and of Artie lying down beside me. "I planned to return tomorrow to feed him, but Artie and the vet had a different plan."

"It's fine with me," Pete said, stroking the dog's head and offering me a hand up. "Were you asking Linette questions about the case?"

"I asked her how to calm Cora's chickens. They don't respond to me in the same way that cats and dogs respond."

"Thank goodness or we'd have a flock of chickens here too." He cleared his throat. "So, where are you on the investigation?'

"Same place as before. The cousin, the real estate broker, the neighbor, and the boyfriend wannabe still seem likely candidates to have killed Jasmine. However, I feel it's less likely that the vet had anything to do with the murder."

"Are those suspects listed in any particular order?"

"No, but I asked Linette if Jasmine owned a gun. She said yes."

"Did the cops say Jasmine's gun was missing?"

"They never indicated that she owned a firearm."

Pete shook his head. "They should've found something by now on her phone or computer."

"Haven't heard a peep about that either."

"Hmm. Sounds like that's all you can do on the case today."

"You got something else in mind?"

"Definitely." He opened his arms for a hug. "Let me take your mind off your troubles."

I melted into his embrace. "You have the best ideas."

Chapter Thirty-Three

Due to a late start on Sunday evening, Patsy and I only baked two of the four batches of cookies for the Island Creamery order. I got up super early on Monday morning, early enough to see the sunrise, due to Artie suddenly barking at the door to go outside.

I took him out on a leash, and the dog leaned on me as he circled the yard the first time. He finally found the right spot to relieve himself, and then we relaxed with coffee on the deck. Artie watched the nearby cats with suspicion. Ivy darted into the woods immediately, but Major sat on the wooden deck railing staring at Artie and communicating in the silent language of pets.

When Major decided to eat his breakfast minutes later, Artie tugged at the leash. By the time I got him settled, Major finished eating and jumped in my lap, purring. Artie sighed and drowsed beside us, and I felt like a real pet mother. Ivy somehow found the courage to eat her breakfast, then returned to her perch on the deck railing.

I made breakfast for Pete a short while later, then he

was off to work and I had two batches of cookies to bake. I left Artie inside the house, and the cats in the yard. The dog barked a bit, but I kept a firm grip on my heart. I had work to do.

Baking and icing cookies calmed me much as lying on a blanket next to me calmed our fostered German Shepherd yesterday. Soon, I had trays of ghosts, pumpkins, and smiling moons. Pete's staff grinned like crazy when they saw today's batch. A tiny slip of a gal said, "These will sell like crazy."

I hoped so. Check in hand for last week's sales, I deposited the earnings in my bank account and motored to the post office. The parking lot was packed. I hurried inside. Ola Mae stood near the mail slot, her face animated as she spoke. She waved me forward.

"You hear the latest?" she asked. Before I could answer, she continued, "Ash Braswell was arrested at daybreak for operating an unlicensed alligator farm. Can you believe that?"

I shook my head to clear the cobwebs from my ears. "What?"

"Heard it on my police scanner this morning. Apparently his gator pen is not very far as the crow flies from Jasmine's property."

The information did not compute. "Ash was raising alligators?"

"Not sure what he was doing with them."

A sudden silence filled the crowded lobby, and I felt the awful weight of everyone's gaze. "I'm stunned by this news. I had no idea, and now I'm wondering if this is related to Jasmine's murder."

Ola Mae pointed her finger at me. "Exactly."

"We shouldn't get ahead of ourselves," I said. "He

could have a perfectly good reason for having an alligator farm."

"Even though they're illegal?" Lizzie Collins asked, her face a stern mask of disapproval.

Having been on the wrong end of people's hasty decisions before, I automatically defended Ash. "With our sheriff's past pattern of rushing to judgment, we can't automatically assume Ash is a killer. Sure, he broke the law by penning up gators. Everyone in this room has made a rolling stop at an intersection or speeded at times. We're not stone cold killers and until we know the entire situation, we can't say that Ash is guilty of anything else."

"He's too handsome to be a stone cold killer," Deb Haversmith hollered from the doorway. "Those eyelashes of his would stop any woman's beating heart."

Everyone chuckled. "Who's gonna post his bail?" Ola Mae said. "Far as I know he's got no family round these parts."

There was a muttering of conversations, and I took that opportunity to duck through the crowd, collect my mail, and escape. Outside in the bright sunlight of a warm fall day, I saw I'd missed a call from Deputy Gil Franklin.

Talk about serendipity. I wouldn't need to invent a reason to call him. I hit the call icon and waited for him to pick up. Unfortunately, the call shot straight to voice mail. My message to him was short. "Call me."

"Our future sheriff got anything to say about all this," Ola Mae said from over my shoulder.

I turned to greet her and shook my head. "Can't reach him."

She studied me intently. "You think Ash isn't the killer?"

"I don't have enough information, and at this point, it's likely the cops don't either. For instance, I don't know if he owns a gun or if he knows how to use one. He cared for Jasmine, so why shoot her? But again, I don't know where their relationship stood. It's my belief Jasmine was married to her search for that rare plant. She didn't have the time or interest for a personal relationship."

Ola Mae seemed to chew on that for a long moment. "Poor Ash. Got no people. Got his heart stomped by a woman. Now he's in the pokey. You heading over there to spring him?"

"Nope. Gotta help Rosemarie clean the rental cottage. That always clears my head."

"Gal, you got more energy than three power plants. I don't know how you do everything."

"I always have a lot to do, so I'm thankful I don't run out of energy," I said. "I meant to ask you earlier. How's Valerie?"

"Getting better every day. She'll be great after I stop at Island Creamery and buy her some cookies and ice cream. Your husband was smart to connect with Holloway Catering. That place is hopping every time I drive by there."

"I'm glad it's working out for both of us. Catch you later." With a wave, I threaded my way through the crowded parking lot to the van. A page of paper fluttered under my windshield wiper, same as on most of the other cars. I grabbed it, saw it was a "Re-Elect Sheriff Vargas" flyer, and tossed it on the passenger seat to recycle at home.

The page landed upside down, and spindly writing caught my eye. I picked up the flyer again. The words read, "Stay out of it."

My mood underwent a sea-change from becalmed ebb tide to that of a hurricane-churned surf. Quickly, I locked the doors of the van and scanned the parking lot. No one in sight. Even Ola Mae was gone.

Should I take this warning to Pete or Deputy Franklin? How serious was this threat, and what did this person want me to stay out of? Since it was inscribed on a campaign flyer, it could be about the upcoming election. Sheriff Vargas had to know I wanted a different sheriff.

But I wasn't actively advocating my choice of Deputy Franklin for sheriff. That only left the case. No way could I stay out of that. Jasmine needed justice, and the official investigation moved at a snail's pace.

I just had to do things smarter, that's all.

~*~

I zipped home and made grilled cheese sandwiches with fig jam, Rosemarie's all-time favorite, and something I'd developed a hankering for.

With nineties music blasting, we cleaned and rocked out, finishing up at three. Rosemarie squealed with delight when she opened her late lunch surprise. "My favorite! Yum."

As we ate, I told her about our new foster dog, Artie.

"Artie. I know that name." Rosemarie snapped her fingers a few times before grinning and pointing her finger at me. "Duvall Shannon has a dog named Artie. Wonder if it's the same canine."

"Shy German Shepherd, who's a bit needy, loves to lie down touching me, and is recovering from a fatty tumor removal?"

"Sounds like the same pet. Did you know he's a retired police dog?"

My brows rose. "Get out! Pete's been looking for a dog like Artie for us. This is unbelievable."

"How's he doing with the cats?"

"So far so good. The vet warned that he'd be my shadow and that happened immediately. It nearly breaks the dog's heart when I go to my commercial kitchen, and he can't follow."

"Maybe you'll get to keep Artie. Duvall's lungs are bad, and he's no spring chicken at 95."

"We'd love for it to work in our favor, but it will be hard to let him go. I enjoy having him around, except for his sleeping on my pillow."

"I can see how that would take some adjustment."

Our conversation drifted for a bit, then Rosemarie asked if I'd heard about Ash's arrest and arraignment.

"Heard about his arrest this morning but not an arraignment. How do you hear all this so fast?" I asked. "I have a call in to Deputy Franklin. You'd think I'd be on top of the news. Tell me."

"My boyfriend's cop friend told him that Ash broke down in tears when he went there to feed his gators at daybreak. Cops swarmed the place, and then Trapper Joe from Savannah seized his gators."

"What happens to them?"

"Don't know," Rosemarie said, "and don't care."

"Why would Ash pen them up anyway?" I asked, not really expecting an answer.

"Meat. People eat gator meat. Also skins. Companies buy hides to make alligator leather everything."

"So, it could've been a second job."

"Not hardly." Rosemarie's eyes glittered. "A TV crew ambushed him on the steps when he made bail. Ash broke down in tears and apologized. Said he couldn't release the nuisance gators Critter Control removed from people's yards because they'd just become a nuisance again. Apparently that happened a half dozen times before he realized he needed a different solution. So he built small, fenced ponds and kept them." She named the TV station. "Be sure to watch the evening news when they run the clip again."

"How'd they discover the gator farm?"

"Your cop hired a tracker who followed the gator prints from Jasmine's yard to the farm. Anyway, they staked the place out and nabbed Ash when he came to feed the gators."

"This is so bizarre. I never imagined a gator farm on Shell Island. Are they legal in Georgia? And if so, doesn't Ash need a license to operate one?"

"Certainly and he didn't. Get this. Some high-priced lawyer paid his bail. That twist has the cops scratching their heads."

Ash couldn't afford a high-priced anything. Not unless he'd been socking away cash from his illegal alligator enterprise. "That is interesting."

Rosemarie gave a telling smirk.

"There's more?" I asked.

"An anonymous donor paid his bail and his lawyer."

"Wow. That's impressive. The Angel Donor strikes again. He or she must be a real crusader for social justice."

The Angel Donor started helping people in our community six months ago. Nobody had any idea who could afford this level of charity, much less operate so secretly.

"Wow is right," Rosemarie said. "It's never a dull moment on the island. Can't wait to see what happens next."

~*~

Pete and I watched the evening news on the sofa, kitties nestled atop the unused sofa cushions, Artie lying across our feet. Finally they reached the segment they called Gator Boy. A tearful Ash Braswell wearing a vintage navy blue T-shirt proclaiming 1990 as his birth year stared directly into the camera. "I'm sorry. I tried to do the right thing. I couldn't kill them, and I couldn't let them go. Either way, I broke the law. I thought if I kept them fed and out of sight, everything would be okay. I had no clue that gators could climb fences, and I sincerely apologize for the gator breakouts. Truthfully, I'm glad it's over. I couldn't afford enough food to keep them fat and happy without calling attention to my site. Rehoming those gators is best for everyone involved."

The reporter ended the story, and we switched off the television. Seeing was believing, and I had an irresistible urge to visit Ash's gator operation. "I'd like to find that gator farm. We know the cops found it by starting in Jasmine's back yard."

"Neither of us have animal tracking skills," Pete pointed out.

"That was my first thought," I said. "Then I realized we had access to a bona fide tracker. Artie is a former police dog. I bet he can track gators."

"It's not as easy as point and click," Pete said. "We'd need something with a gator's scent on it."

"Something like Jasmine's bed linens?"

He hesitated then nodded. "I see where you're going

with this. You propose that we trespass and steal an item that doesn't belong to us."

"Sounds bad when you put it that way."

"It is bad, and Deputy Franklin won't like you wading into his case."

I hadn't heard from my cop friend all day. "Deputy Franklin can kiss my grits."

Chapter Thirty-Four

Deputy Franklin called late Tuesday morning when I was pulling home-baked dog treats from my oven. My foster dog and new shadow, Artie, sniffed the air appreciably and kept a close eye on my activity.

"Sorry to have been out of pocket. Lots going on at my end," Franklin began.

I clung to the phone, not wanting to miss a single syllable. "I heard about Ash Braswell's arrest. He seemed relieved that he no longer had to hide his secret. His tearful TV interview jerked my heartstrings. He sounded very emotional."

Franklin took a long moment before responding. "He's emotional all right, and before you ask, yes, he's still on the suspect list for Ms. Garr's murder."

"How so? He cared for her."

"What if she followed gator tracks to his unlicensed compound? She would've had to report him, giving him a strong motive to kill her."

"Is that what you did?"

"I'm not at liberty to say."

I sucked in air through clenched teeth. "Okay. I understand, but if Jasmine found his gator farm, by whatever means, that would be a game changer. Despite Ash's feelings for her, she would become an instant liability. He might've had to choose between his freedom and unrequited romance."

"Believe it or not, some people choose murder over going to prison."

I eased over to the back door. The cats lay side by side on the deck in a pool of sunshine. "Poor Ash. He has no family left. His adoptive parents have passed, and he's all alone in the world. That's a hard road to travel, but it doesn't make him a killer."

"He's a criminal, River, and he should be in jail. Don't romanticize his actions."

Though I didn't care for the sharp edge of his voice, he was right. I didn't want Ash to be guilty because he'd gone to such lengths to protect those gators. He was the underdog, in my opinion. He needed loving care and friendship. Playground kids told him he was adopted way back when, and from that day forward he called his adoptive parents by their first names. I didn't know that he'd ever searched for his biological parents, but what must it be like to be so alone?

"Listen," the deputy said, "this will hit the radio and TV news soon, if it hasn't already gone viral through the island grapevine. Milton Wainwright is under arrest for real estate fraud and false advertising. He had a handgun in his bedroom with the same size bullets as the one that killed Ms. Garr."

"Ash told me Milton owned a gun, so I'm not surprised. Did the bullet rifling match?"

"Testing is occurring right now."

I drifted over to the kitchen table and sat. "What kind of fraud?"

"He misrepresented properties, omitted negative aspects, promised extras would be done, and generally lied about almost everything. Iris O'Brien was right to be worried about him scamming her cousin. I'm fairly certain that was the case, though you didn't hear that from me."

Some people had no moral compass. "Glad I never had any real estate dealings with him. He sure had me fooled with his fake sympathy and all. Iris called him a sociopath, no, wait, I think she said he was a narcissist. In any event, everything was always about him, a hundred percent."

"In the course of satisfying his need to be top dog, he scammed thousands from every client. His reach is so extensive we've a forensic accountant digging into his financials."

Those poor people. He'd betrayed their trust. "Sounds like a huge mess, and I guess this misconduct didn't exonerate him from Jasmine's suspect list."

"Nope. He's looking good for murder from where I sit."

I gazed out the door at the cats lounging on the deck railing. They seemed unconcerned about everything, even Ivy, whose pet mama got shot. "What about the Chicken Lady? I'm still feeding her chickens."

"No sign of her or her truck. I can't ask her neighbors either, because Jasmine is dead."

"Her mind's sharp, and her body's strong from staying physically active her entire life. I hope she's somewhere safe, but I don't believe she abandoned her chickens. It's more likely that she isn't safe, that someone abducted her."

"Who would take that woman? She'd scratch your eyes out in a heartbeat. I've seen her angry before, and it's ugly. You think she's come to harm. I think she's laying low until we arrest somebody else for Jasmine's murder."

"I respectfully disagree. Maybe she already came home."

"Not there. I have patrols check her house twice a day. She's in the wind."

"No way she willingly abandoned her flock. She wouldn't leave home unless someone threatened her life."

"Let's agree to disagree on the fate of Cora. Watch your back," Franklin said. "This case is reaching the boiling point. People do bad things when they get desperate."

"Uh, regarding that. There's something I should mention. Yesterday, someone left a threatening note on my windshield telling me to 'stay out of it.' Since it was on the back of a flyer for Sheriff Vargas, I thought it was in reference to the election. Then I realized that it could be about the case."

"Good advice," Franklin said. "You should stay out of it."

"I can't walk away. Not now. Jasmine needs an advocate, and I'm all she's got. Let's face it. You can't flush the killer from the suspect pool either."

"No comment," Franklin said with a deep sigh. "What does Pete say about this note?"

"I haven't told him yet. Thought I'd run it by you first."

"The killer is watching you. That's not good. You

should walk away."

"Not happening."

"Then be safe about it.

"Thought you might say that."

After the call ended, I glanced at my pan of dog treats. I'd meant to remove them from the pan as soon as they cleared the oven, but in the distraction of my conversation with Franklin, I'd forgotten to do it.

The pan was empty.

Hmm. The cats were outside, and Artie wasn't glued to my feet. I found him in the living room, racked out on the sectional sofa. His breath smelled like liver. He didn't even crack an eye when I approached.

"Bad dog," I said. His mouth curled into a canine grin.

Lesson learned—a big dog like Artie could easily eat off my kitchen counters. Note to self—don't leave anything on the counter unless I want it eaten.

~*~

Iris and her little ones were at the park after lunch. "No school today," she said, making room on the bench for me, "so there's no preschool either. Seems like every year there are more school holidays."

I nodded in agreement. "Did you hear the news?"

"The news where Ash was arrested for running an illegal gator farm, or the news where Milton got in trouble for being himself? I feel sorry for Ash. He has a good heart, but Milton has always had his hand in everyone's cookie jar. Milton is not a nice person, and if there's any justice in this world, he'll be convicted and serve time."

The news grapevine on this island must be supercharged. "Not vindictive are you?"

She chuckled. "Not much."

We listened to the happy shrieks of playing children. Someday my kids would play here, I hoped. "So what's happening with Jasmine's property? With Ash's gators out of the woods, you don't have to worry about gators trekking through that yard."

Iris sighed. "My lawyer encouraged me to abandon my claim. Said anything I want from the estate will cost less in the long run that way. I don't know what's best for me. For so long, I've wanted that property. Jasmine's ownership of it was a real thorn in my side. Now that she's not around, I feel the need to take action. What if I could somehow manage to hang onto our family legacy for my kids?"

Interesting. I didn't take her as having an ounce of sentimentality. She'd previously indicated that the possession of the Garr homestead was about keeping score. Now she wanted to save the land? That didn't sound like the Iris I knew.

"If you decide to keep it, can you manage the debt load?" I asked.

"I'll figure something out. Look, I know I'm not the most likeable person, and people think I'm vindictive. The truth is I took a hard look at myself in the mirror last night. I'm all out of family. Jasmine's place is where my ancestors lived and walked the earth. If I sell it, my kids will never have that connection."

Her words rang with conviction. "That's a good point. Would you move there?"

She shook her head. "I've pictured us living there several times, and the mental image always blows up like a cartoon explosion. That feels like a strong subliminal message from the universe not to move there. My personal feelings for the house are mixed with my emotions of being a second-class citizen among that branch of my family. But I have to rise above those feelings to keep that doorway open for my children."

"I see what you mean. Maybe you could arrange a long-term lease for the county to maintain the gardens and make them open to the public. As for the house, you could rent it separately."

"But I wouldn't want just anybody there. That would matter to Gram, my cousin, and me. It has to be somebody who understands what this island means, what older homes mean, that sort of thing. Island newcomers today want to live in a beach condo. It would take someone like Jasmine to want to live in the woods."

Wheels turned in my head. "If you took possession of the land, how much would you rent the place for?"

She named a figure, and it sounded decent. "If you need a renter for the house, let me know. I know a couple who might consider living there."

"Who is it?"

"My brother and his wife are looking for a larger place for their family. They have three kids now."

Iris paused and then nodded. "I've always thought Doug was a good guy. Like I said, even though I want the property, it isn't mine. If I win my appeal, I'll need a miracle or two to hold onto it. Nothing's certain at this point, so don't mention it to him yet."

"Sure." I studied a butterfly on the nearby beautyberry bush to ease into my next question. "The Chicken Lady is missing. Have you seen her?"

"Cora is an odd duck. I'm not surprised she's missing. It would help my property value if she and those chickens were gone."

Her statement caught me off guard. I'd been thinking Iris wasn't hardhearted as I'd originally thought, but now she sounded like her mercenary self again. "She's something of an icon on Shell Island."

"She can be an icon elsewhere."

The conversation lapsed, so I said goodbye. As I drove away, I had a blinding thought. Of the people on my suspect list with motive for killing Jasmine, Ash, Milton, and Cora were basically out of commission. Only the veterinarian and Iris remained at large. Since Linette had less to gain than Iris, that meant Iris was the last big dog standing.

Chapter Thirty-Five

Pete and I took some us-time at sunset. It felt decadent to relax and enjoy ourselves. Each of us held an ice cream cone from Island Creamery, butter pecan for me, peppermint stick for him. The new cone wraps he'd created for the shop were distinctive with bold stripes and the company name, and passersby on the fishing pier glanced at our treats with interest.

"You're quiet tonight," Pete said when we reached our favorite bench on the far end of the pier. "What's on your mind?"

"I'm trying to keep this evening about us. I never want you to feel like you're second fiddle to my business or my hobby of finding things."

"Not feeling second fiddle at all, and I'm keenly interested in the investigation."

"With Cora missing, I've been feeding her flock. I wish I knew what happened to her. I started out with five suspects with motive to kill Jasmine. Of these, the vet and the cousin have not been implicated in another crime or haven't gone missing. That's not to say the others still couldn't be guilty, only that they aren't actively benefitting from Jasmine's death at the moment."

"That's my girl," Pete said. "Tell me more about Linette and Iris."

"Linette benefits directly from Jasmine's death, with estate-donated funds earmarked for free pet services, even though she claims Jasmine's gift won't net her repeat customers. On the other hand, Iris stays mad at the world. There's a chance she might win her lawsuit to inherit Jasmine's estate, but she can't afford to keep the property, though she now says it should be a legacy for her kids. Lately I've had this very strange thought. Could our suspects have colluded?"

"That's a different twist on things. I didn't think any of these people liked each other."

I scowled. "Not a good fit, I know, but really, it feels like we're nowhere on the case. There must be something big we're missing."

"You aren't the only one missing it. Deputy Franklin and crew appear stumped as well."

"Let's talk about something fun, like our cookie collaboration."

"The cookie business was a brilliant idea if I do say so myself," Pete beamed. "We're moving more ice cream, pulling more traffic through our doors, and upping our bottom line."

"Seems odd how it took right off. My catering business hasn't worked that way in the past. I've spent years building a reputation to get my repeat customers."

"We're both benefiting from your established customer base and five-star reputation, thank you very much. People love to treat themselves to little luxuries, and dessert is a perfect way to do that."

"To tell you the truth, I was hoping the Monday cookies would fly off the shelves, but they don't seem as popular."

"Monday is a harder sales day all the way around unless it's a holiday. Most people have busy Mondays. We still might develop a Monday customer base, but we could cut back Monday's order to one batch of your most popular cookies. That'd free up your weekend again. Further, you and Patsy could bake Monday's cookies on Friday and freeze them. To maintain exclusivity, we could still stage the production of you bringing them in on Monday at noon."

"Sounds like a plan. I have a weekend catering event coming up in two weeks, so it would be good to focus solely on the banquet dinner."

"People love you and love your cooking."

"Won't they get tired of eating cookies and cakes eventually?"

"Nope. And we have a great mix of locals and tourists who frequent Island Creamery, enough to stabilize our bottom line. You're still happy with our partnership?"

"Of course. I love baking. Tell me your thoughts about the dog."

"Artie is gentle and big enough to deter the wrong kind of people."

"He's also a sneak thief. He ate a whole tray of dog treats I'd baked."

Pete tried to hold in a laugh, and it burst out anyway. "I take that as a good sign. He's relaxed enough to be himself, and he's certainly taken with you."

"It will be hard to give him back." I filled him in on

what I knew of the dog's history.

"Perhaps. Things have a way of working out when you're involved. I'm very glad to have Artie as our watchdog."

"And two watch cats," I added. "Speaking of my cookie business, it's almost time to meet Patsy to start our batch for Wednesday. Gotta get my baking done. My business partner expects every delivery to be on time."

Chapter Thirty-Six

Wednesday morning started off with an early wake-up call from customer LaShaundra Delight, the retired entertainer. I fumbled for the phone and managed a throaty hello.

"River, honey, you got to wake up. I have an emergency on my hands."

It was still dark outside. "LaShaundra? Are you all right?"

"No. I'm not all right. I just realized a gaggle of friends are passing by today on their way to St. Augustine, and I need to feed them lunch and your Death by Chocolate Cake. Please, please tell me you can help me."

Pete hadn't moved beside me, and a dog-sized weight trapped my feet. My very warm feet. I managed to pry them out from under Artie. "Give me a second to get to the kitchen."

"Sure."

I padded silently down the hall. "First, there's a premium fee for a rush job like this. Second, you are limited to whatever entre items I have on hand. Third, if it's a lot of people, I can't accommodate you. I just don't keep a large quantity of perishable food on hand."

"I'll pay the rush fee. There will be eight of us total. The lunch doesn't need to be fancy, it just has to be delicious."

We worked out the fee, the food, and the delivery time. I hung up the phone, grabbed a thermos of coffee, and went to work in my commercial kitchen. For the sandwiches, I thawed out boneless and skinless chicken breasts, cooked them with lemon and dill, and chopped green apples, celery, and red onion. For the dressing, I mixed Dijon mustard and red wine vinegar.

Luckily, I kept a batch of frozen dinner rolls for emergencies such as these. As I pulled them from my freezer, I checked that they were still within the month of preparation for freshness. Satisfied, I made a note to restock the freezer with more dinner rolls. I also made a note that I needed butter lettuce to complete the sandwiches.

Meanwhile, I chopped cucumbers, cherry tomatoes, onion, and feta cheese to create a classic Greek salad. Lastly, I started another Death by Chocolate Cake. It would not be ready in time, but I still had a few hours. I could assemble the cake at LaShaundra's place. That would work out the best, though it would mean hauling more items to her home. Not a problem. The van had plenty of room.

Pete knocked on the door, surprising me with more coffee and an egg sandwich. "Thanks," I said as I downed the breakfast offering. "I hope I didn't wake you. A client called to book a last-minute luncheon today, so I rushed over to get started."

"I missed the call and you leaving. But, you may want to wash the sheets when you finish here. I awakened with Artie snuggled beside me, his head on your pillow."

My face twitched. "Oops. He may need more house training. He must be feeling very comfortable to want to be so close to us."

"It's you he wants to be close to, but I'm fine with that. Though it was a surprise to wake up with his big nose so close to mine."

"Where is he?"

"Fed and watered, like the cats, and now acting as a doorstop for your kitchen door."

"At least he quit howling when I'm cooking over here."

"Whatever you're fixing it smells amazing and lemony, with a hint of chocolate."

"Chicken salad on dinner rolls, Classic Greek Salad, and Death by Chocolate Cake are on the menu."

His eyes brimmed with alarm. "You're not giving away my cake are you?"

"Your cake is safe and ready to go. I'm working on a second one that I'll assemble once I get to LaShaundra's if I don't have time to finish it here first."

"She's becoming a frequent repeat customer."

"She entertains frequently and can afford me. It's a good fit." I washed and dried my hands after eating. "Say, I hope you don't mind if I drop your noon delivery off a smidge earlier. LaShaundra expects her guests at 12:30. I need to be set up over there a little before noon."

"I can take your baked goods with me, if that makes it easier for you."

"I can swing by there, not a problem. Besides, I think you're right. I like the idea of people salivating at the sight of my van at your place. It's good for business."

"Now you're talking."

~*~

The morning and luncheon passed in a blur. All too soon, LaShaundra's happy guests departed, and I had the task of collecting everything to go home.

LaShaundra settled into a chair as I neared the end of sanitizing her gorgeous kitchen counters. If I ever had a house with a kitchen large enough to swim in, I'd pattern it after this one. Everything gleamed and coordinated. "You have such a great kitchen," I began. "If I lived here, I'd never leave this room."

"It's a good space. Johnsy and I cook in here together, so I have fond memories of this room too." The former entertainer made a small throat-clearing noise. "How's the case going?"

"The police are working the case. I'm still trying to determine why anyone wanted Jasmine dead. I'm at the stage now where I know more information about each suspect, but what's relevant? With each investigation, I'm reminded how little we truly know about the people we encounter each day. People have secrets. For instance, Ash operated an unlicensed gator farm, Milton stole from his clients, Iris is broke, and the Chicken Lady went to ground or came to harm."

"You didn't mention the other vet lady, the one with zero personality."

"Linette Nelson doesn't have secrets far as I can tell. Like Jasmine, she works too hard to have personal relationships."

LaShaundra bit her lip.

"What?" I asked.

"She made time for Jasmine. I've seen them together outside of work."

"It wouldn't be unusual for colleagues to grab dinner or a drink together."

"No, more than that. They were in the clubs that Johnsy and I frequent. Got a feeling they were a couple. A *romantic* couple."

I blinked. Never saw that coming. "I had no idea. Was that recent?"

"It was this year, maybe a few months ago."

"Is Linette seeing anyone else now?"

"That's your department, girlfriend."

"I'll see what I can find out."

"While I have your ear, I had another thought. On TV cop shows, the crime solver always ends up back at the beginning, viewing the new evidence through that early lens."

"I can do that."

"You know, "LaShaundra said, with a toe waggle of her crossed leg, "I'm a huge fan of Jasmine's podcasts. I've watched them all, several of them multiple times. I always wanted to find that rare plant too, but I'm no outdoorsman. Not my style."

I crinkled my nose. "Not mine either, though it certainly suited Jasmine. She seemed very at ease in the woods. Not once did I see her startle in the videos I watched."

"Rock solid and surefooted. I asked her to come over here and start a native garden section out back, but she said no. Said she was a vet not a landscaper."

"Sadly, her refusal to make suggestions for your landscaping fits with the feedback I'm getting on her personality. It seems to be fairly unanimous among islanders that her actions were mostly self-serving."

"I knew she was a hard-hearted Hannah, but I thought since she loved plants she might make an exception for me. She turned me down so fast my head spun."

I got sidetracked for a moment by that image. "Be that as it may, much as I appreciate your business, I'm going home. It was a busy morning, and I could use a nap."

"Until next time," LaShaundra said, pinning me with a bold stare.

She said it with such conviction I wasn't sure if it was a promise or a threat.

Chapter Thirty-Seven

Late that afternoon, Pete and I drove to Emmeline Drive to check on Cora's chickens. Major jumped right into the Buick, but Ivy scooted off into the woods and wouldn't come, no matter how much I coaxed her. We left Artie inside our house for good measure as we had no idea how he'd react around the chickens.

The short drive passed quickly. Along the way, I studied Pete's profile, his strong jaw determined, his eyes steady on the road. The fact that he indulged my investigations, even participated in them, made our relationship so much more meaningful.

My bakery products helped him as well. That's what partners did, help each other. Some would say we were lucky to have each other, but the truth is, we'd made our luck. When our careers took us in different directions, we found a way to be together. The change worked wonders in terms of daily companionship and professional interests.

Heck, I didn't know what a business plan was before Pete. I only knew cooking was my thing, and that I had to do it. He'd found a way to make it pay better, and that change wasn't as scary as I'd imagined it might be.

Cora's place had an abandoned air about it, with darkened windows and seed tops waving in the sparse lawn. No vehicles in the driveway, nobody in the house. The flock still eyed me like I was an ax murderer, but they went to the food as soon as I retreated. Major supervised our progress from the car.

I stopped to right a fallen ornamental lawn chicken. "Since we're here, let's cruise by Jasmine's place."

"Thought you might say that," Pete said.

"LaShaundra suggested I go back to the beginning of the case. I know more about Jasmine and her acquaintances now, so reviewing data at her place could spark a new lead."

We motored further down Emmeline Drive and pulled into Jasmine's driveway. At once I was struck by the brooding emptiness of the property. Overgrown shrubs and weedy beds underscored the lack of human presence here.

Pete sat with me on the hood of the car, glancing at the shaggy shrubs and curtained windows. No Trespassing signs were posted on the house. That was new. For once, Major stayed close instead of scampering away. "We're here," Pete said. "Now what?"

"There might be something that was missed before. Let's walk around to the back."

Pete pointed at the signs. "Her estate doesn't want people here."

"Understood, but we're not here to vandalize anything. I need to see the back yard again, to work through the morning when she died. Nobody will ever know we were here."

"Look at you, living on the edge." He strolled beside me on garden paths, stepping out of the way of errant branches, stepping over weeds. "Doesn't take long for a place to start looking forsaken, does it?"

"No. That's why my family kept the landscaping simple around our place." Despite the riot of plants here, their earthy scent centered me. "Jasmine had privacy galore, only what got her killed? The house and land are underwater with debt. She did things for the community, she worked at vet clinics, and she nurtured this two-acre garden, which must have been a big-time drain."

"Not to mention her searches for that rare plant," Pete added. "What was its name again?"

"*Franklinia alatamaha.*" My feet stopped at the site of her death. Major sniffed for a moment, then bounded for the back porch. I turned around in a slow circle. "This spot has a wide visibility. I can see a long ways in most directions."

Pete appeared to study her back yard. "She has no patio furniture. If she enjoyed sitting outside with her coffee in the mornings as you do, she might have wandered down to this raised bed to commune with nature."

Full afternoon sun drenched the back steps right now, so they would be shaded in the morning. If Jasmine wanted to feel the morning sun on her face, she would've walked out here, sat, and faced her house. I thought about how I'd move with a full coffee cup. Jasmine's legs were longer than mine, so it was likely she walked to the closest part of the raised bed to sit.

Turning, I set a pretend cup of coffee on the wooden ledge and hopped on the ledge. Not a breath of wind stirred. A distant woodpecker hammered on a tree. "This feels weird."

"It makes sense," Pete said, "considering she was found over here." He pointed to my left.

I looked around to see vibrant yellow swamp flowers and a narrow trace of a path that led off the property, such as a deer might use.

"Hmm. Would you pace to the tree line and then walk toward me?" I asked Pete.

"Sure."

I sat on the wooden bed, my feet dangling in the air. Pete made no effort to be quiet, and as I heard him approach, I leaned to the left to gaze his way. I immediately lost my balance, and my left hand went into the vegetation as I fell. My fingers glanced off a hard object before they sank into soft dirt.

I smiled my approval. "You're a genius, Pete. Jasmine heard someone, turned, and lost her balance. Since cops often find many murders are caused by a person the victim knows, let's assume she recognized her visitor. Given the outcome of the visit, it's likely they argued."

"The shot wasn't fired at close range," Pete said as we stood toe-to-toe. "The person must've stopped back there, by that old magnolia tree."

"Good theory. Somebody intent on harm or doing something sneaky would seek cover. Maybe he or she didn't want Jasmine to see the gun. Whatever the argument, Jasmine turned her back on the shooter, a fatal mistake as she was clipped from behind. I wonder if the cops came up with this scenario."

Pete grinned. "If only you had an inside track to the investigation."

I parted the flower stems in the bed and beheld a

rectangular object. "Since there's a cell phone in this planter, I assume they didn't work through this. It's probably Jasmine's phone."

"Could be," Pete said, glancing over my shoulder. "Call the deputy."

My shoulders tensed. "He won't like that we're here, especially since those 'No Trespassing' signs are posted. Let's collect the cat and call Deputy Franklin from the head of the road."

"Okay."

We walked toward the back steps where the cat sat staring at us. Soon as he had my attention, Major chose that shining moment to dart over and paw the back door. To my amazement, it slowly creaked open.

Chapter Thirty-Eight

"Stay back." Pete told me as he hurried to the open doorway. "Anybody here?"

No response. I took the stairs two at a time. "Hello?" I called out from beside him.

His exasperated gaze spoke volumes. "I told you to wait down there."

I gestured with my hand. "You did, but no one is here, except our cat."

He stepped in front of me and called out again. "Hello!"

Not a sound came from inside the house, and I was tired of being protected. I ducked under Pete's arm. "Major...Here kitty, kitty."

The cat yowled, and my concern mounted. "Something's wrong. I need to get him."

A shot rang out. My heart stalled and echoes of that shot reverberated in my ears. Pete hauled me down the steps and wrangled me into the Buick. When I could speak, I asked, "What about the cat? We can't abandon him."

"That cat has nine lives. You don't, and we're not dying today." Pete sped away from the Garr property. "Major will hide until help arrives. He's a clever cat. He'll be okay. Meanwhile, call the deputy."

I glanced over my shoulder at the Garr place and swallowed around the lump in my throat. "Thanks for getting us out of there. That gunshot stunned me. I was so sure the house was empty, and Major had found another clue."

"He did. He let us know somebody was in that house."

The seatbelt kept me from digging into my pocket for the phone. "I wish we had the cat too."

Pete pulled into Cora's drive, and I unbelted and called Deputy Gil Franklin.

"The back door of Jasmine Garr's house is open," I began, "and my cat's inside the house. Pete and I called his name from the doorway. Then someone fired a shot inside the premises. We drove over to Cora's place and called you."

"On my way," Franklin said. "I'm nearby. Hang tight."

Pete and I stared at each other. "He didn't yell at us for trespassing," I said to fill the silence.

Pete turned the car around to face the road. "That'll come later."

"I wish I knew Major was safe."

"Before he claimed us, Major roamed the island. He's a survivor, and he would've followed his instinct and hidden."

"I sure hope so."

A patrol SUV shot past us and zoomed down the road. "What should we do?" Pete asked.

"Follow that car!"

Pete eased out of Cora's drive and followed at a safe distance. We clambered out of the Buick, at the property line, but Franklin motioned for us to stop.

"I'll check this out," Franklin said as he stood beside our vehicle, gun in hand and pointed to the ground. "Stay in the car."

He circled the house, gun in the firing position. Seconds ticked by at the speed of molasses. "Come on, Major, show yourself," I said.

Pete took my hand in his. "The cat's tough. He sought cover."

I took comfort from his grounded certainty, but I'd be relieved when I saw my cat again.

Franklin rounded the back of the house. "Intruder's gone, and the cat's fine."

"No one passed us on Emmeline Drive. This road's a dead end. How's that possible?"

"The culprit came on foot. He or she tossed the house. Drawers are dumped, cupboards and closets ransacked."

"What were they looking for?" I asked. "I doubt Jasmine kept any valuables in the house, not as broke as she was."

"It had to be something lightweight since the intruder came on foot."

"Maybe they wanted Jasmine's phone."

"I'd like to find her phone," Franklin said. "They're gold mines of information. Now, what were you two doing on private property?"

"We were recreating Jasmine's last minutes. We figure she must've come out to that flower bed beyond the back steps to sit in the sun and drink her morning coffee. That's where I would've gone to sit if I lived here.

We knew she was found to the left of that bed, so Pete went out about fifty or so steps on the path and started walking toward me. When I twisted around to see who was coming, I lost my balance and fell off the bed. Which reminds me. I found a phone in the flower bed."

"Show me," Franklin said.

So I did. "My fingerprints may be on it now. I accidentally brushed it when I fell. We think Jasmine knew her visitor who approached on a deer path. Since she was shot in the back, I assume they talked, and then she turned to walk to her house."

Franklin stared at me, phone bagged in his hand, the cop gears in his head turning. "You got all of that from looking at the back yard?"

I shrugged. "Pete helped. We're a strong team."

"Huh."

"Wonder where that deer trail goes?" Pete asked.

Franklin scratched his head a moment. "Ash Braswell's alligator compound isn't far from here as the crow flies. If you know the right turns, the trail leads there."

A nearby gator farm explained how a gator got trapped inside Jasmine's house earlier. "Ash is out on bail," I reminded him. "He could've been in that house just now."

Major came up and rubbed against my legs. I gathered him in my arms. For once, my independent kitty didn't struggle to get down. He seemed to need the cuddle as much as I did.

"Pulled a bullet out of the wall when I was inside," Franklin said. "I'll compare that to the kill shot. It occurs to me that the intruder might've been looking for her phone, which we now have. I'll fast-track the phone analysis."

"You think it's Ash?"

"Could be," Franklin said. "Ash and Milton look good for this. Hell, it could be Cora Radley for all we know. So far nothing about Ms. Garr's death indicates brute strength."

I frowned, disliking him casting aspersions on my friend Cora but knowing in my heart that he was right to include her. "Yep, our suspect pool is alive and well."

"Mark my words," the deputy said. "This case is heating up."

Chapter Thirty-Nine

We left Emmeline Drive, stopped by Nature's Bounty for grouper filets, and headed home, Major safely in the back seat. Artie and Ivy watched us arrive, Artie looking ever hopeful through the door windowpane that there would be treats, and Ivy's little white face peering through the bushes before she scampered out to greet us.

After a dinner of grouper fingers, coleslaw, and roasted asparagus, I cozied up on the sofa to resume watching Jasmine's podcasts. She hiked and lectured nonstop. It felt weird to see and hear her so animated, but soon I focused solely on the content. Her voice rang with enthusiasm as she identified plants, lectured on riverbanks, and waded through swamps.

She had a knack of facing the light, something I'd discovered was important when I briefly took up photography. There was an art to framing a photo, to make a subject compelling by catching the right blend of light and shadow.

Midway through a podcast, I realized the more recent

podcasts paid less attention to light and framing. Not only was somebody filming Jasmine's podcast, they weren't the camera artist Jasmine was. Everyone and their brother thought they were photographers these days due to the popularity of cellphone cameras.

Because of Jasmine's passion for her topic material and her attention to detail when she shot the videos herself, I concluded she demanded perfection from herself and others. Though I hadn't noticed her obsession with this plant in my dealings with her, I understood her passion and dedication as I approached my business the same way.

At some point, Jasmine lowered her quality standards for her podcasts. Though I didn't know why, it represented a change in how she'd acted. Her videos attracted about 500 views each, so she'd found a niche viewership, but no podcast had gone viral.

Jasmine spoke with poise and confidence in the podcasts so it was easy to keep clicking to the next video. I started rooting for her to find this lost plant.

~*~

Early the next morning, Linette called after I put dough balls in the oven to rise.

"Any way you can give me a lift from Island Tire and Auto to the clinic right now?" the vet asked.

Much as I hated leaving a mess in my commercial kitchen, I wanted to speak with Linette. "Sure, I'll be there in ten minutes."

"Thanks. My ride fell through at the last minute. I'd postpone the service appointment, but my vehicle keeps stranding me. It needs help."

"I'm coming."

"Great and while you're here, I'll tell you my news."

I bustled around getting ready and when I headed outside, Major and Ivy gazed at me hopefully from atop the Buick. Artie barked from inside the house. I quickly reconsidered my vehicle choice and opened the kitchen door for Artie. He bounded to the Buick and waited for me.

Artie rode shotgun, tongue lolling out the window, while the cats claimed the entire back seat. "Good thing Linette likes pets," I said.

This time of morning, traffic was light, so I passed quickly under giant oak boughs and beneath towering pines. In no time, I pulled into the garage parking lot.

Linette burst out laughing when she saw my companions. "You have such a way with animals. I've never seen Artie looking so pleased with himself. I'll share the back seat with the cats."

"I can put Artie back there," I offered.

"No, this is fine." Linette got in and closed the door. "Your cats are really into each other."

In my rearview mirror I saw the cats nestled together, eyes on the veterinarian.

"I'm lucky they're so compatible." I eased onto the main drag and accelerated toward the clinic. "You made me curious about the news you wanted to share. What's up?"

"It's a good news-bad news scenario. Last night I received a call from Artie's owner, Duvall Shannon. He doesn't have long to live. His son already moved him to a care facility in South Carolina. Anyway, Duvall relinquished ownership of his dog to a good home. Artie is yours if you want him."

My hands jerked on the wheel. "My goodness. That is dual-edged news." Inside I was doing cartwheels, but the reason for my unexpected blessing was sad. "While I'm sorry to hear Mr. Shannon is doing poorly, we've fallen in love with his dog. I say yes to adopting Artie. Pete and I are glad to keep him. He's been a perfect dog, well, except for him sleeping on my pillow and snarfing down a whole tray of dog treats when my back was turned."

"Sounds like he's settling in just fine. Ivy didn't hiss or bolt when I sat beside her. You've done wonders with her too."

I couldn't hold in a smile. "She still has timid moments, but Major is a strong guiding force for her. Say, how's it coming on your search for another veterinarian?"

"Still looking. I've love to find a single female fresh out of vet school."

Her female reference jogged another memory. "About that. A customer mentioned she'd seen you and Jasmine at a private, special interest club."

Linette opened her mouth, closed it, and swore softly. "I wondered if that would get out. Look. We went out a few times. After a few dates I made a pass at Jas and she shut me down. That's the real reason I didn't attend her awards ceremony. It was awkward between us. I was embarrassed that I'd misjudged her so completely."

"For what it's worth, I don't think she was into guys either. Jasmine marched to her own beat."

"That's one way of putting it." Linette paused until I cleared the next intersection. "She was a light burning brightly. I should've realized she would flame out quickly, as super-talented folks often do."

"I see." I pulled into the clinic parking lot. "Does Deputy Franklin know?"

"He does. I'm out of the closet, but I don't advertise my sexual preferences. Franklin commiserated with me. Both of us agree that dating sucks."

For some reason that tickled my funny bone. "Maybe he'll end up with a menagerie of pets like me."

"You got a dog, two cats, and a husband. You're set now."

"I never considered the deputy was lonely."

"I'm sure he is. I certainly am. Do you know what it was like to work with a love interest who doesn't return your affections? And that damn plant, the Franklin tree. Every time Jasmine spoke she laid it on thick about that plant. I swear she was obsessed with it."

"Obsessed?" That rang a bell. Somebody mentioned that word and Jasmine recently.

"Yeah. She searched for that extinct plant on every day off, despite the swamps and marshes having poisonous snakes and gators. The thrill of the hunt, you know. I'm terrified of alligators, and even though she invited me along on her treks, I turned her down every time. She fixated on the plant and that darn scrapbook fostered her plant obsession."

I nearly fell off my shoes. "Scrapbook? What scrapbook?"

"Her mom made it for her. It has all the original plant discovery information, photos of leaves, and photos of Jasmine giving talks about the plant to various clubs. Good grief. That plant was all she talked about. Tell you the truth, I'm glad she wasn't into me. I would've had to listen to her gab about that plant day and night."

Jasmine was obsessed with the plant. That rang true. Why hadn't I heard about the scrapbook before? "This is the first I've heard about a scrapbook. I wonder where it is."

"Good riddance to the book I say. I never want to hear about that plant again."

I processed the new information. There was a scrapbook that Jasmine treasured. She talked about the Franklin tree nonstop to her associates. And, most interestingly to me, both the deputy and Linette were looking for romantic relationships.

"I won't mention it again. On the other hand, good to know you and the deputy are looking for someone to date. I'll keep my eyes peeled for singles."

"No weirdos. I've met enough of them through those online dating apps." Linette opened the door. "Thanks for the lift, Pet Whisperer."

"That's Caterer and Pet Whisperer to you."

Driving home, I mulled over the conversation. Linette may have been embarrassed by Jasmine's rebuff, but she didn't seem to harbor a grudge. My earlier conclusion about the vet still felt right. Linette didn't seem the murdering type. I'd have to look elsewhere for the killer.

Chapter Forty

That evening, Doug, Viv, and the kids came for dinner. Nothing fancy, just burgers and dogs on the grill, along with the prerequisite chicken nuggets. Harry couldn't stop talking about his Halloween costume. This would be his first time ever to go trick or treating. Viv adroitly grabbed her phone while nursing the baby and recorded Harry's excitement. She played it back for me a few minutes later, after Harry had dashed away to show us how fast Buzz Lightyear ran, Little Harry's voice competed with a football game televised in the next room, and I realized the importance of a controlled environment for taping.

Background noise. Many of Jasmine's podcasts, especially the later videos, were shot when she was walking and talking about various plants. Most of the time, there were no competing noises on Jasmine's podcasts, except I'd heard something once.

"You've got that look." Viv handed me the baby to burp while she stood and stretched. "Did something happen with the investigation?"

I cuddled Ginger Belle close, loving the smell and feel

of her in my arms. "Not exactly, but as I listened to Harry's excitement on tape, I realized we have background noise here. Most of the time on Jasmine's podcasts I hear nature sounds in the background."

Viv sat again. "I noticed the same thing as I listened. I've heard woodpeckers and songbirds. Once I heard an owl."

"Yes, I heard rain falling in a video."

"I watched that one too. She was totally committed to finding that plant."

"Something's hovering at the edge of my thoughts, worrying at me. I heard a stray noise that didn't belong on a podcast, but now I've watched so many videos I don't remember where I heard it."

"It would've been so much better if the person videoing the podcast spoke once in a while, but that person is singularly mute," Viv said.

"Exactly. I wonder if that was by design."

"Could be. Jasmine can't tell us, and the videographer certainly hasn't stepped forward."

"What about her camera? Deputy Franklin hasn't said anything about finding a camera."

"Maybe she used her phone. It's relatively lightweight, and it's something most people would carry with them wherever they go."

"True, and we should know more about that soon."

"What? You found her phone?"

"I did." I filled her in on our visit to Jasmine's place yesterday, the open back door, and the shot fired.

Viv's eyes rounded. "Someone tried to shoot you and Pete?"

"Not sure what the shot was about. After our black cat dashed inside the house, we heard the shot."

Viv looked around. "Is the cat okay?"

"Cat's fine. We're fine. Deputy Franklin dug the bullet out of the wall. So he has two new leads to follow, the phone content, and the bullet comparison."

"Why would someone be in her house? Isn't Jasmine's will being challenged and the estate disposition in limbo?"

"Yes to the estate in limbo, and I don't know why someone was there. Maybe they wanted the *Franklinia* scrapbook Jasmine's mom made for her, I don't know. If the bullets match and it was the killer, he or she must've been searching for something. If it's a random burglar, we'll find out soon enough. Chances are we'll find new prints in that house."

"Hmm." Viv reached for little Ginger Belle, and they settled together like two halves of a whole.

Despite my baby-envy, I was proud of my friend's accomplishments in her new role as mother of three kids. "You're so easy with her. It's like you suddenly have this wealth of maternal knowledge."

"You'll have it too, once Project Baby happens for you and Pete." I must've made a sad face because she grinned at me. "When are we going to meet the d-o-g?"

Harry dashed in. "O is for Olaf."

I must've looked puzzled because Viv piped up with, "A popular snowman character in a kid's movie."

Pete strolled in on Harry's heels. "Did I hear d-o-g?"

Viv nodded. I reached for Zoey, who had pulled up on a chair, afraid she might tip the chair over. Our plan to discuss the case after the kids were fed and calmed fell flat because Harry and Zoey got energized after dinner.

With both the tots on the couch between Viv and Doug, Pete brought Artie in on a leash. Zoey cried and hid her face. Harry turned to Doug and said, "Will he eat me?"

"Artie is very gentle," Pete explained, "so you must be gentle around him. Treat him the same way you treat the new baby."

Harry nodded solemnly. "I can't jump on him or yell near him."

"Exactly," Doug said as Pete squatted beside a sitting Artie. In a matter of minutes, Harry and Artie were fast friends, and little Zoey squirmed off the couch and crawled over to the dog.

"Y'all okay with this?" I asked Viv and Doug.

"She's fine," Viv said. "Just watch her hands. She doesn't understand her own strength and loves to smack things with her open palm right now."

I caught the little hand just in time and redirected it to petting the dog's fur. The dog got Zoey's scent, Zoey saw the dog wouldn't eat her, and all was well in my household.

Despite a lovely evening and wonderful company, my thoughts veered back to Jasmine's videos as I prepared for bed. If only I could remember that out-of-place background noise I'd heard. Surely that departure from the norm had some greater meaning.

As we settled in bed, I shared my realizations with Pete about an out-of-place noise on Jasmine's podcasts and the mute videographer.

"Can't help you with the noise, but I had a thought about your camera operator." He covered his mouth to hide a big yawn. "Were there credits in the video clips?"

"No."

"Sometimes you have to go back early in the broadcasting to find mention of the film person," he replied.

Though my eyelids dropped, I made a mental note to search those early videos again, especially the ones shot by another person. Because of taking the night off from Holloway Catering, I'd be super busy baking early tomorrow. Sleuthing would have to wait until tomorrow afternoon.

Chapter Forty-One

Deputy Franklin stopped over at half-past eleven the following day. "Thought you'd want to know. I put a rush on the bullet analysis, and the results are in." His eyes glowed with horrible knowledge. "The one fired into the wall matched the bullet that killed Jasmine. Be very careful in whatever you do."

"Got it. The killer knows I'm looking for him. Any new fingerprints in the house or on the busted door lock?"

"We didn't find anything new, but I say that because I didn't hear any news about a match."

Took me a minute to process that. "Who owns the house now?" I asked. "Has the estate been settled?"

"Good question," Franklin said, gazing longingly at my boxes of cookies and cakes. "Until we solve this case, it's in limbo."

"I gave Linette a ride yesterday. She said Jasmine obsessed over finding the Franklin tree, and she had a treasured scrapbook about the plant. The way Linette talked, Jasmine flaunted the scrapbook at her acquaintances. Have you seen it?"

"Can't remember a scrapbook in the inventory of items we took from her place. I'll double-check when I return to the office. Meanwhile, I'll hang out with you this morning and follow you to Island Creamery."

"I appreciate the escort, but just so you know, every bakery item in here is bound for the ice cream shop. No samples available today."

He made a sad face. "Pity."

~*~

Pete noticed my police escort when I pulled into the back alley of Island Creamery.

Once he heard about the bullet match, he became my shadow for the day, sending the deputy on his way.

He followed me home for a quick soup and sandwich meal. While we did the dishes afterward, he asked, "What's on your calendar this afternoon?"

"I planned to watch more of Jasmine's podcasts. With the security system, the dog, and the cats, I should be fine locked in here. You should go back to work."

"Not a chance. Someone will call and off you'll go. We're sticking together. I can access everything at the office on my home computer and phone."

"Lucky you."

I settled on the sofa, Artie lying on my feet and the cats on either side of me, and began watching Jasmine, paying attention to the camera movements. At first Ivy seemed interested in Jasmine's voice, but then she lay down and dozed like Major. After I viewed four videos shot by the mystery videographer, I had no new information about her film crew, but I brimmed with knowledge about the lost plant. The *Franklinia alatamaha* had been extinct in the wild since the earliest 19th century. A father and son botanist team found it in a sand hill bog. Specimens from their expedition survived, and the tree existed today as a cultivated ornamental tree in various botanical gardens.

My phone buzzed. Iris. I took the call.

"Can you meet with me privately?" Iris asked.

"What did you have in mind and when?" I replied.

"Now. Come to my place."

Not a good idea. I sought another possibility. "Can we meet at the pier?"

"There are lots of people at the pier."

"Not many all the way at the end."

Iris sighed. "You won't come over here?"

"No. I can do the pier today. That's it."

"All right. I'll run a quick errand and meet you there in fifteen minutes. I have to pick up the kids soon, so please be prompt."

She hung up on me. I saw Pete watching me from the threshold. "You were right," I said. "Iris called and wants to meet me privately."

"She's on your suspect list." He stared at me and if I had two heads. I rushed to fill in more information. "It's not what you think. You and Artie are coming along, and we're meeting at the pier. She wouldn't shoot me in a public place."

"You never know what people will do, but that plan sounds reasonably safe. Let's go."

~*~

As she approached with a companion, Iris shook her head at me, Pete, and the large dog. "This is a private meeting," she snapped.

"You brought Milton," I said, waving her over to the semi-private bench Pete and I favored at the south end of the pier. Once the four of us sat, I asked, "What's this about?"

"Milton's got a buyer who wants to build a solar farm on Jasmine's property and will pay top dollar, but he has to move on it fast or they'll look elsewhere. Can you use your influence with the cops to get the property released?"

"It's not up to me or the cops. It's a legal issue, and I have no connections to lawyers or judges."

"How can that be? Haven't you fed everyone in the county by now?"

I wanted to say something snarky in reply, but I exercised restraint.

Iris must've realized what she said. "I'm sorry. That didn't come out right. You're so popular. I was so sure you knew everyone in the whole county."

"I can't help you with this, Iris. You're on your own."

"Milton says the Nature Coalition doesn't want the property now. There's too much debt associated with it, and they're afraid they won't break even."

I shot a glance at Milton, and he nodded. "Did they write a letter to the judge withdrawing their claim or refusing the bequest?"

Everyone looked at Milton. "No. Should they do that?"

"Yes," Iris said. "You made me think I was the hold-up in us getting our money. Instead, it's you. Go write that letter and turn it in. The clock is ticking."

He glanced at his big, shiny watch. "It's two-thirty on a Friday afternoon. I can't get something drafted and approved through the organization's board before close of business today. The courts are closed over the weekend, so the earliest anything could happen would be on Monday. My buyers won't wait that long."

Iris turned to me. "Can't you do something? You're always fixing other people's problems."

Iris was projecting her inadequacies on me. Apparently she thought I was a super-woman. Time to bring the focus back to her. "Did you find any record at the courthouse of an earlier will, like your grandmother's, that said the property was to stay in the family?"

Iris made a fist. "Why is everything on me? I've got little kids. I can't manage much more than my kids."

"Ask your lawyer to do it."

"Then I have to pay him more."

I'd heard enough. She wasn't serious about resolving her problems. I rose. "This is your issue, Iris. You have options, but you have to implement them to get results, and there are no guarantees. However, and this is my unschooled opinion, without an older will that shows the property is to be inherited by your grandmother's descendants, the judge will most likely rule for the current will."

She tugged me back down to the bench. "Even if the Nature Coalition refuses the bequest?"

I didn't like her hands on me and twisted away. Before I could speak, I had to forcibly unclench my jaw. "I don't know the answer, but anything that runs contrary to the current will delays settling the estate."

"We don't want that," Iris shrilled. "How many different times in my life can Jasmine screw me? This is beyond ridiculous."

Artie started howling in response to her sharp voice. I bit back a smile because I wished I could howl and be done with this meeting.

"I need help," Iris said, "and no one's going to help

me."

"This is a legal matter and your attorney can offer legal solutions, if there are any."

Milton's phone rang. He checked it. "Gotta take this. Excuse me."

Iris swore under her breath. "That man makes me crazy, getting me all lathered up over some big fish he has on a line. I shouldn't have let him get to me today. I should've realized that he was all hot air."

Brushing the wind-tossed hair from my face, I stood next to Pete, jostling Artie off my feet. "We need to go."

Iris checked the time and yelped. "Me too. School pickup's in five minutes."

Pete and I watched as she hurried away. "That was interesting," I said.

"No kidding. Think the Nature Coalition will waive their ownership if they know a solar farm is going in there? Everything green on that property will be clear cut."

"Gosh, you're right. Getting those native gardens installed was hard work. Jasmine's legacy should be preserved. I've seen solar farms in other places, and it's mile after mile of solar collectors thrusting out of gravel. Those solar farm people probably want Cora's place too."

"Good luck with that. Cora's still out of pocket, right?"

"Yes." I tried to clear the case from my thoughts, but Iris bobbed back like a fishing cork. I turned to Pete. "It occurs to me Iris's problems would be solved if she got a job."

Pete snorted. "Like that's going to happen."

Chapter Forty-Two

Pete and I dropped Artie at home and continued to the library because I'd remembered old newspapers were stored in microfiche format. It took about thirty minutes to figure out how the machine worked and locate Mr. Radley's obituary.

Boyd Radley of Shell Island's Emmeline Drive died in 1990 at age 40, a shooting victim of an armed home invasion. He'd worked at the mill for 22 years and moonlighted as a yardman for nearly as long. He left behind his wife Cora Radley and was buried in Lot 4D-138 in the Whispering Dunes Cemetery.

"Look at this, Pete," I whispered. "Boyd Radley was shot. That can't be a coincidence."

Pete read for a few moments then whistled under his breath. "Franklin needs to see this."

"Absolutely."

I printed the obituary, snapped a photo of it with my phone, and texted it to Deputy Franklin. He called as we were leaving the library.

"Did not know there had been a Mr. Radley," Deputy

Franklin said. "This is very interesting, especially the part about him being shot at home. I'll search for the police incident report of his death."

"You think the bullets will match?"

"Not likely, given the amount of time that's passed, but stranger things have happened."

"Makes me wonder how old Cora was when she and Boyd tied the knot. She must've married him right out of school. I wonder what the attraction was."

"Ask her when you see her. Anything else?"

If I saw her. I hoped she was okay wherever she was. "Iris asked me to meet her about an hour ago. She wants to sell Jasmine's property to a solar farm company. Milton convinced her this deal will solve their money problems."

"It's not hers to sell."

Pete's truck looked odd as we approached. Eggshells dotted the windshield, the hood, and the sides of the truck. "Not my truck!" Pete swore and hurried to his vehicle.

"What's wrong?" Franklin asked.

It felt like spiders were crawling on my neck. I scanned the lot fearfully, seeing nothing unusual. "Someone egged Pete's truck while we were in the library."

"I was right," Franklin said. "This case is heating up super-fast. Any witnesses?"

"None that I see." Pete was already picking the shells off his truck. "Do we need a picture of the egged vehicle?"

"Wouldn't hurt. But you have to come to the station to make a report. I'm off duty and this evening, the patrol deputy has double-duty covering the island and a section of the mainland. She's handling a traffic incident out on the interstate right now. Be careful. We're short-staffed at the moment."

After I snapped photos of the egging, we hit a car wash and then drove over to Whispering Dunes Cemetery. Many of the graves were overgrown in this burial ground, but the plots were clearly marked with bronze plaques attached to corner slabs. We figured out which way to go and headed to Boyd Radley's final resting place.

"Sorry about your truck," I said, as we eased past headstones and statuary.

"My truck will be fine," Pete said as we crept along a pine-straw covered lane. "We got to it soon enough that it didn't mar the finish. Because eggs were used, could this be about the Chicken Lady?"

I braced as we bounced through a wallow in the road. "Hard to say. Egging is usually a teen prank, but no other vehicles were egged. Most likely it's related to the investigation. I wish I knew why. It bugs me I can't figure out who took the videos of Jasmine. Of the people on my suspect list, I am certain it wasn't Iris. She's not the outdoorsy type, and neither is Milton. If he'd been behind the camera, he would've plugged his real estate company. Lovestruck Ash fits the bill as an outdoorsman, but he worked two jobs so he would've been busy. Linette staffs her vet clinic six and sometimes seven days a week, and she was sick of hearing Jasmine talking about the Franklin tree. By default, the person with the most availability was Cora."

"Sounds like the Chicken Lady just moved to the top of your suspect list."

"I hope not. Stop the truck. This is the right section."

We got out and paced the plot with seven headstones. Most of the gravestones were ornate, but one grave had a very plain marker. I read it aloud. "Boyd Radley 1958 to 1990." I studied the other markers and didn't recognize any of the names. "Wonder where his parents are buried."

"Not here, that's for sure. Boyd was the only Radley we saw in the newspaper obituary index search."

Another mystery. Without consciously thinking about it, facts rearranged in my head, only they seemed too preposterous to voice. At the same time, I felt uneasy, which was unusual for me because I usually felt comfortable when I visited cemeteries.

"What?" Pete asked.

"Given how little we could find about him and given that I've moved Cora to my top suspect, something completely random occurred to me. Maybe she hated his guts, shot him, and made up the home invasion."

"Not a snow cone's chance in hell you can prove that."

The need to leave intensified, and I gestured toward the truck. "There are no answers here. Let's go home and start dinner."

~*~

After we grilled veggie skewers, I watched more of Jasmine's podcasts on the sofa. Finally I caught the sound that caught my ear before. Chickens squawking. The faint sound was undeniable.

"Found it," I told Pete who sat beside me reading the newspaper on a tablet. "Cora's chickens followed her everywhere. You guessed correctly. She filmed those videos of Jasmine."

"Seems like we're saying her name a lot today. Why'd

she disappear?"

The spillover of kitchen light gave the living room an intimate glow, despite the night-darkened windows. "Everyone wants to know that. Darn. It's too late to call Deputy Franklin and update him. It'll have to wait until morning."

Pete got a sly look in his eyes and drew me into his lap. "I've been hoping you'd finish your research soon. How about a little us time?"

"Thought you'd never ask."

Chapter Forty-Three

On Saturday, I awakened early, dressed, and downed my first cup of coffee. Pete dragged into the kitchen after me. "Breakfast first, right?" he asked.

"Working on it." I handed him a cup of coffee, then I cooked the beaten eggs, chopped spinach, and diced Swiss cheese into omelets.

Soon as we were fed and caffeinated, I called Deputy Franklin. "I have news."

"Let's hear it," he said gruffly.

I gave him the rundown about the grave and the chicken squawks on Jasmine's podcast. "Interesting," Franklin said. "I've made headway as well. Since you gave me the lead about Boyd, I'll share it with you. The bullet that killed Boyd Radley is the same caliber as the one we pulled from Jasmine."

I had to remember to breathe. "Cora shot her husband?"

"Didn't say that, though Sheriff Vargas is ready to arrest her based on the coincidence. We need to know more about her. Who are her friends? Her family?"

"I've never heard her mention her family, and I'm not sure who her friends are. Perhaps her egg customers?"

"Who are they?"

"I don't know, but we didn't search her place for personal information before."

"I'm headed there now. You and Pete want to meet me there in thirty?"

"Roger that. I should feed and water the chickens again."

~*~

Pete and I arrived after Franklin. "Come on in," he said, waving at us from the open doorway.

I hurried across her spotty lawn. Chickens squawked and flew out of my path. "Her door's usually unlocked in case you're wondering. That way if her customers need eggs and she's out, they can get them and leave money on the counter."

"Doesn't look like she's been here." Franklin led us to the kitchen. "No money on the counter, and no eggs in the fridge."

Her place looked the same to me. "I'll collect the eggs from her chicken pen when I feed them in a few minutes. Find any bullets or guns?"

He shook a small ammo carton. "Same caliber as both kill shots. No gun on the premises though." He set the carton on the counter. "We have enough evidence that I can assign a techie to review those posted vids of Jasmine's search for the *Franklinia*. Meanwhile you two stick together."

"Will do."

~*~

A few hours later Franklin called. "We have a GPS location of the last podcast. It's deep in a wetlands area.

I have a campaign event in two hours, so we'll check it out tomorrow."

"Pete and I could take a look today. What are the coordinates?" I asked, reaching for a pen and paper on the kitchen counter. Quickly, I scribbled them down. When Franklin hung up, I turned to Pete. "You up for a hike in the woods?"

"Absolutely."

Pete entered the coordinates in his cell phone and off we went, decked out in deep woods gear and boots. We went down dirt roads until they ended.

"Ready?" I asked as we parked in tall grass.

"Yes. I wonder what we'll find."

We taped our pants to our boots and applied bug spray. Pete handed me one of the two backpacks he'd prepared. Inside the packs were pocketknives, flashlights, water, energy bars, matches, clothesline, and insect repellent.

When Pete grabbed a machete from behind his seat, I became alarmed. "You think we'll need that?"

He locked his truck and nodded. "You never know what you'll run into in the woods. We're about to follow GPS coordinates through an unpopulated area. There may not be a trail. With this blade, I can hack through vines and brush if needed. It also works to dispatch dangerous critters."

I thought he'd been safety conscious in preparing our packs. Now I realized he'd put a lot more consideration into our trek. "Gotcha. Glad you thought of it."

After ten minutes of steady hiking through wetland forest toward our goal, we passed an active snake nest, and I barely held a scream inside. Snakes may be part of the ecosystem but I didn't have to like them.

We kept going. A while later, I heard guttural noise. "Hold up, Pete. I hear something."

"I hear it. Sounds like a gator."

"I hope he's going the other way."

Pete grinned. "I'll protect you."

He hadn't broken a sweat during the hike. He seemed energized, like he could do this all day. I wasn't nearly as comfortable in these heavy clothes and trail boots, but this was the smart way to travel through unfamiliar wooded areas. No way would I complain, though. I truly wanted to see what Jasmine saw, to stand where she stood.

Finally, Pete halted. "This is where Jasmine shot her last video."

Mosquitoes orbited my head, not venturing closer due to the super-charged bug spray I had applied to my clothing and ball cap. Flexing my calves, I realized moisture from the spongy ground was nearly covering my toes, so I moved to stand on dry ground. The sparse understory in this shaded, meadow-like area must be due to a thick canopy overhead.

Unsure of what was important, I filmed a short video with my phone and snapped some photos. One small tree caught my eye. I photographed its leaves. Jasmine stated in her last podcast that she still hadn't found the elusive *Franklinia*, but I wondered if that were true. If she'd found it, one other person knew. Her camera operator.

Seemed to me that if the videographer also sought the extinct tree, a find of that magnitude could be motive for murder.

Meanwhile, the grunting noise ceased.

"How'd Jasmine even find this place?" I asked. "Did

she just head out on exploratory hikes in any direction? From my research on the plant, it used to occupy the margins where wetlands met with dry areas. She referenced a topography map several times. What if it had the with lowlands marked? What happened to that map?"

"The cops didn't mention finding a map at her place. This location isn't by a stream or road. We didn't follow a straight path from the truck here, and if not for the GPS pin on the phone, we wouldn't have stopped here."

"Her search for the plant must've blunted her good sense. Speaking of which, we're lucky those snakes weren't out on the trail. I'm dreading going back that way."

"You want to keep going instead?" Pete asked, gesturing in the direction we'd heard that deep animal sound.

Chasing a gator noise seemed risky at best. I was hot and sweaty, and a shower sounded great right about now. "Let's go home. I need to look at my photos and see what I've got. Oh, and see if you can route us way around snake central this time."

He grinned. "I can do that. Follow me."

"Right behind you."

~*~

Franklin left a phone message while I was in church on Sunday. He said there was nothing to see at the site. I hurried home and compared the leaves in my photo to reference images of the *Franklinia*. Looked similar to me, but I was no botanist. I messaged the deputy a photo of the leaves I took from the location and called him.

"I sent you a photo. Jasmine may have found the *Franklinia alatamaha* there."

270

"You took this photo?"

"I did. Pete and I canvassed the podcast's GPS location yesterday. If the camera person cared about the quest, finding the plant would've been a very big deal to him or her as well."

"That remains to be seen. I have a BOLO out on Cora Radley."

I sent up another quick prayer for her safety. "I hope you find her soon. Speaking of suspects, I haven't seen Ash since he made bail. Have you seen him?"

"Nope, but I have no reason to seek him out."

"I usually see his truck around the island, but I haven't seen it these last few days. I'm not Ash's relative, so am I allowed to request a welfare check on him?"

"Sounds like a good idea. Zillo's riding with me today. We'll check Ash's place in twenty. I'll call if we locate him."

"Heck, I can meet you there as a concerned citizen."

"Only if you wait until we clear the property."

"Sure thing."

Ash's place was unlocked and empty when Pete and I arrived. As the deputies toured his home and called his name, Pete and I sat in his truck, windows open. Ash's truck slumbered in the drive. Calls to his cell went to voice mail and nothing rang in our vicinity during the calls.

Deputy Franklin approached the passenger side of Pete's truck. "We checked the house and yard. He's not here."

"Couldn't have gone far on foot," I said. "What about his alligator farm? Would he go there?"

"Good idea. We'll check that next," Franklin said.

"May we accompany you?" I asked.

"Same rules as here. We can't have civilians interfere with our work. If you wait with the vehicles, I will return for you if it's safe to join us."

I swallowed my protest. "All right."

We crossed the island, circled through a forested section, and pulled up at the end of a crude lane. The long grass appeared to have recently been matted and smushed. The deputies departed, and time crept by. It was worse than waiting for a pot of water to boil. The longer I sat, the antsier I became. "They've been gone a while, and we didn't hear gunshots," I said. "I've never seen a gator farm. What would it hurt if we followed them?"

"It won't hurt if no one is lying in wait out there."

His logic erred on the side of caution, and I understood it, but I really wanted to follow the cops. "This site is such a longshot at finding Ash. I mean, how would he get out here? We're easily seven miles from his home."

"Some truth to that. I don't like waiting either. Okay, let's do it."

Pete and I shouldered the all-purpose packs we'd used yesterday. He grabbed the machete again. The man was always thinking of safety precautions.

We paused to douse ourselves in insect repellant. I heard the hollering before we'd gone twenty steps in the woods. "Someone's in trouble," I told Pete. "It might be Franklin or Zillo."

"I want to know what's going on." Pete checked his watch. "Let's approach slowly and as silently as possible. If shots are fired, run for the truck."

I nodded. "Sure."

"It might be bad. I can't imagine a person hollering like that if he wasn't in dire pain."

I steeled my nerve. "I can take it."

He caught my chin. "No running ahead when your big heart for others starts pounding. You are my world, River."

I squeezed his arm. "Promise."

Chapter Forty-Four

Pete interlaced his fingers through mine, making it clear that we would stay together. We inched toward the direction of the noise, careful of how we stepped, my ears straining to hear the conversation. Every snap of a twig sounded thunder-loud. Black flies swarmed us, making me grateful for my protective clothing and insect repellant.

The foul smell hit me first, ripe and sharp, as cloying as sewage. Eyes watering at the stench, we crept forward, careful to stay concealed behind trees and bushes. At last we gained a view of fenced enclosures. Ash's alligator farm looked primitive with fence posts leaning in every direction. Dark water puddled in each enclosure. A rough-hewn hut stood nearby, walls of stacked logs on three-sides and a similar rig of branches on the flat roof.

Ash cried out in pain, and my gaze followed the sound. Ropes bound him to a pine tree inside an enclosure. I froze. Franklin and Zillo stood nearby, guns aimed at Ash.

My God. What was going on?

I shrank back reflexively into Pete, and his arms held me tight. His steady heartbeat lent comfort and reassurance. He leaned close. "Remember, we aren't supposed to be here. Don't make a sound."

With a nod, I turned back to face the horrific tableau. The odor here verged on putrid, and tears flowed down my cheeks as I forced shallow breaths. If I were to imagine a level of hell, this would be it.

"She's crazy. Batshit crazy," Ash shouted, his eyes wide. "She tried to kill me. Said I was weak. Please, help me. I need water. I'm so thirsty."

"Who did this to you?" Franklin asked, weapon aimed at Ash.

Zillo turned her back to Franklin and aimed her gun at the perimeter, repeatedly sweeping the area as Franklin spoke to Ash.

Pete and I hovered at the tree line, in a terrible limbo of hearing the scene play out but not being part of it. I noted that Ash had dried blood on one leg. What on earth happened out here? Why weren't the deputies cutting him down?

"She stabbed me in the thigh, tied me to the tree, and smeared honey on my wound," Ash cried in a keening voice. "Ants and flies are tearing me up but that's not all. She said I'd wasted my life and that I'd turned out worthless. She said I deserved a slow, agonizing death."

"Who?" Franklin asked again. "Who said that?"

Ash groaned and strained against the ropes, his head hanging low. "The Chicken Lady. Please, cut me loose."

"Not buying that. She's been missing since last Friday."

"She did it. Help me. Please, I'm begging you."

"Where'd she go?" Zillo asked, her weapon now centered on Ash.

I leaned close to Pete and whispered, "Why aren't they helping him?"

"They want information," he whispered back.

"But he's hurt."

"You believe his crazy story?"

"Yes. Otherwise, it makes no sense. Ash needs hydration and medical attention."

Pete pulled me close so that his whisper spoke volumes. "We're eavesdropping, remember? You're not a cop. Don't blow our cover."

"He's hurt," I restated.

"The cops must believe something's off with his story. I've been leaned on before by cops and bad guys. You reach a point where you'll say anything to end the interrogation. They want Ash to reach that point."

Personal safety and compassion battled in my head. "It's inhumane to leave him like that."

"Does Franklin tell you how to bake cookies? No. We wait. The cops need information first."

"She's hunting gators," Ash sobbed. "Said I should be part of the ecosystem, like my dad. Get me out of here."

Neither cop moved to help him.

"What are the 55-gallon drums for?" Zillo asked, pointing to the cluster of barrels with her weapon. "You processing gator hides again?"

"Not me. It was never me. Cora does it. That crazy woman thinks I'm her son."

Chapter Forty-Five

"Clear the perimeter, Zillo," Deputy Franklin ordered.

At that, Pete and I hunkered down into people-sized balls, hoping our tree gave us cover, as did our green and brown clothing.

Zillo strode into the woods, weapon in a shoot-to-kill position. I waited and waited until every ounce of my patience frazzled. A man was hurting. I needed to help him.

"We need to get that man down. This isn't right," I whispered to Pete.

"Hold fast," he whispered back.

The seconds grew more onerous. Franklin glanced around and muttered to himself. He said something to Zillo in a low voice, and she melted into the woods. Then he reached for his phone.

An instant later my cell rang in my pocket. My gaze met Pete's. "Busted. Should have silenced the ringer."

"Should've known you'd follow us." Franklin pocketed his phone and raised his voice. "River,

Merrick, show yourselves," Franklin yelled. "I need another set of hands."

I unfolded and trotted over, Pete right behind me.

"Either of you got a pocketknife?" the deputy asked.

"I do," Pete said, reaching in his pocket.

"Cut this man down while I stand guard. Then we'll move him to that shelter."

"Where's Deputy Zillo?" I asked.

"Making a perimeter sweep." Franklin said. "Good thing I radioed for backup soon as we saw this place. "Be on your guard. We need to assume Ash's attacker will return soon. Stay alert."

"She's crazy," Ash muttered with his head down and eyes closed.

I noticed he was still wearing that navy blue "Made in 1990" T-shirt he'd worn when he was interviewed on TV after his arrest. I've seen that date elsewhere recently, I realized, but where?

Pete cut Ash's bindings, then he and Franklin carried Ash to the three-sided hut. Inside was a rustic stool, a mud-caked three-ring binder, a few walking sticks, and a tarp. Jasmine's face peeked at me from the binder's dirty front. The space felt crowded with four of us in the hut. Overhead, the roof of smaller branches gapped, allowed narrow beams of sunshine to illuminate the place. "What can I do?" I asked, feeling like excess baggage.

"You and Pete stay with Ash while I find Zillo. Give him water if you have it. Don't budge until I return."

"Got it." I reached for my small pack and offered Ash some water. He drank greedily from the bottle I held, then his eyes closed. "Stay with us, Ash. Tell me more about Cora's claim that she's your mother."

He didn't awaken. My hand brushed his face, and the warmth of his skin surprised me. Ash was burning with fever. I checked the scratches I'd seen on his arms a few days ago. Their bright red color and puffiness indicated infection.

"Wish I had antibiotic cream in my pack," I told Ash. "I'd coat you in it."

When Ash didn't respond to my voice, I patted his face. "Ash, you in there? Wake up."

He didn't reply. I glanced at Pete. "Maybe he's unconscious. I can't rouse him."

"He's breathing, so that's good. Must be exhausted after being lashed to that tree. See if you can get more water in him."

No matter how I tried, the water ran off the side of his face. "No luck."

While Pete kept a lookout from the open side of the hut, I moistened my bandana and tried to cool the injured man's head. "This seems surreal. I can't make sense of it. Ash is hurt. Cora vanished. She has always been such a nice person."

"People change," Pete said.

"But Ash said she did this to him and that she's his mother. If he's right, I never knew Cora at all. I had no clue she ever bore a child. The person that did all this isn't the woman I knew. What changed? Why would she hurt anyone? It doesn't make sense."

"She wanted you to like her." Pete knelt beside me on the ground and rubbed his shoulder. "When I was in California, my so-called friends and allies nearly killed me. I have no trouble doubting anyone's public persona now."

"Sorry. I didn't mean to stir up painful memories. I

can't wrap my head around how Ash was strung up and intentionally wounded. That's torture. On Shell Island. It takes my breath away. I thought Cora was a good person, but I misjudged her. Setting my feelings aside, the logistics of who had time to take those videos of Jasmine fit Cora's lifestyle the best. Given her outdoorsy persona, it isn't a stretch to believe she had the gator curing skills Ash claimed."

Pete flashed a fleeting smile. "I'll make a conspiracy theorist out of you yet."

Deputy Franklin returned, his arm around Zillo. The female cop walked haltingly and appeared dazed.

I stood alongside my husband. "What happened?"

Franklin walked Zillo into the hut where we waited and sat the deputy on the crude stool. "She has a knot on the back of her head. Says she was struck from behind. Found her on the ground, and her service weapon is missing. She needs medical attention."

"So does Ash," I said. "He's in no shape to walk. He fell asleep as soon as he drank a sip of water, and he's feverish. How can we get both of them back to the vehicles?"

"If Zillo's weapon wasn't missing, Pete and I could carry Ash, and you could assist Zillo. That missing gun is a game changer. The assailant is now armed. It would be reckless of me to have my gun hand out of commission."

"So we wait for back up?" I asked, gesturing to the open side of the three-sided hut. "Anyone who's a fair shot could pick us off from across the clearing."

"Three sides of protection is more than we'd have out there. I have my service weapon so we're not defenseless. Either of you know how to make a stretcher?" Franklin asked.

I glanced around the hut, seeing the tarp and poles in a new light. "I can make one with that tarp and poles and the clothesline in my backpack."

"Go for it," Franklin said. "I'll stand watch."

"I'll help River," Pete said.

We cut the tarp and lashed it to the poles using the clothesline from my pack. Zillo lost her balance on the stool, and Pete caught her head as she slid to the ground.

"That does it," Franklin said. "We can't carry two unconscious people out of here. We wait for back-up."

Chapter Forty-Six

Leaves rustled nearby. Suddenly, baby alligators rained into the hut. *Must've come through the gaps in the roof*, I thought as I tried to leap to higher ground and instead banged my head on the crude roof. "Ouch. Ouch. Ouch. Oh, my God!" I shrieked and used my backpack to herd them away from me.

Pete picked me up and kicked in the direction of the hatchlings. They scattered, but two headed toward Ash. "I'm okay. Put me down. They're going for Ash. He can't defend himself."

Pete held fast, his gaze quartering the small hut.

Ash screamed, and I saw he was under attack from a tiny gator. I pushed against Pete. "Look! One is biting him! We have to help him."

Pete lowered me to my feet, bent in a fluid motion, and gripped the reptile behind the head. The critter released Ash and tried to bite Pete. Just as quickly, Pete, flung the small predator out of the hut, and it splashed in the nearest pond.

"My hero," I said as I gave him a kiss.

Meanwhile, Deputy Franklin herded two baby gators outside with leftover poles. "Where'd they come from?"

"Through the cracks in the roof," I said. "I saw them fall to the ground. Someone's out there."

Pete bent to retrieve the machete he'd dropped, but instead he swore aloud and knelt beside Ash, his hands gripping Ash's thigh.

"Uh-oh, that leg is bleeding faster. A thigh wound can be life threatening," I said, fingers digging into my palms. "We've got to get him to a hospital."

"No time for that. Make a tourniquet," Franklin said.

"Use my belt, but someone else has to take it off me," Pete said. "I can't risk him bleeding out while I do it."

I knelt and unfastened the belt. "Now what?"

"Cinch it tight as you can above the thigh wound," Franklin said.

Ash moaned when we lifted his leg. Blood oozed through Pete's fingers. Finally I had the buckle threaded and the belt cinched as best I could. "Is this good?"

"Ease the wound pressure and watch for seepage," Franklin said.

Pete opened his grip and we saw blood. "Nope." Pete pressed against the wound again, stopping the flow.

"Tighter, on the belt," Franklin said through clenched teeth.

It took several rounds of tightening before we staunched the flow of blood. My hands throbbed from the effort.

"Got it." I shook feeling into my hands.

"Help's already on the way from the mainland," Deputy Franklin reminded. "Here's our plan. River will monitor Ash and Zillo's health status, while Pete and I keep a lookout for our assailant."

This situation felt decidedly odd, as if I'd been transported to a horror movie set. Any second now someone would yell cut, and Ash and Zillo would be fine. Only neither was waking up. Ash's paleness concerned me. Would he die despite our efforts?

Poor Ash. If we hadn't arrived when we did, those baby alligators would've eaten him alive, one bite at a time. The very thought made me shudder.

I glanced overhead repeatedly, fearing more falling predators. "Gators live on the ground, and they're known for conserving energy. If the bloody scent drew them, wouldn't they have entered through the open side of the shelter?" I asked. "Instead, someone dumped them through the roof."

Franklin nodded and stepped out of the hut. "Makes sense. That same someone struck Zillo on the head. Assuming it is Cora Radley, she must be spying us, waiting to make her move. I'll find her. Stay put, you two. And I mean it this time."

Minutes pooled like slack water. I felt on edge before this happened but now I wanted to run far away from this place. My gaze ventured to that dirty binder in the corner. I sat down and thumbed through the heavily obscured pages. A map stuck out of the back.

Even so, an icy chill shivered down my spine. The subject of this notebook was the *Franklinia alatamaha*, the rare plant Jasmine had been hunting. It contained a collection of reprints, essays, photos of her public appearances, and her topography map. "I know what this is," I told Pete. "This is Jasmine's scrapbook. Linette Nelson mentioned it to me. Someone marked it up, blotting out all reference to Jasmine. Her photos are nearly unrecognizable."

Pete spared me a glance from his guard duty. "Two people knew of this place before the raid, and neither the book nor map were here then, or they would be in an evidence box now. You thinking Ash or Cora defaced the photos?"

I placed the binder where I found it and moved closer to Pete. "Seeing how incapacitated Ash is, it has to be Cora. I didn't want to believe she had a mean streak in her body, but now I see her actions from another perspective. She's been asking me questions from the start. Every time I saw her she wanted an update on the investigation. She wanted to know what I knew. Maybe she planned to kill me all along. I sorely misjudged her."

Pete did another visual sweep of the perimeter before he looked my way again. "Perhaps your openness saved your life."

"Could be, but I feel so disconcerted now, I don't know which end is up. I thought I was a good judge of people, but my pride in that judgment might get us killed. I don't see how Ash can be her son, but that's what he said. Bottom line: Cora's the killer, which means we aren't safe here. Ash warned us she'd gone to collect gators, and then gators dropped through the slatted roof. She's playing with us. This place is her turf. The longer we stay put, the more likely we are to lose this round."

"We don't want to lose at all, but something feels wrong again," Pete said, checking his watch. "It's been ten minutes. Where's Deputy Franklin?"

I called his phone. No answer. Worse, I didn't hear it ringing either. "I can't reach him." I strained to listen. Not a single insect or bird chittered or called. My breathing sounded noisy. A cold certainty crept over me. "He underestimated her. Heck, we all did. Think about what we know about her. For starters, Cora is an experienced woodsman."

"For what it's worth, I agree with you about Cora. She's behind this. She blended into the fabric of the investigation like a chameleon."

His voice sounded flat. Heck, mine probably did too. Though I'd befriended the eccentric woman, not once did I glimpse her true character. The way she cared for her chickens led me to believe she cared for all living things.

Shame etched my cheeks, branding my face with emotion. She'd duped me. "It's the only solution that fits. She had the opportunity as Jasmine's next-door neighbor, and judging by what happened to Ash, the means to kill. Still don't know what set her off, though I keep going back to the extinct plant."

A shot rang out nearby. Instinctively, Pete and I ducked and crouched on the ground. "You okay?" Pete asked.

"Yes," I whispered back. "I hate cowering in here. Cora knows our location, and she has the advantage of mobility and a lethal weapon. We're blind on three sides. Your machete and our pocketknives are no match for a gun. Even if we hightailed it out of here, she'd pick us off. Our best chance of survival is to reason with her."

Pete's low voice turned sharp. "You think she's rational? A sane person wouldn't weaponize alligators or harm others for no reason."

Certain that this was how I could save us, I squared my shoulders. "The woman I know is trapped inside whoever she's become. I need to bring out that caring side of her nature, the side that shows kindness and mercy. It's our best chance of survival until help arrives from the mainland."

"I don't like it. I want you in here, safe with me."

"This hut offers relative safety, but consider this, she penned us in here, same as she caged the large gators she and Ash raised. In huntress mindset, Cora will kill us. Without the deputies protecting us, we're easy pickings here. As I see it, engaging her in conversation and appealing to her humanity is our only chance of survival. I talked you in to coming out here. I'll reason with her."

"River! No," Pete whispered.

"We have to save ourselves," I whispered back. "This is the only way."

I stepped into the clearing before the hut, hands in the air. "Cora?" I asked. "It's River. I mean you no harm. Please, talk to me. Let's figure this out."

Silence sleeted around me like sharp kitchen knives. Despite the nervy wobble in my knees, I turned slowly in a circle, knowing she was out there, watching. "Cora, you've had multiple shocks lately. It must be hard to make sense of everything. I've been caring for your chickens, and I want to help you. Won't you speak to me?"

As the silence lengthened, doubt crept in, but I stood my ground.

"Why should I believe you?" Cora eventually said in a raspy voice. "People lie same as they breathe."

"I've never lied to you." I oriented to her voice and gulped at her straight line-of-sight into the hut. "We're strong women who help others."

A prowling tension filled me. At least I knew where

she was, and she wasn't firing her gun. All of a sudden it stuck me where I'd seen the date 1990 recently. On Boyd Radley's grave marker. Ash's assertion that Cora claimed to be his biological mother could be true. Perhaps if I appealed to her maternal instinct, I had a shot at reaching her. "Ash is your son, isn't he? You helped him build this place because, like you, he has such a kind heart for animals."

"Yes."

The acknowledgment was soft, but I felt a tiny surge of victory. I'd reached her. I strung a few more facts together. Parents helped their kids, trained them in certain skills. This gator farm could be her way of helping her son. "You wanted to make amends for giving him away."

Fall-hued leaves moved where Cora was hiding. She mumbled something I couldn't understand. "What's that? I couldn't hear you," I said.

She sighed. "No mother should have to do that. Boyd paid for what he did."

"What did he do?" I asked, genuinely curious about her late husband.

"Said I couldn't stay if I kept the brat. Said it cried too much. I couldn't make the baby stop crying. Couldn't afford a doctor. Found out later he had a dairy allergy."

"That must've been hard."

She snorted. "You don't know how hard. I lurked in the shadows of my boy's life. Just recently I taught him a new trade, but he's a disappointment. 'Got no bottom' as Boyd used to say. Like sand in the dunes, he varies with the wind, too weak to stand his ground. Can't even form an original thought."

Out of the corner of my eye, I saw Deputy Zillo

crawling out of the hut. She made a circular motion with her hand for me to keep talking. I gave a slight nod.

Thank goodness, Zillo was conscious now. My role was to distract Cora until Zillo stopped her. "Why'd you hurt your son?"

"No matter what I did, Ash hated me. Called me crazy to my face. Nobody does that. I smacked him, good. He turned on my chickens, too. He nearly murdered Mrs. Wiggles, and he chopped up Birdie Sue and fed her to his gators. He did that to hurt me. I brought him into this world, and I can damn well take him out."

I winced at her harshness. "I'm sorry he did those things. Those Braswells must not have raised him right."

"He shoulda had it better with a couple that wanted kids...but he turned out sorry and no account, like his daddy. Give either of them a boat and a fishing pole, and they're deadwood for weeks on end."

"I know you loved your baby, and you must've loved Jasmine too, to tape all those podcasts she made."

There was a long pause before Cora muttered, "How'd you figure that out?"

"You had the free time to accompany her. It made sense to me."

"Jasmine had her chance to do the right thing. Multiple chances, actually. Thought she knew everything because she had three college degrees, and I dropped out of high school."

Took me a moment to parse her last statement. "You didn't like her? I thought you were friends."

"Jasmine could scorch paint off a barn with her fiery tongue. She was a good vet because animals recognized her alpha female nature, but I couldn't do it. I swore I'd never bow to another bully again. She told me to take my theories about the *Franklinia alatamaha* and go to hell."

"If you didn't care for her, why help her with the plant search?"

"My husband used to tromp through the woods looking for the plant. Boyd's enthusiasm lit a fire in me. Later, Jasmine caught *Franklinia* fever from me, and then she narrated all those podcasts like she was the world's leading authority on the rare plant. Even worse, she stole the *Franklinia* books from my house so I helped myself to her things."

"You shot her for petty theft?"

"No. I shot her because she discovered Ash's gator farm and intended to report him. That was before I knew him for who he was. I took care of business for Ash and what'd he do? He fed my chickens to gators, that's what. He terrorized me and my chickens."

"Given his love of most animals, he must've been very angry to do that."

"I don't care if he was upset. He had no right to touch my biddies. They were my only family, aside from his sorry hide. He sealed his fate when he harmed them. Nobody touches my chickens."

Cora's thin grip on reality must've slipped when Ash took out his frustrations on her flock. Best to change the subject for now. "Did you take Jasmine's computer?"

"I hid it in the chicken coop eaves until the heat died down. I filmed those podcasts. Jasmine didn't deserve them. I'm the true authority on the Franklin plant."

"What about those dog prints you saw near her body?" I asked to keep stretching out the conversation.

She cackled. "I made that up for misdirection.

Everybody knows I don't have a dog because dogs chase and kill chickens."

"And the kayaks y'all used for some of the podcasts? Where are they?"

"I hid her kayaks and then sold them once Jasmine was out of the way. That's my way, to take from others who have too much. The strong survive, you know."

What was taking Zillo so long? I had to keep Cora talking. "Did you shoot Deputy Franklin?"

"Nah. He never harmed me. Just coshed him on the head same as I did that other deputy. But now I got me another problem. You and that husband of your'n know too much. If I run, you'd keep looking. I'd never be free. I won't live in fear again."

Her surety fueled my desperation to survive. "Being on the lam is no way to live, Cora. Tell the cops and lawyers what you told me, and they'll be fair with you."

"Not happening. I've gotta have room to flap my wings. There's no future for a free-range bird like me in prison."

"There's always a future, Cora. Focus on your blessings. You have your health and your friends. You'll have time to earn your GED, or even college degrees, if that's your desire. You can read to your heart's content, maybe even write your own book about the *Franklinia*."

"Good pep talk, River, but I have a different plan. Don't bother running from me. I can drop you where you stand. Any last words?"

I noticed the red laser dot on my chest and gulped. "Yes. Please don't do this."

"River!" Pete called. "Duck."

I hit the ground. The bushes shook, and Cora fell face first toward me. Zillo followed her out of the shrubs, thin wires connecting her to Zillo's gun. Must be Taser leads, I thought. I hurried over to check on Cora. Her eyes rolled up in her head, and her chest stilled.

"Call an ambulance!" I attempted to take her pulse and immediately gaped at Zillo in disbelief. "There's no pulse. She's dead."

Chapter Forty-Seven

"Not possible." Zillo dropped to her knees beside Cora. The deputy doublechecked for the woman's pulse and shook her head. "I used stun mode. That's not enough juice to kill."

She spoke into her hand radio and requested another ambulance. Then she started CPR on Cora, the whole time sing-songing at a fast clip the words "staying alive." After one long sequence of chest pumps Zillo said, "Don't ruin my life by dying, Cora Radley."

"Let me spell you," I said when she labored for breath.

"Sure, I need a break," she panted. "Do the compressions at the same beat of the staying alive song."

"The tempo seems so fast," I managed between pumps.

"Trust me," Zillo said. "It's right." She rose and staggered over to where Pete guarded Ash. "You okay in here?"

"The tourniquet is holding," Pete said, coming out to

be with me. "He's still breathing. How's the head?"

"Good, except for a killer headache." Zillo stomped around me and swung her arms. "Y'all got this? I need to check on Franklin."

"We got it." I kept up the fast-paced staying-alive compressions. Pete spelled me when I slowed.

"Franklin's breathing, but he's still unconscious," Zillo said upon her return. "I'll stay with him to make sure nothing takes a bite out of him while he's down."

I rocked back on my heels. This was exhausting work. Further, I couldn't do it as long with each iteration. Pete slowed, and we each cycled through the process again. At long last, Zillo's radio squawked.

She trotted through the clearing. "Keep going. I'll guide the team here. Be right back."

Time stretched and bent and fractured as we kept pumping. Suddenly six uniformed people swarmed out of the woods. An EMT I didn't recognize took over for me, and I crawled toward my husband. "Pete Merrick. You're a hero. You saved Ash's life today."

He drew me close. "I did what anyone would've done, and we all helped. And look at you, bravely talking to an armed killer, getting her to confess to murder." He glanced over at Cora, and his breath hitched.

I followed his gaze, saw that they'd quit working on her, and cried out in anguish. "It wasn't a lethal charge. Deputy Zillo said so. I don't understand."

The rescue focus shifted from Cora to Ash, and the medics used their portable stretcher for him. The one I'd made with a tarp, poles, and rope was used to haul the Chicken Lady out in a body bag. Simultaneously, other paramedics assessed Deputy Franklin and carried him to an ambulance.

With guns and people accounted for, we hurried to the vehicles. Ash and Franklin were transported to the hospital, and the Chicken Lady went to the morgue. Zillo, Pete, and I were bustled to the law enforcement center. After a long wait in a stuffy interview room, I had the pleasure of being interviewed by Sheriff Vargas himself.

"You again," Vargas said, pacing the small room. "My well-ordered world turned into a swamp once you began investigating. Why can't you stick to baking?"

His question sounded rhetorical and sexist, so I didn't respond. This man had an ugly way of looking down his blade of a nose with disdain and enough swagger for three sailors. I'd rather not arm him with any extra information about myself.

"I can't even be hopeful Franklin's injury will cause him to drop out of the sheriff's race. He's my best deputy, and I need him for this case wrap-up. Who knows if he'll get his mojo back after this? The doctors say the whack on his head might cause a brain injury. Start at the beginning. Go."

I stared at my interlocked fingers on the table. "We looked for Ash at his house and then the gator farm—and found him and Cora as well."

He dropped into a chair across from me. "You found them all right. Keep going."

I recited the sequence of events. "I can't remember Cora's exact words, but she killed Jasmine. She admitted it out loud. We all heard it."

"She killed her over a shrub? Not buying that."

Regional pride filled my chest, and I glared at him. "That's partially true, but it isn't just any shrub. Finding the *Franklinia alatamaha* growing in the wild again would be historic, epic even. It would be like finding the pot of gold at the end of the rainbow. It would be a huge deal for our community."

His eyebrows rose. "There's money involved?"

"Indirectly. If someone discovered this rare plant growing in the wild, people would flock here. Botanists would come to study it. Books would be written. That sort of thing."

He shook his head. "Still doesn't track for me as a homicide motive."

"Well, Jasmine found Ash's gator farm weeks ago. She planned to report him. Cora shot her before she had a chance to mess up Ash's life. Cora is Ash's birth mother. She was protecting her son. That's why she killed Jasmine."

He snorted. "Some mother. She nearly killed him too. Those soft tissue issues were severe. That man will limp for the rest of his life because of her."

"He's alive, and so are deputies Franklin and Zillo, so she only killed one person, though I wish she hadn't killed anyone."

"Why do you do this?" Vargas asked punctuated by finger taps to the table.

"I care about the people involved. In this case, I cooked for Jasmine's mom for most of the summer. I wanted justice for her daughter."

"That's my job. You campaigning for sheriff too? The field is already too crowded for my taste."

"No way. Catering is my thing."

He stared me down for a long minute. It felt like I had a sniper's laser beam on my chest, and I had trouble drawing a full breath. The message came through loud and clear: don't mess with Vargas.

He rose.

I took that as my cue. "Am I free to go?"

"Not until I talk to Merrick and Zillo. Stay put."

The door shut firmly behind him. He didn't intimidate me. Not that I'd intentionally rile him, ever, but I couldn't stop being River Holloway Merrick. He had to accept me the way I was.

Hours later, Pete and I headed home. Franklin lay unconscious in a hospital bed, while Zillo was suspended from the force pending an investigation of Cora's death. I thought I'd feel happy about solving Jasmine's murder, but all I felt was spent.

I wanted a shower and my bed.

Chapter Forty-Eight

Two days later, I bumped into Ola Mae at the Post Office. "Did you hear the news?" the senior asked.

She vibrated with excitement, and her sister Valerie sat pretty on a motorized scooter. Both ladies wore fall colors, a rich gold for Ola Mae and a burnt orange for Valerie.

"What's the scoop?" I asked, pushing my letters through the mail slot.

"Deputy Zillo is reinstated, that's the good news," Ola Mae crowed. "Cora Radley had an underlying medical condition that caused her to die when she was Tasered."

"They said something about underlying conditions when she skipped out of the hospital early. Did she have a bad heart?"

"Nope. The coroner called it an electrolyte disorder. Something called metabolic acidosis messed up her kidneys. Seems Cora had a recent medical documentation of both conditions that she ignored. Getting zapped changed her zip code permanently."

"I've never heard of that," I said. "I'm sorry that she

died."

"We heard you were there," Valerie said. "She have any parting words?"

"None that I heard. After being hit with the Taser, she stopped talking. Just pitched forward onto the ground. Deputy Zillo started CPR, then Pete and I spelled her. You wouldn't believe how tiring that is, and then Cora didn't make it."

"Why'd she kill Jasmine?" Ola Mae asked bluntly. "Some kind of neighborly rivalry?"

"Jasmine found Cora and Ash's gator farm and threatened to expose them," I said. "It was all rather sad."

"How'd Ash fit into all this?" Valerie asked. "I keep hoping we'll get a gator in our yard so he'll come over, but no such luck."

At Ash's request, we were keeping the secret of his biological parentage. He wanted nothing to do with Cora in life or death, and who could blame him? "He's in plenty of trouble with the law for his unlicensed gator farm, but he's no killer. If you recall, he took the heat for the gator farm and Cora skated. Anyway, he's getting released from the hospital today."

Ola Mae shook her head. "I had no idea our Cora had such killer tendencies. She had her quirks, but who doesn't?"

"The Chicken Lady sure left her mark on the county. That spread the reporter did of all of her chicken statues surprised me. I wonder how he accessed her home after the cops locked it up."

"Reporters are sneaky that way. Any word on our next sheriff?"

"Assuming you mean Deputy Franklin, nothing yet.

Yesterday they put in a drain to relieve the swelling in his head."

The sisters exchanged a look of alarm. "He's still in the hospital?"

"Far as I know."

"We'll get people on his election committee to sit with him. Can't have him cocking up his toes now. Vargas is on the ropes."

I shuddered, well remembering the man's intensity. "The sheriff still has a lot of bark in him. Don't count him out."

~*~

The next afternoon I was invited to Ash's house. Pete accompanied me. After we exchanged hellos, Ash handed me a phone. "This is for you."

"It isn't mine."

"It was Cora's. Believe it or not, she had a will. In it she left her property to me and her video library to you. She didn't have a computer, just this phone, so I assume everything is on her device."

Cora had Jasmine's computer earlier but now the cops had it. "Okay. Thanks, I guess. I wasn't expecting anything. What does your future look like?"

"Some jail time and a big fine for the unlicensed gator farm. I'll sell Cora's property to pay the bill."

I thought back to the nice size of her property, about an acre or so. "How much you want for it?"

He grimaced. "It isn't worth as much as I thought. Because it's landlocked, there are no waterfront views. And, given her eccentric nature and killer tendencies, the real estate agent I spoke with said I shouldn't count on an offer at any price. She quoted me a figure that's much lower than comparable properties. I don't really care though. It'll cover the fine, and I'll be on my way to being a free man again."

"When does it go on the market?"

"Possibly tomorrow, as that's when I told the agent I'd get back to her."

"And your asking price?"

He named a figure, and I got excited. "I know someone who might buy that property from you today and save you the hassle of listing it. My brother and his wife are looking for a fixer-upper, and Cora's place qualifies. Plus it gives their three kids room to grow."

"There are chickens everywhere," Ash warned.

"Shouldn't be a problem. Let me see what I can do."

Thirty minutes later, Pete, Doug, Viv, and the kids joined me in checking out the Radley place. I unlocked the door and showed them inside the house. "What do you think?" I asked Doug.

"It would be easy to expand this place, similar to what we did at your house, except we'd keep this place on one level."

"Viv?"

"It works for me. I'd love a new kitchen but we need bedrooms for the kids. If everyone had a room, that would make my life easier. I probably need a big laundry room more than I need a big kitchen. These kids go through more laundry than you can imagine."

"And the chickens?"

"We'll rehome them. I don't want to take care of one more living thing right now."

I nodded. "Understood."

"You think the bank will loan me the money?" Doug asked me.

I glanced over at Pete, thankful that we'd discussed

this possibility on the way over. "They will if we co-sign the loan," Pete said.

My brother's face lit up. "You'd do that for us? Thanks."

We followed Doug and Viv to the real estate broker's office. Doug offered full price for the property. Everyone was all smiles, and the contract sailed through the acceptance process.

On the way home, Pete said to me, "That was nice how you found Doug a place to live. He's a quality craftsman, and he'll do a great job fixing it up. That will be a good location to raise children."

"It will and one day our kids can play with theirs."

He shot me a toe-curling look. "We should focus on Project Baby when we get home."

"Fine with me."

Chapter Forty-Nine

What with one thing and another, I didn't look at Cora's video library until a week later. I was surprised at how sad she sounded when talking about her life and her verbally abusive husband. I wished I had the power to give her a do-over in life.

Feeling the need for closure, I invited Doug, Viv, their kids, Patsy, and Deputy Franklin to dinner, and everyone accepted the invitation. Doug and Viv said they wanted it to be adults only and got a sitter. Gil Franklin hedged until I told him the kids weren't coming.

The menu included veggie lasagna, sautéed shrimp, baked apples, steamed carrots, green salad, and a spice cake. As soon as people arrived, we served our plates from the kitchen island and sat down to eat.

Viv inhaled a plate of food and then scowled at me. "I was doing great getting my pregnancy weight off, and now I want seconds on everything. You better hope your brother likes his women on the heavy side."

"I love you any way you are, Viv," Doug said. "May I

refill your plate?"

Viv swatted his hands away and rose. "I'll get my own, thank you very much."

The deputy glanced across the table at Patsy. "How are things at the vet clinic?"

"We're good," Patsy said, color rising in her cheeks. "It got exciting when Iris stormed the clinic and demanded the money from her inheritance. After the deputies removed her from the property, Dr. Nelson wanted to ban Iris from the clinic for life. I convinced her Iris was overwrought because she'd lost her appeal. We've already got our first free vaccination clinic on the calendar."

"Is Dr. Nelson having any luck recruiting another vet to join the practice?" I asked.

"No one's jumped at the offer so far."

"Well, I'm glad that they can't afford you full-time. I rely on you for Holloway Catering. Baking for Island Creamery could become a full-time job for both of us at this rate."

"We haven't hit saturation in the market yet," Pete said. "But creating a sense of scarcity inspires people to rush over and get their sweet fix before we run out. Your freshly baked items have taken my bottom line to the next level."

"Glad it's working out for both of us." I took a moment to finish my baked apples, savoring the rich cinnamon flavor. "Ola Mae figured out why the Garr estate was so heavily in debt. Holly Garr bought her beachfront condo at the height of the market, and then it was damaged by a hurricane. Lizzie Collins said Holly didn't use the insurance money for repairs, so she got black mold in there and sold at a horrific loss when she got sick. That plus her round the clock nursing care on Emmeline Drive ate up all the equity in the property. The note is for more than the land is worth. What will happen to it?"

"The Garr estate will declare bankruptcy and the mortgage holder, Island Bank, will take ownership of the property," Franklin said. "They'll ask top dollar for that land at first."

I digested that news. "All those gardens will run amuck."

The cop shrugged. "Happens."

He seemed okay with all that work going to waste, but it irritated me. Best to change the subject. "On another note, I finished viewing Cora's video library. She wanted Jasmine and Ash to marry, but that didn't happen. As Jasmine's podcast star ascended, Cora grew envious of Jasmine's alleged expertise."

"That was my thought, too," Franklin said. "We kept copies of her phone files. My take was she hoped Ash would join her in searching for the *Franklinia*, but he had no interest in doing so."

"What's this about Ash?" Patsy asked.

"Cora developed an interest in him as he grew, even willing her property to him because he was also alone," I added, sticking to the don't-tell policy about Ash's biological mother. "He didn't appreciate the attention at the time, but her estate money is helping with his legal problems."

"I understand what happened," Viv added. "I don't understand how the Chicken Lady was such a bad ass. Was she married?"

"Yeah." I shared what I knew about Boyd Radley. "That newspaper reporter found someone who knew

Boyd all those years ago and recounted how Boyd had been an expert trapper. He taught Cora how to skin animals and tan their hides, skills which Cora later tried to teach Ash, but Ash hated doing that."

"It's possible she shot Boyd, based on the size bullet, but no one prosecutes a dead woman," Franklin said with another fond glance at the lasagna pan.

Patsy reached across the table and scooped up his plate. "Let me get you a second go-round."

Gil beamed at her. "Much appreciated."

Pete and I shared a smug glance. Maybe we had a talent for matchmaking.

"But why'd she shoot Jasmine?" Doug asked.

"Jasmine planned to report the gator farm," I said. Deputy Franklin nodded in agreement, so I continued, "Despite her odd outlook, Cora wanted her protégé to thrive. Ash wasn't a self-starter and his lack of initiative annoyed her, though he did her biding for the alligator farm. Jasmine dismissed Cora's ideas about the *Franklinia*, along with anything romantic having to do with Ash. The scrapbook Holly Garr made for her daughter must've started old hatreds simmering. Jasmine received the recognition Cora felt she deserved. It must've been the final straw for Cora when Jasmine found the gator farm. Luckily, Deputy Zillo taped Cora's confession in the woods, so her own words convict her."

Scenes from that terrible morning flitted through my head. The horrible smell. Ash's mistreatment. The baby gators. The injured deputies. Talking down a killer. It wasn't something I'd forget anytime soon. Ash, Pete, and I had spread Cora's ashes around the island. Seemed only fitting that a little of the Chicken Lady would be everywhere.

"What happened with Jasmine's place?" Viv asked.

"Her furnishings were auctioned off, yielding five grand for the free pet clinics, " I said. "Iris purchased her family portraits and china for pennies on the dollar and was glad to get them. She phoned and told me she's decided to sell real estate. I'm glad she finally accepted the terms of the will."

"If you say so. Iris is a nasty piece of work," Patsy said. "Speaking for myself, I'm thrilled with Jasmine's donation to the vet clinic. So many animals will be helped."

"What about Ash?" I asked Franklin. "How much trouble is he in for gator farming without a license?"

"Ash hired a good lawyer," Franklin said. "They're working on a plea deal for him. He may serve minimal time, pay a fine, and start over."

"I wonder what he'll do next?" I mused. "Would anyone hire him to remove their nuisance animals?"

"I'd call him," Viv said around a mouthful of shrimp.

"I'd call him too," Patsy said. "He provided a valuable service. Besides, there's no one else around that does his kind of work."

Franklin cleared his throat. "Most people call the emergency number and dispatch routes the appropriate people their way to address their issue. Patsy's right, though. Ash is the only business on our referral sheet for small animal removal. Long as he's licensed for that, we'll use him. Otherwise, people will pay a fortune for someone out of Savannah or Jacksonville."

Patsy glowed at Franklin's praise.

As the conversation ebbed and flowed around me, I

relished the strong bonds of family and friends. My personal life and business direction were heading in the right directions and everything felt right. I hadn't given up on having a baby, but it would come, in time.

I'd finally come to terms with a change in my business model. The change had been less scary than I expected, and I was making a living wage from catering, something I hadn't achieved until this month.

Sometimes I felt the need to pinch myself for all the blessings in my life. Nothing had been handed to me, and I'd worked hard for everything, even my relationship with Pete when he lived across the country.

This year, I'd married Pete, renovated our home, taken on extra catering commitments, and adopted two cats and a dog. Everything clicked, even my sideline of solving crimes and I couldn't remember ever being happier. Nobody knew what tomorrow would bring, but today was darn nice.

"River?" Pete drew me out of my musings with a gentle caress. "You ready to cut that spice cake? I can't wait to taste it."

I beamed, squeezed his hand, and rose. "Coming right up."

About the Author

Southern author Maggie Toussaint writes mystery, suspense, and dystopian fiction. Her work won three Silver Falchion Awards, the Readers' Choice Award, and the EPIC Award. She's published twenty-plus novels as well as several short stories and novellas. The last book in her paranormal mystery series, *All Done with It*, released August 2020 and book one in her new culinary cozy series, *Seas the Day*, debuted in April 2020 quickly followed in November 2020 by book two, *Spawning Suspicion*. Maggie served on the national board for Mystery Writers of America, was Chapter President of Southeast Mystery Writers of America, and is Co-VP of Low Country Sisters in Crime. Maggie and her husband live in coastal Georgia where live oaks and heritage cast long shadows. Visit her at https://maggietoussaint.com.

More Books by Maggie Toussaint

Thanks for reading Shrimply Dead, Book 3 in the Seafood Caper Mystery Series. I hope you'll try my other books. A list of my books follow.

Seafood Caper Mystery series, culinary cozies
Seas the Day
Spawning Suspicion
Shrimply Dead
Dreamwalker Mystery series, paranormal mysteries
Gone and Done It
Bubba Done It
Doggone It
Dadgummit
Confound It
Dreamed It
All Done with It
Lindsey & Ike Romantic Mystery Novella series, cozy mysteries
"Really, Truly Dead"
"Turtle Tribbles"
"Dead Men Tell No Tales"
Cleopatra Jones Mystery series, cozy mysteries
In for a Penny
On the Nickel
Dime If I Know
"No Quarter" (novella)
Single Title Cozy Mysteries
Death, Island Style
Murder in the Buff

Mossy Bog Romantic Suspense series
Muddy Waters
Hot Water
Rough Waters
Single Title Romantic Suspense
House of Lies
No Second Chance
Seeing Red
The Guardian of Earth Futuristic Mystery series
G-1 (writing as Rigel Carson)
G-2 (writing as Rigel Carson)
G-3 (writing as Rigel Carson)
Short Stories
"High Noon at Dollar Central" (a Dreamwalker story)
"Sand Dollar Secrets" (a Cleopatra Jones story)
"The Trouble with Horses" (a Seafood Caper story)

River's Greek Pasta Salad

Ingredients
2 cups seashell pasta
⅔ cup fresh squeezed lemon juice
⅔ cup extra-virgin olive oil
2 tsp oregano
2 tsp minced garlic
Sea salt and pepper to taste
12 cherry tomatoes, halved
1 small red onion, chopped
1 c artichoke hearts, chopped
½ cucumber, sliced
½ cup sliced Kalamata olives
½ cup crumbled feta cheese

Heat a large pot of lightly salted water to a rolling boil over high heat. Stir in the pasta and return to a boil. Cook uncovered, stirring occasionally, until the pasta is still firm to the bite, about 11 minutes. Rinse in a colander with cold water and drain well.

To make the dressing, whisk the lemon juice, garlic, oregano, salt, pepper, and olive oil. Set aside.

In a large bowl, add pasta, tomatoes, onion, artichoke, cucumber, olives, and feta cheese. Gently stir in vinaigrette. Cover and chill for at least 3 hours before serving.

River's Iced Sugar Cookies

<u>Ingredients</u>
Sugar Cookies
5 and 1/2 cup flour
2 tsp baking powder
2 tsp salt
3 sticks butter, room temperature
2 cups granulated sugar
4 large eggs
1 TBSP vanilla extract

<u>Icing</u>
1 cup powdered sugar
1/2 teaspoon vanilla extract
2-3 tablespoons milk, to desired thickness
Food coloring

<u>Cookie Instructions</u>
In large bowl whisk together the flour, baking powder, and salt.

In another large mixing bowl cream the butter, add the sugar, and mix until light and fluffy.

Add eggs one at a time mixing in between. Mix in the vanilla.

Slowly add in the dry ingredients, until dough is mostly formed. Remove the dough and place on floured nonstick surface. Knead dough gently with hands.

Separate the dough into three equal portions. Use a floured rolling pin to roll the dough out until ¼ inch thick. Place the dough onto parchment paper on a cookie sheet.

Repeat with the other sections of dough, stacking all atop the first layer, remembering the parchment paper dividers. Place another parchment sheet on top of the dough. Place the cookie sheet with the dough in the refrigerator to chill for at least 2 hours.

Once chilled, remove one section at a time, cut with cookie cutter, and place on a parchment paper lined cookie sheet.

Bake at 350 degrees for 9 minutes. Remove from heat while edges are still white.

Allow the cookies to set for a few minutes then transfer the parchment paper to a wire cooling rack.

Icing Instructions

In a small mixing bowl, stir together the powdered sugar, milk, vanilla extract, and a few drops of food coloring. Spread icing until cookie top is covered.

Allow icing to dry before stacking cookies.

River's Boom Boom Shrimp

<u>Sauce Ingredients</u>
1/2 cup mayonnaise
1/4 cup Thai sweet chili sauce
1/4 tsp sriracha sauce
Mix ahead of time. Refrigerate until ready to serve.

<u>Fried Shrimp Ingredients</u>
1 pound medium or large shrimp, shelled and deveined
canola oil for frying (other oils are acceptable)

<u>Batter ingredients</u>
¾ cup cornstarch
¼ cup flour (for gluten-free batter use a GF alternative)
1 tsp baking powder
½ tsp salt
¼ tsp pepper
½ cup water (or use club soda or beer)
1 egg, slightly beaten
Mix dry ingredients, then add the water and egg. Stir until smooth. Use immediately.

<u>Fried Shrimp Instructions</u>
Dip the shrimp in the batter. Place dipped shrimp on a plate. Heat a thick saucepan on medium high and add about 2 inches of canola oil. Once the oil reaches 350 degrees, add the shrimp individually. Cook until lightly brown, about 1-2 minutes on each side. Drain shrimp on paper towels, then serve with the sauce.

www.ingramcontent.com/pod-product-compliance
Lightning Source LLC
Chambersburg PA
CBHW060359260626
47160CB00006B/2372